Shooting the Moon

D1407099

ROBERT FANNIN

Shooting the Moon

HACHETTE
BOOKS
IRELAND

First published in 2009 by Hachette Books Ireland
First published in paperback in 2009 by Hachette Books Ireland
A division of Hachette UK Ltd.

1

A CIP catalogue record for this title is available from the British Library.

ISBN 978 0340 98019 4

Typeset in Sabon by Hachette Books Ireland
Printed and bound in Great Britain byCPI Mackays, Chatham ME5 8TD

Hachette Books Ireland policy is to use papers that are natural, renewable
and recyclable products and made from wood grown in sustainable forests.
The logging and manufacturing processes are expected to conform to the
environmental regulations of the country of origin.

Hachette Books Ireland
8 Castlecourt Centre, Castleknock
Dublin 15, Ireland
A division of Hachette UK Ltd.
338 Euston Road, London NW1 3BH

www.hachette.ie

To Luke and Aoife

In the days before satellites and GPS receivers, an ocean navigator relied solely on his sextant and a clear view of the sun and the horizon to get his position. If, in bad weather, the sun or the horizon was obscured for long periods, the navigator would be forced to consider taking a moon sight. This is a much more difficult proposition, partly because it has to be done at night but also because of the extra calculations that are needed with the moon's erratic orbit around the earth. For this reason, most navigators would have to feel they were close to losing their bearings before they considered 'Shooting the Moon'.

Prologue

Fortunately Roland couldn't pull in. All he could do was slow to a brief stop. I said goodbye as I stepped on to the kerb and didn't look back because I knew he'd be leaning over the passenger seat giving me one of his don't-do-anything-stupid looks. When I did turn I saw the tail end of his car disappear behind a bus.

The front of the Wills Building is large and sections of it protrude, creating corners, places in which a person can lose themselves with ease. I leant against the wall under a plaque and put one foot up against the brickwork so that my knee was pointing outwards. I folded my arms and looked at the ground. I didn't want to see anyone I knew and a lot of people were passing. In fact, it often surprised me how seldom I bumped into acquaintances, especially clients, in what was basically a small city. Quite where they all disappeared to after they left me was a mystery. But one thing I was sure of: I didn't want to see any of them now.

From time to time I glanced up at the passing faces, mostly young and preoccupied. No one paid any attention to me.

I looked at my watch. She was now five minutes late. Maybe she'd been detained, maybe she'd had second thoughts. Just as well, maybe. How long would I give her? Another five. How would I feel about walking away alone? Thoroughly rinsed with relief. Right now I would give anything to get off this wall, join the flow of faces and just disappear.

Thoughts bounced into my head from the past, ribbons of images and words that had no apparent meaning. My stomach was a bag of rancid liquid. This was torture.

I checked my watch again – eight minutes beyond the appointed time: I could go now, I thought. It's early, but fair's fair.

Chapter 1

Bristol, March 2008

I leant on the railings of Redcliffe Bridge looking downriver. A chilly wind rippled the water with ghostly footprints, forcing the swans to face into it. On the left bank, by the boatyard, a collection of craft was tied to the dock. Over them, still and silent, hung the arm of the dilapidated crane used to lift the boats from and put them into the river. Further on down the quay there were more boats – yachts, trawlers, narrow boats, the assortment that gathers when sea and river meet.

For a moment the sun appeared. It lit the buildings in sharp lines and deep shadow. I closed my eyes and let its weak warmth fall on my face. When I opened them I saw swans emerge from under the bridge beneath me. From this angle they were feathery parcels of white, propelled silently by black feet. If I were to spit now it would land on one. Was spitting on swans against the law? The Queen owned them, so maybe it would be seen as a political act. On they came, this carpet of white. Were they monogamous? If so, it was probably because they didn't speak to one another.

Dogs began to bark and I saw a figure leave the boat shed and move towards the yard gates. He was clad in navy overalls and walking with a swagger, his head down as though vexed by some recent event. It was Roland. He went to the edge of the dock and clambered down on to the first of the moored boats, then made his way across them to a yacht that lay on the outside. There, he opened a cockpit locker, fished out a key and, with it, opened the saloon hatch and disappeared below.

I felt a pang of guilt. He had phoned some time back, months ago probably. I'd said I couldn't talk just then, I was busy, but I'd call him back. I never did. Perhaps that's how friends finally separate, nothing violent, nothing dramatic, just a slow drifting apart with the current of events.

He reappeared in the cockpit, took out a bilge-pump handle, then stooped and began to pump. I looked at the boat: she was a classic double-ended ketch, white hull, wooden masts, small bowsprit. A pretty boat, well kept, 1930s maybe. It was time to break the silence.

By the time I got down there he had finished pumping, put away the handle and was in the cockpit, reviewing the city as though he had just sailed into it.

I waited under the arm of the crane. He didn't see me until he was about to step back on to the dock. He smiled in genuine surprise and walked over, extending a hand. Ordinary objects, like a pint of beer or a shifting spanner, substantial in anyone else's hand, were dwarfed in his. Shaking hands with Roland was a matter of trust.

'Still looking after your harem, I see,' I said.

He was smiling, shaking his large, bald head. 'Where have you been hiding?'

'Don't ask.'

'How's Lynn, the kids?'

'Everyone's fine.'

12

'Listen,' he looked at his watch, 'I have a thirst on me you could take a picture of. What do you say we go for one?'

'I've got clients at six.'

'It's only half four now.'

'Yeah, but . . . Come on, let's go.'

The back room of the Shakespeare was quiet. We perched on two stools by the bar. I ordered. When his pint came, Roland lifted it, held it in front of him in a moment of silent homage, then lowered a good quarter of it into himself. 'Jesus, that's better,' he said, wiping his mouth on the back of his hand. He turned towards me, 'So, are you about to tell me what's going on?'

'What do you mean?' I said, holding my glass of juice.

'I don't see you for months and when you turn up you've got a face on you like a plate of dead fish.'

'Marital problems.'

Roland laughed. 'That's good, I like that. You should be on the stage.'

'What do you mean? I do have marital problems.'

'Yeah, but you're a marriage guidance what's-it – you can fix any problem you have easy as I can fix a boat.'

'Except one is structural and the other is emotional.'

'Yeah, well, don't blame me for that.'

'We had a huge row just now – I don't even know how it started. Something about how I treated Mark this morning. All I know is suddenly we're both shouting and then she threw a sleeping bag at me.'

'A sleeping bag!' I could see him trying to keep the smile down.

'Yeah, well, it was the only thing she could lay her hands on.'

'I see.'

'Weird thing is, we haven't rowed for ages – maybe years.'

'Everyone goes through bad patches.'

'I'm beginning to think maybe it was a good thing. Like, at least it was passion of a sort.'

'Hey, play your cards right and you might be able to translate it into a bit of how's-your-father.'

'I'd forgotten exactly what depth you can bring to a conversation.'

Roland ordered the same again and began to recount the latest episode in his battle to raise enough money to build a Bristol pilot cutter. He had wasted all the time he was going to filling in forms for council grants and EU funding. 'It's a palaver designed to get a man precisely nowhere. Whatever you start out wanting to do you end up being a form-filler, a pen-pusher. Not me. No more.'

'So, what, then?'

'Simple. I have an ad going in next month's *Boats and Yachting* for someone who's serious about wanting a new Bristol pilot cutter and is prepared to put some money up front.'

'That's great, Roland. I hope it works.'

'Bound to, man. People want these things and I can build them, I just need a break to get the first one going. Once that's done, I'm away.'

'What about the boat I saw you coming off just now? Nice-looking craft.'

Roland stopped mid-thought and focused on me. 'Jesus, why didn't I think of it before?'

'What?'

'She's yours, if you want her.'

'What are you talking about?'

'Listen, I was replacing a couple of planks on her for this old boy, nice chap. Next thing I know, he stops coming around, invoices ignored, all that. So I phone him at home, and his daughter answers, real posh, and tells me she's afraid Daddy's passed on. Just like that – heart. She wants to know if I can sell the boat for her, "Just get what you can for it, sell it to someone who'd appreciate it. Daddy'd like that." That's what she said. And you're the man, the perfect man.'

'Wait a minute, Roland, hold on, how much are you talking about?'

'Ah – it would have to be sensible. She's forty-two feet on deck, spars are good, she's being beautifully maintained, worth eighty thousand without a doubt. I wouldn't have the final word but I'm sure she could be yours for somewhere around thirty.'

'Lynn would have a fit if I went back and said we were going to spent thirty grand on a boat.'

'Tell you what, take her down to see it. She'll fall in love.'

'That I'd like to see.'

'No, seriously, that's a lovely boat there, she'd be an investment, and down below . . . I mean, she's not modern, no air conditioning or any of that, but she's a beautiful boat, anyone who's gone aboard her has fallen in love. She's a peach.'

'I get the impression here that you like her.'

'Fuck off, she's a lovely boat and if you don't want her there'll be plenty that does. I just thought of you because, you know, you're into boats, you been around boats.

'I can just see Lynn's face.'

'Come on and we'll go and see her now.'

'No! Are you mad? I've got clients in . . .' I looked at my watch. 'Christ! In forty minutes!'

'The keys are in the gas locker. Have a look any time you like. Take her for a spin, get a feel for her.'

'That's kind of you, Roland, seriously it is.'

At 6 p.m. the deep tone of the doorbell echoed down the narrow hallway. The couple I saw when I opened the door were nothing like what my imagination had conjured from the one brief conversation

I'd had with the male side of the partnership. Speaking to him, I'd had the impression of a rather bland pair in their mid-thirties. But the two standing in front of me looked as if they'd stepped straight from the pages of a society magazine. He had dark hair and stern features. She was a mass of blonde curls, blue eyes and a smile that radiated calm.

I ushered them past me and told them that the room was at the top of the house. He let her go first and they climbed the carpeted stairs in silence.

At this stage of the proceedings, when nervousness gives everything edges, one or the other of the couple will sometimes make a comment, something in the nature of 'This must keep you fit.' I was happy that these two stayed quiet. I wanted to get down to the business of introductions without the leftovers of polite chat.

The room in which I see my clients has three straight-backed chairs. I arrange them within the natural pool of light from the window. I always sit on the same chair, the one closest to the window, and leave the couple the choice of the other two. There is a third option – a couch by the wall. In reality, it's a single bed covered in velvet with two large cushions leaning against the wall – this gives it the impression of being a couch. It's about six feet from where I sit.

When we entered the room I went to my chair, and they assessed their options, flashed each other a look, and took the couch.

There is a moment, when a couple first comes to see me, when I can observe them without a word having passed – it's a moment that will often reveal what words will later try to hide.

She tilted her head to one side and stared at me with large, unflinching eyes. He was nervous: sitting forward, peering from beneath the shadow of his thick eyebrows, he scanned the room before allowing his gaze settle on me.

The silence increased his anxiety; strangely, it seemed to relax her. When he began to rub his hands, I broke it.

'My name is Seán Farrell,' I said. 'Originally from Ireland, as I'm sure you can hear. And you are?' I was looking at him.

'Peter Reed,' he said quickly, and glanced away.

'Kate.' She smiled. 'Kate Wren.'

'OK,' I continued. 'The first thing we need to do is find out how you want to go ahead with your relationship. And to do that, we need to find out where it's at now. So, I suppose, a good place to start is if you tell me why you decided to come here.'

He fixed his gaze on the far wall. She settled her head against the cushion behind her. 'Peter wants to split up.'

'That's just it. I don't.'

More silence. I got the feeling that whoever spoke next was the loser in the other's eyes. He rested his elbows on his knees and began once more to rub his hands together.

'Was there any particular incident that made you decide to seek help?'

'He was unfaithful,' Kate said.

'We've been together nearly three and a half years now,' he said, 'and things have changed.'

'Changed?' I prompted.

'Well, you know, sex and that. Like, when we first got together it was great – not just the sex, everything – but now it's not like that.'

'What is it like?' I asked. I could see him strive to answer, then decide to close off. He put his hands into his pockets and muttered, 'Boring,' to no one in particular. I repeated it, looking at him.

'Yeah!' he said, casting a glance at her.

'Would you like to tell me why?' I asked.

She crossed her legs away from him. 'Peter thinks I'm boring because I don't want to sit around backstage smoking dope and drinking till dawn. Talk about boring!'

'She never wants to go anywhere.'

'You can talk to one another,' I reminded them.

They stayed silent.

'Tell me how you met,' I said.

Kate spoke: 'I was at university here in Bristol. Peter was a friend of my flatmate. We all just hung out.'

'You and Peter?'

'There was a group of us. Then one night Peter and I went to bed together and that was that, really.'

I turned to Peter.

'I had my own place. A couple of months later Kate moved in.'

'That's where you live now?'

'Yeah.'

'Do you both work?'

'I'm in the music business,' he said. 'Kate's looking for a job.'

'I have a degree in philosophy,' she said.

After they left, I went to the office to jot down a few first impressions. But I felt unable to. I needed to eat.

I went into the kitchen. There, Geraldine was attempting to open a can of tuna. The serrated wheel of the opener wasn't catching the underside of the tin so there was no pressure on the blade to cut through the lid.'Christ!' she said. 'Not even the can-opener works.' She abandoned the tin and the opener on the draining board and went to the table where a copy of the *Guardian* lay open at the sports page. She placed her plump hands on either side of it and leant over the print.

I connected the opener to the tin and squeezed the arms together. The smell of cat food hit me so I knew I'd pierced the lid. All I had to do now was keep the pressure on and turn the handle.

'Everton lost to Sunderland. Can you believe that?' she said.

'Your tin's open.'

'Thank you, Seán. Sorry to be such a pest.'

'We need a new tin opener.'

'That's not all we need.'

'Oh?'

'You amaze me. I've just sat up there for the last hour with a gale rattling the windows. I was freezing. My clients were freezing. And look at this kitchen! We need to spend some money.'

I went to the fridge, took out a container, removed the cardboard lid and put it in the microwave. 'I'm all for spending money.'

'Good. Let's have a meeting.'

'Let's.'

She looked up from the paper. 'Seán, what's wrong?'

The rectangular tray circled behind the glass door. It was beginning to bubble at the corners.

'You'll tell me when you want to,' she said.

'There's nothing wrong.'

'Fine.'

The microwave pinged. 'Geraldine, there's nothing wrong.' I lifted the container out and dumped the contents on to a plate. 'Sometimes,' I said, forcing a little lightness into my tone, 'I like to escape into a windless fog and just float. Nothing wrong with that, is there?'

'You need to see what's-his-name.'

'Who are you talking about?'

'Your counsellor – what is his name?'

The image of Philip jumped into my head, small, bald and cheerful.'If you ask me, you're the one who needs counselling.'

She tutted over the paper.

'Well, you and your little Everton chaps, I mean, what's behind that?'

'Oh, do shut up. Sunderland, of all people!' With that she drifted into a rant about the new manager, the old manager and their latest signing – a worthless, overpaid piece of shit.

I realised she was being kind in so far as she was leaving me alone

19

while indulging herself in her favourite pastime – ranting about Everton Football Club. But, as usual, in her effortless, intuitive way, she had detected signs of my ragged state of mind. Where it was coming from and what enabled it to occupy so much of me I didn't know. But I didn't want to think about it. I had a lasagne to eat.

Afterwards, I went back to the office and tried again.

I felt that she, Kate, was, or had been, comfortable in Peter's shadow, but now she was getting ready to emerge from it. Peter felt threatened by this. I had caught him using a series of verbal belittlements in an attempt, I presumed, to undermine her. Perhaps his infidelity had been part of this. But they had come to seek help, and, as I had discovered, at Peter's insistence. Clearly, of the two, he felt he had most to lose.

I filed the notes and got ready for the next couple, a middle-aged pair who had been coming to me for more than three years. Despite my familiarity with them and their situation, I pulled out the notes I had made after our last session. As I tried to concentrate, Kate's image wandered into my head. It was her eyes, a combination of earnestness and intensity, and her expression – trustfulness that made you want to make everything all right for her. Christ! What was I doing entertaining ramblings like this? I forced myself to focus on my next clients.

After the session, I walked home, glad that the night air was cool. Dread came over me in waves as I neared the house. I didn't know how the residue of this afternoon's row had fallen. Might there be a kiss, a smile, an apology waiting? Hardly. It was much more likely to be icy silence or more of the same.

I slipped the key into the front door and let myself in. It was strangely quiet. When I poked my head into the living room, Lynn, in her dressing-gown, was half lying, half sitting on the couch, a column of exercise books on the floor beside her. She glanced at me over the rim of her glasses.

'Kids out?' I asked.

She shook her head. 'No, Ali's here.'

'Lynn, it's nearly half past nine.'

'I'm dealing with it.'

If an Apache helicopter had flown through the front door it would have been less of a threat to our kids than Ali. He was a sultry sixteen-year-old who sought the company and flattery of Mark, our son, two years his junior. He'd sit on the couch, remote control in hand, flicking through the music channels. When he found one he liked he'd describe every image he saw as 'uncool' or 'wicked' in a series of grunts. Mark and Karen stared up at him from the floor, nodding at his wisdom. I was sure Karen, now twelve, had a crush on him. Lynn had smiled away my concerns, saying they were just kids. For her, any situation could be rendered harmless with the application of the word 'just'.

I had almost forgotten about Kate Wren by the time their next appointment came round. When I opened the door, the sight of her sent a sudden sensation to my chest. It was heaviness, a longing. I promised myself I would speak to Philip soon.

They sat in the same seats as before. Peter produced a diary saying there were several days when he'd be unavailable in the coming weeks. We slotted an appointment between them.

At the end of their last session I had given them an exercise to do. I had asked them to write separately, and privately, a list of what they would remove from their relationship, what they would add to it and what they would keep. Now I asked about this.

Kate produced a sheet of paper from her bag. Peter sat looking at me. 'I didn't get a chance,' he said. 'This week's been murder. I could tell you, though.'

'Peter, the exercises I'll give you here are important.'

'I'm sure they are, but my feet haven't touched the ground since I was last here. I've been thinking about it, though, and I'm happy to tell you.'

'Go ahead.'

He wanted more sex, more freedom, more fun, less hassle, less grumpiness and fewer rows over domestic trivia. He would keep their basic view on how they saw the world.

As Kate listened, she crumpled her list into the tight ball of her fist.

My intention was to ask how she felt about what she had just heard. When she looked at me, waiting for me to speak, the words I was about to use became derailed. I turned sideways and stared through the window at the buildings opposite, shadowless beneath a low grey sky. This was ridiculous. I was forty-nine years old and I had been counselling for most of my life, the last fourteen with couples, and all that had been blown out of the water by a glance from a pretty woman half my age. Either this had to stop or I had to stop this. I took a breath and turned back to meet two pairs of eyes.

'Would you like to read what you have?' I asked her.

'No, not really.' She seemed angry. After a moment, she said, 'Peter says he loves me, it's all "let's just have fun", but it's not as simple as that, is it? I don't just want sex and drugs and rock and roll. I want something that means something. What we have now, well, it's shallow.'

'Kate doesn't see anything but what she wants to see,' Peter blurted.

'Tell Kate.'

He inhaled and shook his head, looking at the floor. 'It's not like that. It's really not.' He looked at her. 'Sometimes I think you see it that way because you're the one who's shallow.' He was silent for a moment, and when he spoke again his anger was gone. 'I'm the one who's out there doing the business, and I'm good at it. I do love you. We have a nice life. I don't see what the problem is, I really don't.'

'That is the problem – that's exactly the problem.'

'What – the problem is that there is no problem? Well, fuck me pink, that's easily fixed, isn't it? I'll just go out and organise a few.'

'You already have.'

'Oh, Jesus Christ!'

A silence followed.

I observed Kate, as a counsellor now. Her declaration that she wanted something to mean something was a very solid statement. My instinct told me that now might be a good time to explore her past, her childhood. I didn't want to ask her directly because it might come across that I was aligning myself with Peter.

'I'd like you to tell me, if you would, about your backgrounds.' I made sure I was looking at them both when I said it.

Peter glanced at Kate and shrugged. 'You go ahead.'

She drew a deep breath. 'Well,' she said, 'I'm an only child. I was brought up in Manchester. My parents split up when I was four. I stayed with my mother but I spent a fair amount of each summer with my dad, Spain mostly. He lives there.' She stopped. 'That's all, really.'

Her eyes welcomed you, trusted you.

'Tell me about your mother,' I asked.

'Mum? She's a film-maker. I think she was a bit of a wild child when she was younger, bit of a hippie, always in trouble. At some point she ran away to Spain with my father. They hung out in Morocco for ages, and then they came back.'

'You were born in Spain?'

'No! Manchester. We lived in a shared house, a commune, I suppose, till I was two. I don't remember it. I just remember the house in Alice Road. It was a Victorian terrace with a garden. We had a pond. It was nice.'

'But then your parents separated.'

'Well, I don't know exactly when they did. There weren't any raging rows, nothing like that. To be honest, I don't think Dad was there that much, so when he was gone it wasn't exactly devastating. It just felt a bit odd at school and that. My best friend had a dad and a mum and sisters – everyone had some kind of family 'cept me.'

'You had your mother?'

'Yeah, I did, but she wasn't very motherly. She was so busy. There was always people round, endless meetings about money and scripts. It was a bit frantic and I just let her get on with it.'

'Let her get on with it?'

'Yeah, her life and that. I mean, she was a good mother. She never left me at the school gate and my uniform was always washed and ironed. And there was Gran. Although she and Mum never got on. Gran was one of those fierce women – she owned boutiques, went to mass.'

'Did you spend much time with her?'

'A bit. But she was more like this figure hovering in the background. Once we all went on holiday together. She rented this beautiful place in Wales but I don't think anyone enjoyed it much.' She became quiet. 'Gramps was there too. He was a nice man. He played the Jew's harp and his shoes were always shiny.' Her eyes suddenly filled with tears. Peter, who had been staring at the floor, reached for a box of tissues that I had left by the side of the couch. He passed it to her without a word. She took one and blew her nose. 'They were both bitches, really,' she said.

'Why do you say that?'

'Because neither of them gave a fuck about anyone but themselves. They were exactly the same. The only difference between them was what they did for a living. That's all. They were both selfish.'

24

Chapter 2

I was on the kitchen phone, trying to make an appointment to see Philip, when Lynn came in. She put her bags down and picked up a piece of paper Mark had left on the kitchen table – it was information about a school cricket tour he and I were to go on. Her expression darkened.

'I do have a gap,' Philip was saying, 'this coming Wednesday at eleven a.m. Would that suit?' I told him I'd see him then and hung up.

'What's all this?' Lynn asked, holding the piece of paper.

'Information about Mark's cricket tour. Why?'

'And you're going on it as well?'

'That's the plan, yes.'

'It's on the weekend of the twenty-first!' she said.

'Yeah?'

'Look!' She marched to the calendar. 'Look what it says in black ink across that whole weekend – "Mum's watercolour weekend". That means me, in case you hadn't noticed. I wrote it there back in February. I know none of you thinks I have a life outside these four walls and work but I do, or at least I'm going to. So just tell me who'll be here to look after Karen while you and Mark are in bloody Swansea, or wherever it is.'

'Lynn, calm down, we can work something out.'

'No, you can work something out because I'm sick of this. Everyone just expects me to be here. No one ever considers that there might be something I'd like to do.' She opened the dishwasher door and began evicting its contents on to the work surface. 'It's just always presumed that Mum, the machine, will be here to cook, clean, iron, never complain, just produce the goods on demand.' She took out the cutlery container, walked to the drawer and fired knives and forks into it. 'It doesn't matter whether it's a clean shirt or a late-night fumble, the machine just has to produce. Well,' she looked at me, 'not this time. This time you might have to come down off your pedestal and actually get involved.'

I didn't say a word. As she turned her attention to the pots and pans I went upstairs and sat on our bed. Sunlight poured through the bay windows. It lit the dust on the discoloured rugs, created crisp shadows in the clothes that lay scattered on the floor and illuminated a delicate downpour of tiny fibres that floated through it.

I lay down and was glad the house was big enough that I didn't have to hear those pots and pans crashing about in the kitchen as I knew they would be now. In former times, in smaller houses, I had listened many times to that symphony of anger. It was how Lynn declared that, despite everything, she was at her station, still working, producing the comforts that her family would consume without thought or thanks.

Her comment about me and my pedestal was unfair, but then, nothing about the outburst was fair or reasonable. I didn't organise bloody school cricket tours. I didn't even like cricket. But Mark did, and he was our son and I was supporting him. What was 'on your pedestal' about that? I could feel anger grow, a little knot turning in my guts. But, unlike in years before, it did not make me want to go down to the kitchen and have it out with her. Now I would stay away, take refuge in fantasy. I was lying on sand, Kate above me, the sun behind her, backlighting her hair; she's laughing and soon will bend down and kiss me, planting a hand on my bare chest.

I was sitting in Philip's office, a much grander affair than mine, talking to him about my new clients, when my eyes drifted through the window behind him and into what I could see of his garden. I was suddenly filled with an awareness of what the world feels like in spring – heavy with combustible wetness. The rain that had fallen on it during the winter lay there now, fuelling a slow and certain explosion, one that would throw everything up to the surface with a vibrancy that could shatter brickwork and rip up roads. Spring was a time when farmers and gardeners got busy trying to control this explosion.

It was a strong but fleeting feeling that I dared not put into words to Philip. If there was one thing that frustrated me about my counsellor it was his preoccupation with words. They were, to him, like sweets to a child. He'd unwrap each one, excited by the delights that might unfold. But sometimes words were just words, a means of moving information from A to B.

He was now waiting for me to continue. I had been telling him about this emerging infatuation with Kate but I'd lost my train of thought.

'How are things with Lynn?' he asked, breaking the silence.

'Fine.'

This was the other part of the problem with Philip. He knew what I knew about relationship counselling and he knew I knew it.

'"Fine." Well, that's good, then, isn't it?'

'Philip, whatever this Kate woman's undoing in me, I don't think it has anything to do with my relationship with my wife.' I sat back on the chair and looked at him. 'All right, my relationship with Lynn isn't fine, far from it.'

He continued to stare at me.

'Philip, if you're going to suggest that I live my life in such a way that I can have nothing but fucked-up relationships, you're wrong. Lynn and I have grown apart. We were never really that close. But I have a great relationship with my kids, my colleagues and friends.'

'I'm delighted to hear it. How are the kids?'

'Fine.' That word again. I didn't want to look at Philip. I knew he'd pick up on it too. 'Growing up can be a messy business.'

'Interesting,' he said, and put his hands together as though he was about to break into prayer.

Everything about him now was annoying me. I felt that there was something else associated with my feeling about this new client, something other than the old ground we had been over in previous sessions about my wife. But he sat there, content and smiling, the dome of his bald head shining and his stupid fucking garden ready to burst into bloom behind him.

'May I suggest,' he said, 'that Kate is offering you a glimpse of the potential you once saw in your relationship with Lynn?'

I scratched my forehead. It was at times like these that I wondered had counselling any value whatsoever. We were all trained in slightly different schools of thought, we all leant towards the teaching and theories of this or that philosopher in our field, but we all came out with basically the same brand of blandness. And sometimes it just didn't work. In fact, more often than sometimes.

'Let's cut the crap, shall we?' he said, smiling.

I was astonished. I had never heard him say something like that before.

'What have you found to be the most common problem among the couples who come to see you?'

His tone was condescending and I hadn't come here to be

interviewed. But I was curious to see where this cut-the-crap approach would lead. 'Generally couples will begin having problems when the individuals who make up a couple are having problems with themselves. They transfer the frustrations on to their partner, thus straining the relationship. With some couples, that can begin a process in which the whole thing starts to slide.'

Philip was nodding.

'Why are you asking me this?'

'You and Lynn.'

'Me and Lynn?'

'Not only do people transfer their frustration, anxieties and feelings of failure into their relationship but also their hopes, aspirations and passions on to someone else. You and Kate.'

'You're way offside here, Philip.'

'Sit down,' he said. I realised my hands had gone to the arms of the chair. 'I don't think I am. When you first found Lynn you had just qualified, you were over your self-abusive tendencies, you were in love and secure for the first time in your life. What happened?'

Now I was sitting back in my chair. He wasn't meant to do this. He had no right to do any of it. 'I don't like what you're doing here.'

'Of course you don't. What happened?'

'Nothing happened!' I was angry.

He stared at me and, as the moments passed, my anger fell away, leaving me feeling little except that I didn't want to be there. He read my mind. 'You can go if you want to.'

I didn't move. Neither did he.

'You said just a minute ago that growing up was a messy business. Why? What happened?'

'Jesus Christ, Philip, we don't have to unravel every incident of my past to find out what quirky piece of dirt is contaminating my life now.'

Philip, the master of the expressionless stare, was giving a perfect performance of it now.

I turned away from him. 'I got expelled from school and I became a fisherman.'

'Why a fisherman?'

I inhaled deeply. We'd spoken before about this. Did he really expect me to go through it again?

'Why a fisherman?' he repeated.

A feeling swept over me. It was hard to put a name to it. 'I wanted to embarrass my father.' Suddenly I felt nothing. I was as numb as if he had injected me with an anaesthetic. 'He was a yachtsman. Yachtsmen and fishermen shared the same pier, the same facilities, but they despised one another. We're talking about the mid-seventies here. Social demarcation was much stronger then, even in Ireland. Especially in Ireland. My father hung out in the yacht club with his friends and I wanted to rub his nose in it.'

'In what, exactly?'

'Well, yachtsmen thought fishermen were not much more than a tribe of waterborne knackers. Looking at it now, I suppose all I wanted was his attention.'

'And what happened? You were what age?'

'Seventeen.'

'And this was in your home town?'

I nodded. 'Howth, just outside Dublin.'

'So what happens to this seventeen-year-old who goes wandering off into a different social tribe?'

Chapter 3

Howth, 1976

I was pulling my oilskin leggings over my sea boots when I caught sight of the skipper in the doorway. He was grinning, airing his prominent teeth, holding a gutting knife. 'Hey you! Want a haircut?'

I could think of nothing to say to this.

'I'll have no long-haired cunts on my boat.' His smile was solid. His tone was gathering pace.

I straightened and smiled back. I hoped it would say, 'Fitz, I've no need to be scared of you. We're men, you and me, shipmates.'

He came towards me, the blade making small, tight circles, catching the blue, pulsing with flashes of sunlight. 'Come on now, boy, I'll give you a haircut.'

Fitz took a swipe. I ducked. He grabbed a fistful of hair. I felt him raise his other arm, the one holding the knife. I reached for his wrist but instead my fingers closed around the blade. He pulled away the knife and I felt metal scrape bone. Blood raced around a knot of knuckles and fell to the deck. We looked at one another. He was breathing hard from the exertion.

I opened my hand. Blood flowed upwards until it hit the reflection of the sun, then separated into streams and took the easiest path it could to the deck.

'Fitz, you'd better haul this gear and get me ashore.'

His face froze. Then he stormed inside. Seconds later, the crew came tumbling out. They looked at me and the pool of blood I was standing in and went forward. The engine revs dropped back. I sat. Fitz was hauling the gear. The tough man had frightened himself.

I went below to the sleeping quarters, my hand wrapped in a tea towel. We were heading in. No matter what the circumstances, there was something magic about that.

Hours later, the sound of the engine fell away again and I climbed up on deck. The others had gutted and boxed what fish were in the net when they'd hauled. Now they stood, sharing cigarettes, watching the harbour open up as we steamed through the mouth. It was mid-afternoon and the quay wall was almost deserted. They lowered the tyres we used as fenders over the side, then went fore and aft to tend the mooring lines. They were pissed off, maybe with me, maybe with Fitz. I didn't know. To them being 'in' meant they weren't earning. That was all that mattered.

A lorry driver and his helper stared down at us from the quay. Fitz, framed in the small window of the wheelhouse, nodded at them. 'Young cunt hurt hisself,' he said, in explanation of our presence.

'We must report all incidents involving weapons to the police.'

'I'm a fisherman. I cut myself mending nets.' The lady behind the hospital's reception desk shrugged. Later, the doctor who was sewing up my fingers smiled. 'They said you got this mending nets. I believe you – you stink of fish.'

*

Two days later, Saturday, I walked down the harbour. The entire fleet was in. And because wages and thirty-six hours of freedom were on their way, the place had an air to it you'd find at no other time. The work to be done was maintenance. But it was done at an easy pace, banter, grumbles and insults fired broadside between crews. Retired hands muttered unwanted advice as they watched nets dragged the length of a deck or spread out on the quay wall to be examined for damage. Engineers hauled drums of oil back and forth from their engine rooms. Cooks stowed the week's provisions and cleaned. So, for a few hours, down below smelt of something other than diesel and dead fish.

At noon the skippers began arriving back from their meetings with the agents. Each carried a large brown envelope of cash and receipts – the week's work translated into money. Their return was watched by all, their expressions read like bank statements. They disappeared below and the first to be called down was the mate. He'd sit in front of piles of brown fivers, blue tenners and green wads of ones, as the skipper explained how that week's money had worked out. Most boats ran a share system. Food and diesel were taken out and the rest was divided into shares. The boat itself took half of these, the skipper took two, the men got one each and the boy, if there was one, got a half.

Because of our departure from the fishing grounds by Thursday, this week would not be a good one.

Joe, our cook, leant against the winch watching me as I descended the chain to the level of the deck. 'He's below,' Joe said, meaning Fitz.

'Right, I'll go and see him.'

Joe gave no indication whether he thought this was a good idea or not, but having said it, I was now committed.

Compared to outside, it was dark down there.

Fitz looked up from the table. 'What do you want?'

'I'm here for my money.'

'You've a nerve coming down here.' He rose, his fists curled on the table.

'I want my money.'

'You're not worth the half share you get, you little fucker. Now get the hell off my boat, and if I see you near it again I'll kick the fucking bollox outa you. Did you hear what I said?'

I held up my bandaged fingers. 'I could have had the law on you for this but I didn't. Now all I want is my money.'

'All it was was the nick of a knife and you go running for your mammy. Next time it'll be more than your mammy you'll be needing.' He made a move as if to come around the table after me. It was a gesture. I was already moving towards the steps. I muttered something but Fitz's attention was back with the cash and papers in front of him.

Chapter 4

Bristol, 2008

Philip's stance had ruffled me. He had plunged straight in. He knew his business so he must have had his reasons. Perhaps it was blatantly obvious to everyone that I was a walking mess. Geraldine had spotted it and Philip seemed to share her opinion. They were both right but, this being life, they were only right in part. There were real problems between Lynn and me, but they were subtle and complicated, and there was no off-the-shelf therapeutic solution.

When I got back from work the following day, Lynn was still fuming.

'Do you think any of this anger could be related to the onset of the menopause?' I suggested. As soon as I'd said it, I realised I'd committed a cardinal sin. She closed the fridge door with a slam and gave me a look that I'm sure had withered generations of schoolchildren. 'How the bloody hell would you know what my problem is? You're so busy running around, chasing your tail, you haven't a clue what's going on. And when something does penetrate, you think all you have to do is put a name on it and off it'll trot, back to wherever it came from. Well, I've got news for you. It won't!'

I left the kitchen silently, not wanting an argument. I slid into the living room, happy to find it empty, and found myself staring at the photographs on the mantelpiece – pictures taken in days when we were younger and smiles beamed from sunlit faces. A saying popped into my head: 'Nothing lies like a photograph.'

There might have been some truth in what she'd said about me chasing my tail. My days were packed. I allowed no space, no idle moments in which I might see time, or anything else, flow past.

From upstairs a throb of booming bass came from Mark's room. That was about all the communication he offered these days. Karen would be in her room too, sitting in a corner, eyes transfixed by a screen on which creatures stalked each other in imaginary worlds. And Lynn was in the kitchen, fuming. Our life was like some modern nursery rhyme – we were all just waiting for the blackbirds to come and pluck off our noses.

Geraldine, with the accountant and I, had carved out a large chunk of the business's finances, and together we planned an assault on our crumbling building. I was given the job of getting quotes. The first thing to be tackled was the roof but, by the time I'd seen the third builder, I knew that would just be the start. It seemed one thing led to another and the whole thing would end up in the basement with a figure many times higher than anything we'd first imagined.

Geraldine, when I told her, shrugged. 'If that's what it costs, that's what it costs.'

'Fifty thousand pounds doesn't worry you?'

'Money's money,' she said, more interested in the cricket results in the *Guardian*.

'What about the disruption? We can't have clients here while the builders are going at it hammer and tongs, can we?'

She looked up, almost smiling. 'No. We'll have to get temporary accommodation.'

'I can't wait.'

In a matter of hours, one day in early May, the scaffolding went up. The poles laid lines of shadow across the carpet, which altered their angle with the time of day. Work was due to start in a couple of weeks and I still hadn't found a place where I could practise.

Lynn suggested the basement.

'But it's full of clutter,' I said.

'Simple. Get rid of it.'

'But it's all my art stuff.'

'What art stuff?'

'My easel, brushes, paints and, well, my paintings.'

'Seán, if you think you have anything down there worth saving take it up to the attic. The rest of the stuff you can dump. There are even companies that'll do it for you.'

'I'm not having a bunch of strangers going through my things and just dumping them.'

'Suit yourself. All I'm saying is that there's a perfectly good space down there, which can't be used because it's full of crap.'

She was right about the space. And she was right about the fact that it contained crap. But it was my crap. That it might have value to me was irrelevant.

When I got back the following evening she told me that a guy called Dave, a mate of her brother-in-law, could come over on Wednesday next week and paint the place; did I want her to call one of those clearance firms?

'No! I told you, I don't want other people just dumping my things.'

'Fine. Let's forget it.'

'I didn't say that. I'll sort it out over the weekend.'

'Great! So you're going to spend the whole weekend clearing the basement.'

'Well, if we're going to use it there isn't any choice, is there?'

'All I know,' she said quietly, 'is it would nice, just for once, to do something together as a family.'

'And all this because you couldn't open a can of bloody tuna,' I said to Geraldine, when I told her of my proposed temporary location.

'I don't know what you're making a fuss about – you'll be getting new offices and an extra room at home. Sounds perfect to me.'

I retold a lot of this to Philip. 'Almost nothing could happen to Geraldine that wouldn't leave at least a small trail of pleasure behind it. She arranges her life like a perpetually blossoming rose garden.'

'And yours?'

The question caught me off guard. 'I just feel like a ghost. I haunt my own life. Sometimes I think it would work fine without me. If I could get an electronic version of me to turn up, nothing would be different.'

'And where would you be while this electronic version lived your life for you?'

'I don't know. Look, I realise how pathetic this sounds when you look at all I have. I ought to be shot.'

'Who's that talking?'

I laughed. 'My father, my mother, every bastard who ever raised a hand or a cane to me.'

'Did you ever retaliate?'

The question rumpled my insides. I had no will, no power, no strength to hit back. 'I fought them,' I said, but it was a lie. All I had ever done was rewrite what had happened and sometimes, if it was plausible, I believed it. In my dreams I had walked back up to Fitz and spat at him, then stood and watched his expression change as my saliva left a trail across his cheek.

Chapter 5

Howth, 1976

Back on the pier, I looked down at the boats. A floating wooden village huddled tight, held in place by curves of woven hemp that looped from bow or stern through the water, then up to the stump of a bollard where they were made fast.

The crews had disappeared now, gone below to count a week's wages and change into their weekend suits.

I stared down the pier – past the shop signs and the steps that led nowhere, past the sand-brown buildings with their dark slate roofs where the seagulls gathered in long lines. At the end of it, the lettering of Findlater's public house was buried beneath neon discs advertising Guinness and Harp. Beyond the pub was greenery. But it was greenery soiled grey by distance. As it climbed to a long, flat horizon, it passed strips of terraced roofs and houses at odd angles. This was the peninsula of Howth and it hung at the end of the pier like a dark picture on the grey wall of sea and sky.

I stepped over the mooring lines and walked the length of it to the bus stop. It had a new logo on its lollipop face. This one had left behind the formal style and now the letters 'CIE' were written in a bold Celtic script. I fingered what coins there were in my pocket. Two tens and one five-pence piece – enough for an entrance fee. I elbowed myself off the wall and walked into the echoing tilework of Findlater's public bar.

Once you opened the door you were hit by the din, the smoke and the moist, mouldy smell of sea salt and stout. I was walking the length of the bar, looking for a place to sit, when a hand reached out and grabbed my shoulder. 'Where are you going?' The hand belonged to John Hutchinson.

'Just called in for a pint.'

He dragged a stool from behind him. 'There you go, rest your bones on that.' The two men he was with looked at me and returned to their pints.

Hutchinson was the only other long-hair on the pier. His was not unlike my own, a mass of tight curls matted well beyond the scope of any brush. It clouded around his face like a fog about to close in. There was something odd about that face too: a smile hovered, but always when you weren't looking.

He was not known as a hard man but the two he was drinking with were. One, small and wiry, in his late thirties, was called Scully. I had heard he had spent seven years in prison in England and I had seen two articles he had published in the *Irish Independent* about fish conservation. The other man, Matty Doyle, was a large, cumbersome lump whose one main feature was that he was good-looking in the Hollywood sense. And he had enough intelligence to know how to mimic it. This I knew from a night spent drinking in his company a couple of weeks before.

As I sat, Doyle ordered four pints, then turned to me. 'Been in the wars?' he said, pointing to my bandaged fingers.

I told them about Fitz and the knife.

'I always wanted an excuse to kick the crap out of that fucker,' said Scully.

Hutchinson's smile was evaporating. 'You're an awful man upsetting poor Fitzie like that.'

'Fitz is one of a breed of men I can't stand,' Doyle said. 'They're loved by the bank managers, the boys at BIM, the agents and all that, but in reality they're scum.'

Scully was studying me. 'Why didn't you kill him?' It was a simple, serious question.

'Fucker's not worth it,' I said, trying to sound as if I'd considered the option. 'Anyway, what could I do?'

'Who operates the winch?' Scully asked.

'I do.'

'Simple, then. Wait till you're unloading, make up some excuse for him to go down into the hold and, when the time's right, drop a couple of boxes of cod on his fucking head.'

The others laughed. I smiled at the thought of it. 'Too late now, he's just sacked me.'

'Right,' Scully said, 'that's one cunt who has it comin' to him.'

Something in the tale had riled Scully and I didn't know why. The West Pier was a rough place. It housed a community of men who had trouble fitting into life ashore. They shipped out in crews of anything between three and seven in boats that varied in size from thirty to eighty feet. Early every Monday morning the fleet steamed out into the Irish Sea and most were not seen again until the following Friday. The only law to be obeyed was the one the sea enforced, and the only rules that applied were those the skipper laid down. Neither could be broken without risking death.

The apparent simplicity of this life attracted an odd assortment of characters. Some came from a life of turbulence, others from a life of boredom. But whether they were ex-cons or ex-bank managers you could spot them as soon as they arrived. Anxious and worn, they'd search among the strange collection of shapes, smells and colours for something to put a little distance between themselves and their former lives. Some faces you'd see only once. Others drifted easily into the routine of the West Pier, its brutality and excesses alienating them further from whatever they had left ashore.

The shore, with its attractions and its trivia, was a place where the reality of life at sea was suspended. There was from noon on Saturday to the early hours of Monday morning to make up for the lacks of life aboard. For most this was alcohol and sex. But, as the weekend washed over them in tides of drunkenness, most desires of the flesh were left to echo unheeded.

Whatever the weekend had given, or taken, the return started on Sunday evening. For some it was from the fireside, kids tucked up warm upstairs. But for most it was from the pubs and, as the night wore on, the arrivals became more and more boisterous, until the last, alone or in pairs, staggered to the deck and then to their bunks. Most would not wake again until they were on the fishing grounds where they would leap at the sound of the throttle being pulled back. Seconds later, they'd crowd out on deck to face whatever conditions existed.

The job at hand was not a big one. The boat was put broadside to the wind and the net was lowered into the water. Two large, rectangular slabs of wood, called 'doors', were attached to its mouth, then shackled to the cables that came from the winch drum. With everything attached, the boat moved forward, leaving the net and the doors to slip beneath the surface. As the boat increased speed, the pressure of the water passing over the doors forced them apart, opening the mouth of the net. With the throttle pushed all the way forward, the drums sang as the cable flew through the blocks, over the side and into the deep. At the six-hundred-fathom mark, the break levels squeezed metal bands and the whirling drums moaned to a stop. Beneath us now, being pulled along the seabed's sandy floor, the net consumed everything that swam before it.

Up on the surface, attached to this moving monster, the round wooden hull tumbled and rolled. Inside, the crew ate and slept and attended to whatever was in the net when it was hauled every four or five hours. Its contents depended on the season. In the summer, it was cod, plaice or any of the varieties of fish that fed from the bottom. In the winter it was herring, fished for at night with two boats dragging the same net. The herring could turn the ink of the Irish Sea into bubbling silver. And the money was legendary. Tales stalked the bars and the summer decks of a year's wages made in a week. These stories were the neon signs, the enticement out into the black winter nights where you swayed, exhausted and cold, waiting for the shout to haul. When it came, hours of sweaty labour followed, filling the hold with silvering fish. The herring, no matter how hard it got, held the excitement of a gold rush. Everyone was poised on the verge of a fortune. Some arbitrary system of selection chose those who won and those who did not.

Between the summer and winter seasons, there were various routes a skipper could take. There were sprats, small, eel-like fish that, like the herring, were fished for in pairs. It was never as lucrative but, a big difference, sprats were caught in daylight. Some of the smaller boats attached heavy, box-like structures to their cables and dragged deep for scallop. But of all the options open to a skipper, one alone spelt drudgery and fatigue like nothing else – the fishing for those little pink delicacies served around the world as 'Dublin Bay prawns'.

A squirming mountain of pink was dumped on deck at the first haul. Hundreds of thousands of prawns. They were mixed with sand, mud, seaweed and some scared flatfish. In trawling for prawns, the footrope, a line that runs across the bottom of the mouth of the net, was weighted with lead so it dug eight or nine inches into the seabed. The net itself was constructed using a heavy twine bound in a tight mesh. Everything that entered stayed inside it.

Once the catch was spilled out on deck the net was reshot. We then had four hours to clear the mountain in front of us before the next haul. The prawns were delivered by shovel to makeshift tables hammered up around the deck. There, red-rubber-gloved fingers worked with mechanical precision, pulling out the prawns, twisting off the heads and throwing the tail, the meat, into a fish box on the deck. Prawns that were too small were swept over the side, along with the other muck, before the next shovelful was delivered.

Before long, the fingers of the gloves went and the fingers that protruded turned the same colour as the prawns they were decapitating. No matter how fast the crew worked, there were always two or three hours still to be done when the order to haul was given again and a fresh mountain was dumped on what remained of the last. And so, with every haul, the mountain grew. When darkness came, it glistened. The shoveller delivered mashed prawns whenever he took them from the bottom. Dawn arrived to reveal the same six or so men wedged into their respective corners, cold and red-eyed, the skipper above in the wheelhouse like a monarch. Meals were the only break.

On Thursday evening, we'd haul for the last time, then close down the engine. In the silence, we'd rock back and forth, working our way through the remaining mountain. Soon after dawn on Friday morning, the engine was started up and we'd steam home. The goal was to have the deck cleared by noon, land the catch and be away by six. And this sometimes happened. But it was more normal to find yourself watching boxes of prawns swing through the night sky on their way from the hold to the lorry.

We were at that stage of the year now, summer's end. Skippers muttered about the advantages or disadvantages of this or that particular type of fishing and who would pair with whom for the herring. The bars were full of rumour. Discontent was aired more openly now than ever.

Such was the mood on this early Saturday afternoon in Findlater's. And as I thought about why Scully and Doyle were so aggrieved by the tale of Fitz trying to rid me of my hair, I figured that they had reached that stage of pint consumption when they needed an emotion to wrap a fist around.

It was all quickly forgotten when a big bald man walked past us on his way to the gents'. 'Right, that's it, we have him!' Scully said.

Hutchinson looked over his shoulder to see who Scully was talking about. 'I find bloodshed too early on a Saturday tends to ruin the weekend. Wouldn't you agree?' This last part was addressed to me.

Scully leant close to Hutch. 'Listen,' he said, 'let one of them in and next thing the whole West Pier will be crawling with them.' He got up off his stool. 'Come on.'

Doyle was standing. Hutch drained his pint and placed the empty glass on the bar. 'Order another half-gallon while we're off about the Lord's work.'

He had turned his back to me and was following the others into the gents' before I remembered I didn't have any money. I sat examining the circular stains on the counter. All I knew about the big man was that he came from Scotland. He had appeared a couple of weeks ago and, as far as I knew, he was now working.

After several minutes, the man returned from the gents'. The only visible sign that he had just survived an attack was his stride – it was slow, as though he was having trouble bending his knee. He sat at the table he'd been drinking at and conversation filled in around him.

Then Scully appeared. He walked back to his stool and spat, 'Fuck,' at something internal. Hutch and Doyle followed. All three bent over their empty glasses, my inability to order staring them in the face.

The aproned curate appeared with four fresh pints. He placed them in front of us and walked away without a word.

I lifted mine. The others didn't move. A lump over Doyle's eye was growing in pulses. Hutch leant forward and picked up his glass. It wobbled in his hand. The side of his face I could see was streaked, deep red blood beneath the surface. The bridge of Scully's nose was expanding like a tyre being pumped. He turned to me as though the interruption had never happened. 'So it's a job you're after?' he said.

'A job! Yeah . . . yeah, I suppose it is.'

'Come down and see me when you're ready.' He was now sounding like a skipper.

'I'm getting the stitches out on Wednesday so I could start the following Monday.'

'Well, whenever, there's fuck-all rush on the *Mary Jo*.' He laughed, got to his feet and said he'd be seeing us. Minutes later, Doyle did the same. They had left practically full pints.

Hutch remained, unfocused in front of his drink. Finally, he stood, dug a hand into his pocket and produced a five-pound note. 'Here,' he said, 'I know you're on the floor.' I wanted to reach out and grab it before he changed his mind but I didn't move. He tossed it on the bar. 'Take care,' he said, and walked with the gait of a man three times his age to the door and the brightness outside.

Chapter 6

Bristol, 2008

I was clearing the basement. Old bicycles went to the dump, along with a bootload of paint cans, a rocking-horse and a chest of drawers whose corners crumbled with woodworm. There were several boxes of artist's oils that had hardened in their tubes. And then there were the paintings. I had remembered them as something good, a sign of a talent that lay within, one that some day I would reignite and head to the Hebrides to capture the light of late summer. But the ten or so canvases I lined up told me without fanfare that I'd be wasting my time. Most were still lifes – books and flowers arranged on a table. There was one self-portrait where my head and shoulders emerged from an eggcup.

I felt a stab of disappointment. There was no evidence here of the artist I had presumed myself to be. I stacked them in the pile that was destined for the dump.

I heard Mark and Karen squabbling in the hall and called them down. The basement had been off-limits to them since the day we had moved in. They entered now in silence, both pairs of eyes drinking in the details.

'This place is cool,' Karen said.

'I'm trying to clear it out. I'm going to use it for work while the offices are being fixed up.'

'Can I have this?' Mark had come to a halt by a massive architect's board with a weighted sliding rule.

'I don't know if it would fit in your room.'

'Please?'

'When I dig it out we'll take some measurements and, if it fits, you can have it.'

'Yes!' he said, forming a fist and bringing it downwards in a reverse punch.

I pulled out a few of the paintings. 'What do you think of these?'

'They're OK,' Mark said. He had eyed a set of drawing instruments under the board.

'Who did them? Did you?' Karen asked.

'Yes.'

'They're not very good.'

'They are good,' Mark interrupted. If he had been looking at them, his argument might have held a little more weight.

'Where did all this stuff come from?' Karen asked, peering into a column of cardboard boxes I'd not yet had the heart to tackle.

'Things stick to you as you get older, like barnacles to the hull of a boat.'

She stopped and looked at me. 'Is there a boat down here?'

'No, I don't think so.'

'Are you two in the basement?' Lynn called from the hall.

Even though I had asked them down and I was standing there with them, they were wide-eyed with trepidation. Lynn's feet moved fast on the stairs. She leant over the banisters and surveyed the scene.

'These are my volunteer helpers,' I said.

'Karen, I've been looking all over for you. It's almost three. You're supposed to be at Mrs Rolt's for your ballet.'

'I don't want to go to ballet.'

'Well, you said you did so you're going, like it or lump it.'

Karen sloped towards the steps. 'It's not fair. Mark doesn't have to go to stupid ballet lessons.'

'Fine,' said Lynn. 'I'll phone Mrs Rolt and tell her that from now on you won't be coming.'

'I am coming.'

After they had left, Mark said, 'I can give you a hand if you want.'

'That would be great, although I'm not quite sure how to continue. What should I do with these pictures?'

'I'll have them.'

'Really? You like them?'

'Yeah!'

'Well, why don't we put them to one side and look at them later, in daylight?'

'I could have them in my room.'

'Mark, we can't take everything from here and just transport it all to your room.'

'You did say I could have this desk thing, though?'

'If it fits.'

'Cool.'

I gave him a job bagging up all the loose rubbish that was littering the area of the floor I had managed to clear. He went at it with a degree of diligence that made me smile. He was alive and had a future, which, down here, was an almost unique claim.

I approached the boxes that Karen had been trying to look into earlier. In the first I found letters, cards and the remains of a cheque book from a bank that had long since been swallowed by a bigger one. There was also a plastic bag containing more letters. These were written on pink paper and gathered in bundles held together by elastic bands. I pulled out one and read the round, even handwriting. 'I don't know why anything is. You, me, those bitches in black. I just don't—' The rest of the sentence finished on the other side of the page. If I pulled it out and continued I'd be swept up in the ebbs and flows of a passion that had long since faded. I put the bundle back into the bag and the bag into the box – fossils from an emotional life long gone.

In the next box there were collections of tattered notebooks filled with urgent, innocent observations. The handwriting was mine. In another I discovered photographs. I skimmed through them, stopping here and there to stare at a face, or group of faces. It was like looking at the promotional stills outside a theatre. My imagination was the only thing that could give these scenes a history or a future. These, too, went back into the dark of the box.

Mark was folding an awkward piece of cardboard into a shape that would fit into one of his plastic bags. Five full ones were lying against the wall.

'You're doing well,' I said.

'Thanks, Dad.'

What was it I wanted to say to him? That life is so full, so meaningless? That the pains and passions of his future would, some day even further in his future, be nothing more than memories trapped in boxes making a spare room unusable?

I slid a cardboard box from an overhead shelf. It was heavy. The sides folded around its contents as I guided it to the floor. It contained framed black-and-white photographs. The first was of a policeman picking his nose in a crowded street, no one in the field of unfocused heads around him noticing. Another was of a large woman in a flowery apron peering from the door of a toy shop, then an elderly man studying the contents of a tray of books outside a bookshop. There were more than a dozen in all.

By evening, the task was done. Boxes waited like taxis at the foot of the stairs. Beyond them the room was clear, which, oddly, made it look smaller.

By the end of the week, Lynn's brother-in-law's mate had painted the place white. And over the following weekend, a mate of his laid a buff cord carpet. All it needed now was some furniture, a few plants, and the place would be fit for clients.

I cleaned up the black-and-white photographs and hung them on the wall by the stairs.

Geraldine had found a space in a tall Georgian building used by a number of her former colleagues. I'd miss our routines. Not that they could have been considered routines: they were coincidental meetings that took place when our schedules allowed. It dawned on me that in all our years of sharing a workplace I knew almost nothing of her personal life. She had a husband, Ralph, who worked in insurance, or used to. She had two grown daughters, neither of whom she mentioned. She had her football, her cricket and her garden. I could hear her saying, 'What more could a woman want?'

I bought a desk. I paid too much for it. Despite that, I bought two chairs and a couch from the same shop. There was something in the salesman's arrogance that compelled me to buy. It was as though I had to prove I was beyond his intimidation. It was a battle only he could win. But the furniture was good quality. Looking at my new room, I smiled. Philip would have approved.

A smell lingered. It was a combination of ancient damp trapped in the stonework, the chemicals from the new paints and the glue beneath the carpet. It hit you as you came down the stairs but it was not unpleasant. I wondered if it would affect my clients. But down they came, took their seats and, for the most part, made no mention of the place or its odour.

*

The dilemma of who would look after Karen while the rest of us were off painting watercolours and playing cricket was solved during a casual conversation I had with the father of one of Mark's team-mates. He said Mark could travel with him. He was taking four of the team as it was, so another wouldn't hurt. When I told Mark, he said, 'That means you won't see me play.'

'Well, no, not this time.'

'That's OK. Mr Cashman's got this incredible four-by-four with seats like an aeroplane.'

When I told Lynn, she shrugged. 'Do what you like. You're in charge.'

It wasn't until some time later that I mentioned to Karen we'd be spending a weekend together. She looked horrified. 'The one when Mark goes to cricket?'

'Yeah.'

'But, Dad, that's the weekend I wanted to go to Ella's house. Mum said!'

'That's not a problem. We don't have to be glued together all the time.'

'Dad, Ella's parents' house is in St Ives.' She added, 'That's in Cornwall.'

'I know where St Ives is. When did Mum say this?'

'Ages ago.'

'So you're not going to be here?'

'Well, not if I'm in Cornwall.' When had she developed the habit of raising her tone at the end of everything she said?

It saddened me to think that the lines of communication between Lynn and me had withered to such an extent that a situation like this could develop. I felt confused, betrayed somehow. I also felt robbed. It was too later now to reinstate myself now into the cricket tour. Maybe some time spent alone wouldn't be a bad thing.

*

Philip's hands were in the prayer position and he had been listening to me for the past fifteen minutes without comment. I had been talking about my relationship with women. I was keeping it broad, waiting for him to choose a target, but as far as I could tell he was strictly on reconnaissance today.

'It's consequences, isn't it? The woman you kiss, the woman you don't, the foetus you abort, the one you don't that grows into someone you'd give your life for. Everything has consequences, and the consequences of your actions join with the consequences of other people's to form the big soup of life.'

'Rendering the consequences of your actions inconsequential?'

'Not quite. But what about the woman you could have chosen to spend your life with but didn't? Can we miss someone we hardly knew, or knew so long ago that they're now fossilised in our memory?'

'Why are you asking yourself these questions? Why now?'

He was wearing a pink shirt, which, I guessed, he thought matched the russet stripe of his pin-striped suit. To my mind it was a mistaken choice. But what did I know about this kind of dress? I had never worn a suit in my life. No, that wasn't true – there had been funerals and marriages, not least my own.

'I don't know. Perhaps because at the weekend I was clearing out the basement and I unearthed remnants of my past. You know, photographs and letters from girlfriends long since gone from my life. I suppose it roused in me a curiosity as to how different things might have been. I'm not saying I'm unhappy about my life as it is – it just gave me a glimpse into how it could be. The decisions we take that turn out to be life-changing are made with the same amount of consideration as putting on the kettle. It's only with hindsight we recognise them to be what they were.'

Chapter 7

Howth, 1976

I picked up the money Hutchinson had left on the bar. Thoughts of Fitz melted away and the weekend opened up like a flower.

I rang Cahill from the public phone by the entrance to the pub and was surprised when he answered. Ever since he had managed to wangle a Yamaha 125 out of his folks he was seldom to be found at home. He explained his presence today by telling me it was part of a new regime his parents had cobbled together to ensure he'd pass his Leaving Certificate next June. He said he was pissed off about it because Carol Malcolm was having a party. A last bash before her and all her gorgeous schoolmates were packed away to boarding school. There'd be stacks of women. When I told him about the fiver, he said, 'Here, fuck the Leaving, I'll see you at your place at eight.' It was like old times.

I got home and had a bath, put on clean clothes and was glad to find, when I got downstairs, that the house was empty apart from Granny and Ann.

My grandmother was a woman of few words. She sat straight-backed in her tweed skirt and blue cardigan staring with grey eyes at the television screen. Ann, my kid sister, had her knees parked under a footstool while she paid homage to her favourite television programme, *The Famous Mr Ed*. I sprawled on the couch, warm in the knowledge that in my pocket was a five-pound note.

Mr Ed, a talking horse, was giving Wilbur, his owner, a hard time about the diet Wilbur was supposed to be on when I heard Cahill's bike pull up outside. I stood up. 'I'll be seeing you,' I said, not taking my eyes off the television.

'Granny, Seán's going,' Ann said. Granny muttered something about it'd probably be another week before they'd see me again.

Cahill seemed fascinated by the fifty-pence piece he had managed to liberate from his ole fella's pocket as he lay drunk on the kitchen floor. He sat there turning it over in his fingers, reluctant to send it across the bar in exchange for pints. Perhaps it was giving him something to focus on. Our conversation certainly wasn't. I couldn't conjure up interest in his tales from school and there was fuck-all point in talking to him about life down the pier. So, the only subject left was women. And he rattled off a list of his latest conquests, so long and elaborate that it couldn't have been true. And it wasn't even hard to look impressed. To be able to dream up this stuff was a feat of a kind. It just didn't do much for conversation. After two pints, we headed for the party.

He was right about one thing: the place was packed with women. And there was no sign of parents anywhere.

The house was close to where I lived but it might as well have been on a different continent. A curved gravel drive hid it from the road. Inside, hallways led to high-ceilinged rooms that tingled with cut glass and cold marble. You could get lost just looking for a toilet.

We headed for the den. Prior knowledge told us that was where the action would be. People were sitting around the floor in groups. Deep Purple pumped from giant speakers. I found a stack of bottled beer and brought one to Cahill. He had aligned himself with two girls who were standing by the bust of a man with long hair. The statue stared past them, looking even more bored by Cahill's banter than the two girls.

I sat on a leather couch. At my elbow, on the other side of the armrest, was a mass of blonde curls. The owner was joking and laughing with friends sitting by the wall in front of her. She had an English accent. This made her instantly worldly, exotic and, to my mind, a thousand times more sexually experienced than me.

Some guy by the wall was rabbiting on about music. He was using words like 'authenticity' and 'integrity'. Blonde Curls, whose face I couldn't see, was having none of it. She told him he was so full of shit his eyes were brown. I broke up laughing at this and told her she was right. He got up and left and we didn't see him again. The others by the wall drifted into a low-volume cloud of their own talk, which left me and Curls together but not together. We began to bounce comments over the armrest. Her observations were good; they made me laugh. I was enjoying the conversation, which was odd. Up to now, talking to women had been a cat-and-mouse farce fuelled by the end desire to achieve orgasm.

Obscured from my direct vision as she was, I could only catch glimpses of her face when she turned to listen or to speak. When, finally, she stood up, I was dumbstruck. She was tall and thin. Clear blue eyes shone from an oval face framed in curls.. It was the sort of face you'd only ever see staring at you from a magazine rack. Except it moved, changed, had expression. Words flowed from it, unaware and independent of it.

She crossed in front of me, then sat and smiled. It was a big, open smile. I said I had to go to the toilet.

Once there, I sat on the side of the bath. If I'd seen her on the street I would have just gazed as she passed. But now, not only had the ice broken, it had melted. And what terrified me was, she liked me. I put my head in my hands to think. She's only a person. She's found someone to talk to, no big deal. Just go down there and carry on the conversation, because in a few minutes some handsome hunk will walk in and she'll smile at me and say, 'See ya!'

When I got back down she was standing in the doorway of the den. 'I thought you must have flushed yourself down the loo,' she said, with a laugh that liquefied my insides.

'There are easier ways out of here.' I was running now on pure nerves.

'You want to go?'

'No . . . I don't know why I said that.'

She leant forward and kissed me. Everything faded as a squall of desire screamed through me. After the kiss, she laughed. It was a light laugh, as though she had surprised herself too. I felt as though I'd been airlifted to a tropical beach somewhere in paradise.

'Would you like a drink?' she asked.

'Yes. Anything.'

When she came back, she was carrying a white wine and a whiskey. She sat down and handed me the whiskey. 'I'm Emma,' she said.

'I'm Seán.'

'I know.' She laughed again. 'Don't get conceited. All we have to entertain us down in St Helen's is talk, so everything gets an airing, eventually.'

'Nice to think I got an airing.'

'Oh, you did.'

'Now I'm getting insecure.'

'Don't.'

We snuggled on the couch and, as our talk flowed easily, I felt as if it was the first time in a long time that I had talked to anyone.

Every word gave birth to the possibility of a whole new subject, and every subject grew so it was like something floating, something you could see all sides of. Look, there's the underbelly, and here comes the funny side, and there's the marching strains of seriousness off to do battle with the buckets in the bath. And sometimes we'd stop and I'd find myself staring at her. Then we'd either laugh or kiss, and if it was a kiss it was driven by something raw and wild, but not dangerous, nothing scary. And it dawned on me that maybe between Emma and me there was a balance. And with balance nothing was to be avoided, everything could be tackled, because if it got too scary or weird there was a counterweight that could bring you back to the centre. So just looking at her, her face, her eyes, made me feel calm and happy. Kissing her was so far from the self-conscious nonsense I had had with other girls that it was like kissing for the first time. Once we found ourselves sitting in silence for a while; we just laughed and I stroked her face.

After some time, she told me that she was tired and heading to bed. 'You sleep here on the couch,' she said, 'I'll think of you.'

After she'd gone, I lay there trying to go over the conversation. I couldn't. Concentration was swept aside by joy and then by sleep.

When I saw her the next morning, she was in the kitchen with Carol. They were in their dressing gowns cutting fruit.

'Look, it's the couch man. He can walk!' Carol said, without looking up. Had she seen my reflection in the melon?

'Sit down – we're going to give you a healthy breakfast,' Emma said. They hovered about me, replacing plates I had just emptied with new ones. I was getting full and having difficulty in communicating with Emma. We shared looks and smiled, but it wasn't like last night. Maybe we were both a bit embarrassed at how close we'd got, or maybe it was the fear that we couldn't recreate it. I felt the sudden need to escape, to get some space. I said I had to be somewhere.

At the front door, Emma said, 'Thanks for last night. It was . . .'
She was looking at the ground.

'For me too.'

'Really?'

'Of course.'

She smiled. I didn't know what to say. I put my arms around her.

'We're not going back until Tuesday,' she said.

'That's the day after tomorrow.'

She nodded.

'Let's meet then, tomorrow, in town,' I suggested.

'Great! Where?'

'Bewley's on Grafton Street at ten.'

'OK. I'll wait outside.'

We kissed, then I turned and walked down the driveway without disturbing a pebble.

The next morning, I got up and joined the last of the rush-hour into town. As the minutes passed and the distance between me and Bewley's decreased, my stomach tightened. I got off two stops early so I could buy a paper, walk, breathe myself into a state of some kind of calm.

I arrived with ten minutes to spare and went inside for a coffee. I sat at a seat where I could watch the door. I took out the paper and looked at the headlines. I couldn't touch the coffee – my fingers were so sweaty I was afraid I'd drop the cup. Why was I doing this? Why was she doing this? Who was she expecting to meet? I wished I could fold myself into my newspaper and be tossed into a bin by some passing customer. When I next looked up at the door, she was there, staring down Grafton Street in the direction I would have come.

She was wearing a white woollen polo neck, a short denim skirt and black boots. She was devastatingly gorgeous and I felt way out of my depth. I left the table and walked towards her. She was a long hallway away, I could easily duck down a stairwell and disappear back into my life.

Then she turned and saw me. I stopped dead. It was too late. She was coming towards me. 'Hi,' she said, casual and pleasant. She was carrying a camera bag.

'Would you like a coffee?' I asked.

'Love one.'

We got the coffee at the counter and took a seat. She said nothing, just smiled. The tightness I was feeling disappeared. 'It's good to see you,' I said.

'You too. How long do you have?'

'All day.'

'Brilliant! Me too. What would you like to do?'

'Well, we could go on the piss, get cultural or just go for a wander.'

'Maybe all three, but in reverse. I want to take some pictures.'

'Pictures of what?'

'Just anything that pops up. I've managed to get out of sport by persuading them I'll be the school photographer so I have to come up with a few projects. It's OK, though, it's fun. We need to capture the essence of the city with this.' She held up the bag.

'Great! A mission.'

'Is it possible?'

'I'm your man.'

We never got to a pub, a museum or an art gallery. We walked the crowded pavements and Emma showed me a side of street life I had never noticed before.

'Do you see that policeman?' she asked. We had just come through Merchant's Arch. On the opposite side of the road, people were gathered at the foot of the Ha'penny Bridge, waiting for the traffic to let them cross. A policeman was standing at the back of the gathering, head and shoulders above everyone else. 'See what he's doing?'

I looked blankly.

'With his nose,' Emma said, with a hint of impatience.

He was drawing his lips down over his upper teeth. Then he'd twitch his nose from side to side.

'He's going to pick it, I know he is,' she said, lifting up a device she had already explained to me was a light meter. She took readings, then adjusted the barrel of the lens. She held the camera beneath her chin and watched him. He looked right, left, then slipped his index finger into his nostril. As he swivelled his hand from the wrist to bury it deeper, the shutter clicked. 'You beaut,' she said.

Half an hour later, we were walking down by the quays when she stopped and looked at the ground. 'Where would you get it?' A pair of trousers was lying on the pavement.

'It looks like the guy just abandoned them as he was walking.' She stepped out into the street, fiddled with the light meter again and clicked.

I glanced back at the trousers as we walked away, still not sure what she had seen.

At other times, things happened fast. We were walking up Tara Street when Emma spotted a large woman in a flowery apron in the doorway of her shop. She folded her arms and bent forward at the hips so as she could get a good view of the street. Emma stepped out on to the road adjusting her lens, then turned towards the woman. She shot off half a dozen pictures, holding the camera at hip level, and never stopped walking. The woman in the doorway had no idea she had been photographed.

By Fitzwilliam Square, I tried to take some pictures of her. She became self-conscious as soon as I lifted the camera so I slipped it on to automatic and, a few minutes later, snapped four or five pictures before she noticed.

It was dark when we leant against the railings to wait for the bus that would take her back to Carol's. It dawned on us both that once it appeared we would not be seeing each other for a long time. We stopped talking and stared at the oncoming traffic. When it came, she squeezed my hand and said, 'Promise you'll write?' We kissed and then she was getting on to the bus.

'I'll see you at Christmas?' she asked, from the platform.

'Before, if I can manage it.'

Her expression changed. 'What do you mean?'

I watched her disappear, holding on to the silver bar, a quizzical smile between the curls.

Chapter 8

Bristol, 2008

As I was sitting around in my new office, it crossed my mind that I might have stumbled, inadvertently, into the type of harmony sought by the disciples of feng shui, despite the faint but persistent odours of damp stone and fresh chemicals. Or perhaps it was because of them. Through this combination I had created an essence capable of putting the soul at peace. Nirvana could be reached in a paint tin and some old basement masonry. It made as much sense as anything else.

But the place was not without its drawbacks. I quickly discovered that when you worked from home you lost the shield that an outside office provides. Once people realise you're permanently anchored to the other end of your home telephone they think of you as a service that will sort out details in their lives that they've overlooked. It could be anything, from picking up kids from football to getting charcoal for a barbecue. Or, worse, they just want to chat. All of this, along with the normal domestic din of washing machines, answering machines and overhead footfalls, combined to click the work button to the 'off' position.

It didn't seem to bother the clients. For the most part, I think they enjoyed the change of venue. Perhaps because it was a different space it prompted most to take a fresh approach. There were exceptions, of course, and among them Peter Reed and Kate Wren stood out.

He appeared sullen when he arrived for their Monday-evening appointment. His concern was for future dates. He was launching a new band, which meant going to the States, so the next two weeks were out. Privately, I was relieved because the noise levels upstairs at that time of the evening were just too high, despite everyone up there doing their best to live on tiptoe.

We arranged a date for three weeks' time. Then Peter sat back. I knew he had come to a point at which the novelty had worn off and was becoming aware of the chore before him. From my point of view this was an interesting stage – he was ripening. He would now either take on what was in front of him or close the game.

Kate began by talking about a row they'd had at the weekend, then drifted into how she dealt with anger. She knew, she said, that in the past she had buried it but lately she was becoming aware that it had Lazarus qualities, as she put it. And when it arose it came out in a much more unsightly state than when it went in. Every so often I'd look at Peter to see if he was involved. He hadn't said a word for more than twenty minutes. All I could detect was disinterest.

When she stopped, I made some general comment to draw him in. He ignored it. I asked him if something was bothering him.

He shrugged. 'I don't think you know what you're doing.'

'I see,' I said.

'Well, like, we've been coming here week after week and we're not getting anywhere. Personally I think we'd be better off spending the money on ourselves, you know, a meal, a holiday – anything but this.'

'What we're attempting here, Peter, is difficult, and it's slow.'

Kate turned to me. 'If we felt we were making any kind of progress maybe it'd be different.'

'Yeah,' Peter said. 'Like a plan, something like that, you know, something where we can see what you're doing.'

At least they were agreeing with one another. 'You both have patterns of behaviour you use because you don't imagine there's a choice. I can't dip into your heads and rearrange them like a mechanic doing your brakes. It's something you have to do for yourselves. I'm here as a guide.'

'And exactly how do you do that?' Peter's voice was heavy with sarcasm.

'By doing what we're doing.'

'I'm sick of this,' he said.

'Peter, stop!' Kate interrupted. 'Look, Peter's frustrated. We both are. I guess we thought that a couple of sessions would be enough.'

'Not a couple of sessions,' Peter said, 'but this is, like, our – what? – tenth? And if you were any good we should have started feeling different by now.'

'So what do you want to do?' I asked.

'There you go again. Do you never have solutions?'

'Peter, I'm not going to produce a colour board of your emotional options. It's your life, your relationship. You decide from the choices you make available to yourself.'

Peter stood. 'Well, I'm going to exercise one of my options right now.' He looked at Kate. 'Come on.'

'Peter, sit down!' she said.

'And what? Listen to more pat answers and sweet little clichés that this guy learnt at the Charlatan School of Therapy?' He strode towards the stairs.

'Wait!' Kate yelled. Then she turned to me and said, 'Sorry,' as she followed him.

I listened to their footfalls in the hallway upstairs, then the front door slam.

The next day I phoned Geraldine to see how she was getting on. She complained about the size of her new space but said that, in general, it was working. It was nice to be surrounded by some old faces. She had taken to going for an after-work tipple at the pub around the corner. 'They do a good lunch there too. Maybe we should meet. You sound like you need to talk.'

'How can you tell?'

'It's called perception, not something men know much about. I can do one o'clock tomorrow.'

'Great, I'll see you there.'

It turned out to be a pleasant place with a small courtyard where we sat in the spring sunshine, watching the lunchtime crowds. Geraldine was drinking a glass of white wine. I sipped Coke. She looked older in raw daylight but, then, she was probably thinking the same about me. 'Us sitting here proves that vampires can take the sunlight,' she said.

'Maybe we should do this more often. Get immune to it altogether.'

'Well, I'll sit in the sunshine drinking white wine any day.' She was holding the glass up, smiling.

'There was a day when I did little else, although whether the sun was shining or not wasn't terribly important,' I said.

'You know, I've always felt there was a drunk lurking inside me and, given the slightest opportunity, he'd be up and out and have me sprawled in a gutter somewhere.'

'Interesting you refer to your drunk as "he".'

'Don't start analysing me, you cheeky bastard.'

The waiter, a pale man squinting in the brightness, appeared and placed the food in front of us. It smelt of garlic and, for a moment, with the sun warming the side of my face, I was abroad. If I closed my eyes I could hear the Mediterranean lapping at the shoreline a hundred yards away. Suddenly it felt like a long time since I had done nothing.

'Things changed, then, since yesterday?' Geraldine asked.

'No, I'm just basking in the ambience of here.'

'I hope it stays fine for you.'

'I had a client walk yesterday.'

Her eyes sharpened. 'I see.'

'There was a time I would have been proud of it, thinking it indicated I'd driven them forward, a little too hard, maybe. This one, though, was different.'

'Probably wasn't. What's different is you.'

'Me?'

'Come on, Seán, you've got problems with Lynn, problems with the kids, and now it's the clients. You're in a slump, you need a break.'

'What are you saying?'

'Seán, you're a wonderful man and an excellent counsellor. If you've any fault it's you try too hard. So stop. You're tired. You need to rejuvenate.'

'And how do I do that exactly?'

'Stop playing games with me. You know what I'm saying is right.'

'Do you have any idea how irritating it is to be in the company of someone who's always right?'

'I've been wrong about so much it's not funny, but I'm right about you now.'

'Geraldine, I can't just get up from my life and walk away. There are thousands of reasons for me to be around.'

'I'm sure there are. And you're hobbling from one to the other unable to do any of them properly. You have a choice, and it couldn't be simpler. Take a break and do yourself and everyone around you a favour.'

'And if I don't?'

'You can work that one out for yourself.'

'No, tell me, what'll happen if I don't?'

'You'll crack up or break down or transport yourself sideways out of the picture. I don't know. Just do it.'

After lunch, I walked her back to her office. We promised we'd do this again soon and I also promised that I'd think about what she'd said. Then I walked uphill towards the cliff face of brickwork that was the council headquarters. Standing aloft on its green copper roof, a golden unicorn shone in the blue. Its head looked at the Central Library while its shadowy posterior stared down upon Unity Street and me.

Listening to good advice is like watching a good film. It happens in front of you but it can't become a part of your life because, in reality, it has nothing to do with you. It's someone else's solution.

I walked to the waterfront, past the media centre then between the giant tulips of the pedestrian bridge. The sun caught the ripples of the water beneath and turned everything into a dazzle of stainless steel.

It was cooler in the shade of the red-brick buildings of Queen's Square. I sauntered in the speckled shadow beneath trees alive with the greenery of their new leaves. It wasn't until I saw Redcliffe Bridge at the other end of the square that it dawned on me I was walking towards Roland's yard.

The dogs came bounding up to me when I reached the gate, both barking. The black one was a scampering young mongrel, all tail and tongue, the other a yellow Labrador, which had fattened since I'd last seen him. Their barking brought Roland to the door of the shed. 'My God, two visits in the same year?'

'Careful, Roland, sarcasm is a sign of impotence.'

'What the . . .? Come here, there's something I want to show you.'

Inside the shed there was a mass of detail, and all of it coated in a fine layer of fawn sawdust. Along every wall, in every corner, benches and machinery stood. In front of me, on the floor, long pieces of curved timber lay scattered like the limbs of a giant insect. Further up, the floor had been cleared and another length of wood was supported on half a dozen blocks.

Roland walked up to it, then turned and smiled at me. 'What do you think?'

'What is it?'

'It's a keel for fuck's sake. What did you think it was? My newest entry for Tate Modern? Imagine an old seadog like you not knowing a keel when you see one.'

'I knew what it was. I meant what's it for?'

He laughed. 'You're more full of shit than Christmas pudding.'

I walked up to it. It was about forty-five feet long, a foot square and an orangey shade of red. 'Nice,' I said. 'What kind of wood is it?'

'Opepe. African hardwood.'

'This is the start of the pilot cutter?'

He nodded.

'So someone came up with the cash?'

His expression faded. 'No. No, not quite. Not yet anyway.'

'So how did you . . .?'

'Took a loan on the house.'

'Allison know about this?'

'I had to do something, Seán.'

'You're a good boat builder.'

'She'll be a fucking beaut.' He put his hands into his pockets and stepped back from the keel. 'So, now,' he said, 'I take it you've finally come to look at your boat?'

It was only then I remembered the white yacht. 'You still have her?'

70

'Yeah. To be frank, I've done nothing about it, been too busy with this.'

'Well, if it's here and I'm here it would be silly not to.'

This seemed to slip him back on to his optimistic track. 'Step this way,' he said and strode out of the shed.

He slid the hatch open and indicated that I should go first. As I made my way down, I was hit by a mixture of rich odours that took me back through the decades, old wood, still air, with a touch of bilge water.

Below, it was surprisingly deep and, looking ahead, seemed very long. I was standing in the galley, which was neatly laid out, everything to hand. Forward, in the next section, I could see upholstered settees and a narrow, highly varnished oak table. The walls were made of a lighter wood and decorated with two framed paintings, a large oil lamp and a bookcase on either side. The pictures were of stormy scenes, in oils. They were good. Beyond the saloon, there was a cabin with a double bed. Here, too, it was decorated with oil lamps and lockers that had carved wooden doors, all of which lay under thick coats of varnish. It was not how I would have done the interior of this boat but there was nothing distasteful about it. It was just that all the varnish down below made you feel like a fly caught in amber.

'Up forward there you've got your oilskin locker,' Roland said, from behind me. 'Still got all the old chap's stuff in it, poor man.'

'Did you not sent it back?'

'She said she didn't want any of it. Even his stores are aboard. Cans and cans of food, charts, safety gear, everything. Come on, I'll show you the deck.'

Roland wasn't long into his tour of the deck before I realised that this was a very well-cared-for boat. Everything, from the hinges on the hatchways to the blocks and levers of the running rigging, had been oiled and maintained. There was even a back splice on the flag halyard.

I interrupted Roland as he was explaining how the anchor windlass worked: 'Look, I can see she's a beautiful boat, and at the money you mentioned she's a bargain.'

'But?'

'Well, I haven't really thought about it much, you know. I mean a boat, especially a boat of this size, isn't something I had in mind at the—'

Roland held up his hand. 'Say no more! Seán, I'm not here to sell you anything, I just wanted to show you around. Look,' he said, producing the keys from his pocket, 'these live in the gas locker. Some time soon come down here, bring Lynn, if you like, sit in the cockpit and have a think about it, take her for a spin. She'll be just sitting here.'

'Thanks, Roland. By the way, what's her name?'

'The boat's name is *Kittigani* – it's African, means something about love or destiny.'

'Interesting. Thanks, Roland, I appreciate this.'

'Not a problem.'

As I walked home I smiled, thinking that, between them, Geraldine and Roland had given me permission and the means to escape. Back home, the house was empty. I had forty-five minutes before my next appointment. And in that time I'd have a go at treating myself as a client. I went down to the basement with the aim of writing down all the ways I could improve communication between me and Lynn. But, looking at the blank page, my thinking mechanism seemed unable or unwilling to engage. I clicked the button on the answer machine and sat back. Kate Wren's voice filled the room, asking me to phone her back.

I returned to the blank page. I wrote 'talking/listening', circled it, then stared at it. This was impossible. Yes, we had to talk, yes, we had to listen, but how? If she wasn't at school teaching, she was at a parents' evening or a meeting, or she'd be sitting on the couch correcting a mountain of homework. And my head was so full of what filled my day that all I wanted to do at the end of it was plonk myself in front of the TV and turn off. Perhaps I was afraid of what I'd say if I did start talking. Or what I'd have to listen to.

The page was filling with doodles, Disney characters impaled on nails. The image of Mickey Mouse's bleeding head caught me off guard. I crumpled the sheet and tossed it towards the wastepaper basket.

I picked up the phone and called Kate. She said she was sorry, Peter got like that sometimes. He could be very impatient. She said she'd like to continue the sessions while he was away. This threw me. Going from couples to singles counselling could have its problems. I was just about to say I'd call her back about it when she said, 'It's just that I feel it would be good to talk without Peter being there. Is that awful?'

'No, it's not.' I scanned the diary. 'OK, can you do two o'clock next Monday?'

'That would be great. Thank you, Seán.'

It was difficult telling Philip about Peter, so I hit it straight on. 'I feel inadequate, and stupid too. Throw in stupid.'

'It's in.'

'Thanks. Geraldine says I need a break.'

He looked at me.

'Philip, I can't. Karen's going to St Katherine's in September, so there'll be fees to pay.' Now I did feel stupid. What was I doing parading information like this in front of him? The only purpose it could have was to distract him. But from what?

'Are you a practising Catholic?' he asked.

'No, I'm a recovering Catholic. I ran a mile from the thing as soon as I could.'

'So why are you sending your daughter to a Catholic school?'

'I don't know. It's Lynn's idea. She's in charge of the learning in our house.'

'It's interesting that you would subject your daughter to an environment that you yourself ran from.'

In the silence that followed it dawned on me what I was trying to distract him from: that I had arranged to take on Kate as a single client. I exhaled. I had to tell him: anything less would render the time I spent here ridiculous.

'Kate Wren has asked me if she can see me on her own. I've said yes.'

Philip stared at me for a long time. Eventually he said, 'This business can be lonely. We're all human . . .'

'So you think I'm back crunching the gravel on the long road to self-destruction?'

'Seán, as you well know, it's not that long.'

Chapter 9

On a Sunday evening, almost two weeks after I'd said goodbye to Emma, I walked down the pier to the *Mary Jo*. It was a good feeling to have a boat as a destination. Since the stitches had come out the week before I had done nothing. All the rhythms I knew of home and Howth had changed. School-friends were wrapped up in a new year, new books and a tightened resolve. The harbour was empty. And so, too, at night, were the pubs. The only thing I looked forward to were letters from Emma.

Every couple of days another arrived, fat and pink. They rambled like our conversations. But, in a way, they were more intriguing because the rambling was not stopped by conversation. Left on her own she became poetical and spiritual, her humour underpinning it all. I wrote back. It was fun. Nothing to stop me but the weight of the pages building. I told her it was possible I was falling in love with her. In her reply she asked me what I based that on: three hours on a couch and a stroll through Dublin with a camera? She said my idea of love was unrealistic and if I didn't watch it I'd land on my arse. That letter was shorter than the rest. She talked about how much she hated the nuns – they were as far from Christians as it was possible to get. In my reply I told her I had to go back fishing so that from now I'd be writing less. But the only good thing was that fishing would give me enough money to go down and rescue her.

Then a package arrived. It was the photographs. They were black and white, bigger than I'd expected. The one of the policeman was brilliant. Everyone in the crowd was blank and bored and slightly hazy while he was in sharp focus, unaware of anything except the excavation of his nose. It was the kind of photograph that made you think, That had to have been set up. As soon as I saw the one of the trousers I knew exactly what she had seen. It was as if the wearer had been sucked up into the sky at such a rate that they had dropped off him and collapsed where he had stood. But the best was the woman in the shop doorway. The detail of her apron mimicked the mass in her shop window and made her look as if she had become part of her shop, or her shop had become part of her. On the back Emma had written, 'Nothing lies like a photograph! Thanks for an unforgettable day.'

The *Mary Jo* had been built in Germany and delivered only months before. You could still smell the grease and hydraulic fluid from her winches. The interior was covered with grey-flecked Formica and it was spotless. There was a toilet, too, in its own cubicle, and a shower, things unseen on any fishing boat up to now. The wheelhouse was space age, with a cushioned leather seat in front of the wheel that swivelled. Switches and knobs in neat rows decorated black panels either side of the compass. Next to them, in one corner, there was a radar, and in the other a sonar. Behind you, as you sat, there was a bank of radios. The VHF was a slim black box with a microphone clipped to one side. There was also a single side band radio that could transmit and receive worldwide. It had a dial the span of my hand, with switches and knobs studded between the slats for the speakers. On deck there was a mass of gadgets that would make life a treat.

The problem with the boat was her skipper. John Grimmer was now in his fifties. He had come from an island on the west coast of Ireland and married into one of the big fishing families in Howth. He had been the golden boy when he'd first arrived on the West Pier – a hard worker who had become popular with the skippers and deckhands.

As soon as he got his skipper's ticket he was given a grant by BIM, the Irish Fisheries Board, and set off into the Irish Sea in a new boat, determined to make rapid repayments. This he did and was given a bigger boat. With it, he broke records for herring landings and, in the summer, landed more cod than anyone else. It was about this time that he married and was seen, for the first time, in the local pubs. He was popular so he was almost always surrounded by pints and company.

When things began to slide, they went slowly. So much so that it wasn't noticed by the people at BIM. They kept urging him into bigger and better boats. So now he was the sole owner of the *Mary Jo*, the fleet's finest. He fished her every day for the first three weeks but he wouldn't stay out at night. By seven each evening she was tied up and he was back in his house, enjoying the comfort of an old armchair and the contents of a bottle of Smirnoff. If he was asked about this, he'd say he was still testing the boat, a reply muttered without much care as to the reaction it provoked in the listener. It was only out of respect for the man's former abilities that no one questioned him further.

After several weeks, the winch packed up, which seemed to validate his approach. So, with hardly a fish scale in her scuppers, the *Mary Jo* sat by the harbour wall while John Grimmer sat in his armchair and picked up a bottle instead of a telephone. When BIM contacted him he told them what he thought was wrong. It was they who found an engineering firm capable of making the repairs.

In all, the *Mary Jo* was out of action for a month. During this time John Grimmer became so lost in alcohol that the West Pier, and the life that teemed on it, became foreign to him. Everything he saw when his wife drove him down there was an imitation and temporary. Soon, order would be restored, the scum that now occupied his crew's quarters would disappear and, in their place, he'd find good men once again.

On the first morning I was aboard, I was woken by the sound of footsteps coming down the ladder to the crew's quarters. The air filled with the warm stench of vodka and tobacco. His hands and face were puce. His eyes, two small knots in heavily varnished wood, were focused on something distant. He made his way across the cabin and stood over Scully. Below Scully, Hutch lay stretched and snoring, a small female face at his shoulder. All were asleep. A phlegm-flapping rattle echoed up from Grimmer's guts, followed by a thick mutter: 'We're not going out today.' He said it twice, then made his way to the ladder and climbed the steps back to his waiting car. I turned over in my bunk, glad of the extra sleep his departure ensured.

After a similar announcement the following morning, Scully declared that he, as first mate, was going to fish the *Mary Jo*. There was a precedent for this, he said. And it was true that on other boats the mate often took over if the skipper was away. But those were boats on which the crews would have worked together long enough to become a unit, everyone knowing their place. Scully could call on the precedent but there was little parallel in our case. He was just bored and broke and frustrated. They all were. In the galley, the shelves were empty. The diesel tank was low, and all that expensive gear on deck was freezing up from lack of use.

As I watched Scully declare his intentions, I caught a glimpse of something that surprised me. It was ambition. Scully's circumstances denied him access to routes open to others. He was known as an ex-con, and a violent one at that. He had some crazy ideas about politics, and the politics of catching fish. All in all, he was too wild for the conservatives down the pier and they ran the place. They were happy to watch him scurry about on boats that would give him neither money nor a chance to prove himself.

And Scully's own mind was never disciplined enough to overcome these obstacles. He could intellectually deride any attempt on his own behalf to better himself. But now, beneath the cover of Grimmer's alcohol problems, Scully had got himself into a powerful position. Although this would not have gone unnoticed, those who might object were far too busy making their own living to do much about it. Whether or not Scully had planned any of this I didn't know. I doubted it. His mind floated far too high above the squabble to plan anything that would need this kind of detail. But he was perfectly capable of taking advantage of an opportunity.

After Grimmer's visit the next morning, when he told us yet again that we would not be going out, Scully sprang from his bunk. 'Right,' he said, 'come on.'

Hutch untangled his fingers from the head of curls that lay beside him, slapped his tongue off the roof of his mouth and said, 'Do you think this is such a good idea, Scull?'

'I'm taking her out. If you're coming you're coming. If not, fuck up on the dock now.'

This stirred Doyle. 'No Captain Bligh shit now, Scully. If we're going out, we're going out as equals.'

'You can be as equal as you like. I'm starting up this engine and whoever doesn't want to be aboard can fuck off.' Scully was looking at Hutch's bedmate. 'She has to go.'

Her name was Claire. She had an accent that was a velvet blend of Scots and Northern Irish. She had come into Findlater's under

Hutch's arm one night about a week before and had set up camp there ever since. In the pub she confined herself to smiles and, aboard at night, she'd send us all into the wilds of fantasy as we lay there listening to the slow, sucking sounds coming up from Hutch's sleeping bag. In the mornings she'd dress as though unaware of her bodily difference. She also seemed unaware of our reaction to it.

Hutch sat up. 'Wait just a minute, old son.'

Claire sat up too, her breasts a distraction to all but her and Hutch. She put a hand on him. 'I'll go, Hutch. It's OK, I'll see you tonight.'

'If we're back tonight,' Scully said.

Concern crossed Hutch's face. He looked at Claire. 'You sure?'

She smiled and nodded.

Doyle leapt from his bunk. 'Right, yiz bastards, to sea, to bollocky sea.'

We slipped between the harbour walls into a grey swell, past Ireland's Eye and off to the fishing ground known as the H and H, where the H line that ran north and south crossed the H line that ran east and west. It was a good place to fish because it was mostly free of snags. Everyone went back to his bunk, except Hutch, who had elected to steer. It would take an hour and a half to get there.

Below, Scully was boisterous. He sat with his back to a bulkhead reading aloud from a copy of *Love Story*. Each sentence was ridiculed into the sentimental goo he thought it to be. Then he flung the book on the floor, declaring it 'total shite'. I laughed, and Doyle slept. As I watched Scully's performance I wondered at the legality of what we were doing. Whatever it was, I was pleased to be part of this breakaway group. We were rebels in a society of rebels.

The day went well. We shot the net just before ten and hauled at two. We shot again and hauled for the last time at six. We steamed home with fourteen boxes of cod and eight of other assorted white fish. By the time we were squared away and berthed up, it was nine thirty.

Claire appeared almost the moment our mooring lines were ashore. We all walked down the pier together that night with salt in our hair and a day's fishing under our belts. It was a good feeling. Drinks came from Claire. Scully was silent. He sat back, observing Hutch and Claire through dark, narrowed eyes. His mind was working, but on what was anyone's guess.

The following morning we were casting off when Grimmer and his wife pulled up in the car. They sat like watermarks behind the windscreen. From the wheelhouse Scully let out a roar. 'Never mind that bollox, slacken off.' It was six in the morning and the sun was coming up over a flat green sea. We were one of the last to leave.

We hauled that evening and were just about to clear the decks for the steam home when Scully lowered the wheelhouse window and gave the order to reshoot. This was met with silence. Shooting the net again meant more money at the end of the week, something nobody would object to. Neither would they object to the work involved. It was the authority the demand represented that had caused the silence. But just at that pivotal point of indecision, Scully spoke again: 'Look, we may as well – it's a lovely evening.' Then he gave one of his laughs. And there was something about the way Scully laughed that put everything into a perspective where nothing mattered.

He drove the boat around broadside into the light evening breeze and we lowered the orange mesh back into the darkening blue.

'Better boil up some fish, Seán,' Scully said from the window, as I was leaving the deck. 'There's some spuds in the locker under the sink.'

This would be the first proper meal eaten aboard the *Mary Jo*. Up to now, cooking had been a joke: jam sandwiches and the promise of pints to come. Although, what I served up that night might not have officially constituted a meal. I forgot to clean the potatoes, so it was mud soup with lumps of fish floating in it. But it was eaten in good humour.

There was no drink aboard. Scully deemed it out of the question. To my surprise, the others agreed. They had agreed to his other conditions, too, when they had been talked about over pints. But those conversations had had a theoretical flavour. Nothing had been discussed since the boat had been taken over. Scully's basic idea was that the share system was good, it was a motivator, but the skippers took too much. When he ran things, the boat's expenses would be taken out and the rest of the money would be divided equally between all the crew.

He sat there now, forking mud into himself, his black hair against the grey-flecked Formica, smiling his rat smile, a cross between Fagin and Jesus. But, whatever role he was playing for himself, the rest of us were not being cooperative extras. Hutch was in the wheelhouse cursing the compass light. Doyle was using a fork to dig at a lump in his hand, and I was busy controlling the contents of the table as they slid back and forth with the motion of the sea.

'What are we going to do about Grimmer?' I asked.

'What do you mean?' Scully said, annoyed at being dragged from thoughts far superior.

'I mean money. Are we going to give him any?'

'Are we fuck. He'd have us rot by the quay wall.'

The subject raised Doyle from his task. 'How are we going to split it?'

Scully's face, half hidden now in shadow, broke into a smile. 'Well, it's like this. On Saturday morning, I'll have it, and youse'll have to fight me for it.'

Doyle put down the fork and looked at him.

Scully said, 'All men get an equal share.'

'Yeah, but that's just the point. We're not all men, are we?'

Scully's eyes went from Doyle to me. 'You mean Cunthooks here?'

Doyle nodded. 'There's no way I'm giving my money to a fuckin' kid.'

'You think he works less than you?'

'I'm telling you, there's no fucking way.'

Scully's tone turned serious. 'Shut the fuck up now or you will be fighting me for it.'

'That'a boy, Scully,' roared Hutch, from the wheelhouse.

'And you can shut the fuck up too.'

Doyle was silent.

Scully looked at me. 'Marvellous thing, greed. It's the weight that stops the human race soaring. Without it, Communism would work and Catholicism would have been forgotten long ago.'

'Fair play to you, Scull, indoctrinate the little bollox,' Hutch's voice said, from the dark.

'Just fucking steer, you.'

While I was washing up, Hutch came into the galley and asked if there were any leftovers.

'You can't possibly want more of that.' I said.

'I do.'

'Well, there's a load of it in the pot.'

He fished out a plastic bag and angled the slush into it. 'Bring us up a cup of coffee when you're finished,' he said and went back to the wheelhouse, taking the bag with him.

I made two coffees when the galley was squared away and gave one to Hutch. We sipped and stared out of the window in silence. So far, the night was moonless. The sea and the sky were separated by one long straight line. A cluster of lights bounced some distance off to starboard – the Clogherhead fleet heading in. Off our bow, by many miles, were two cargo vessels, one heading south, the other north.

There was something comforting about being in the wheelhouse at night. The muted red from the instrument panel gave the place warmth. And there, fingers wrapped around a hot mug, you were free to wander in speech or thought.

'Where's Scully?' Hutch asked.

'In his bunk, I'd say.'

He lowered his voice. 'Right. Now listen. Take this bag of culinary delights here down to the hold, will you?' He was holding out the bag. I stood, staring at him. 'Claire's down there,' he said.

I knew he was serious. 'Why?'

'Scully won't have a woman aboard, it's bad luck, and she can't stop ashore.'

'Right,' I said, and took the bag. I walked out of the aft door to the deck. There, I watched the black furrows of the waves roll away behind us. The two parallel lines of the cables, as taut as iron bars, stretched out into our wake to the net far below.

I worked my way along the side of the wheelhouse, an obstacle course, swaying in the motion. At the hatch, I removed the cover boards and stared into the darkness.

Each time the net was hauled, the fish that were kept were gutted and sorted into boxes by size and type. These were then lowered into the hold where they were treated to a shovelful of ice and stacked into one of the pounds. Twice today I had been down there, once with Doyle and once with Scully. How had we not unearthed her? And what would have happened if we had?

I climbed down the ladder, whispering her name. It was a hell of a place to house a human. The pile of slowly melting ice in one of the pounds meant it was always cold and damp. The floor was a slimy mess from the leaking fish boxes.

At the end of the ladder, I called her name again. Silence. I wondered how much noise I could make without it travelling through the bulkhead to the sleeping Scully. I flicked the light switch and the place suddenly leapt into the damp, colourless hole it was. The sound of movement came from the far end.

'Seán? Seán, is that you?'

'Yes.' I followed the sound. She was crouched behind the boxes we had stacked earlier. 'I have some leftovers for you.'

She looked faded in the harsh light. The sleeping bag she was huddled in had been a bright nylon green, but now it was dark from the wet and the dirt. She peered at the food and smiled. 'Thanks,' she said. 'Are we not going back in tonight?'

'No.'

She started to eat, surprisingly dainty. 'I didn't know you were down here,' I said. It was a stupid thing to say. 'Would you like a cup of tea?'

She looked up from the bag. 'Oh, yes! Coffee would even be better, if you have some.'

'I can do that. Look, I'd better turn off the lights. But I'll leave the hatch open so at least you can get some air and watch the stars.'

'You're very sweet,' she said. I didn't know what to say to that. It was not what I was used to hearing in the hold of a fishing-boat.

'I'll see you in a minute.' I headed for the ladder.

'And, Seán?'

'Yeah?'

'I'd love a cigarette.'

'No problem.'

As soon as I got back up on deck I looked at the wheelhouse windows. Black plates speckled with salt. I could make out Hutch's features behind one. He was alone. When I got back to the galley, he was standing there.

'Is she all right?'

'Yeah, I think so. I'm making her a cup of coffee and she wants a smoke.'

'Do you think you could take the wheel for a couple of minutes and I'll bring it down to her?'

'Yeah, OK.'

When it was ready I took it to the wheelhouse.

'You've taken a watch before?' he asked.

'Not really, not with the gear down.'

It's very important for a fishing boat trawling a net to know its exact position so it can avoid dragging it over one of the many wrecks or other obstacles that lie on the seabed. These are marked with a large red X on the chart. Running the net across any of them meant it would 'come fast' and you'd lose the lot. To avoid this, most boats used the Decca navigation system. It consisted of a series of radio signals that criss-crossed the Irish Sea. These were picked up by a receiver and identified by a letter, then further divided into numbers.

Hutch looked at the two illuminated lines of the Decca readout. On both, the letter H appeared, followed by a line of numbers. He translated them into a position on the chart, then drew a line with his finger from our position along the path we would travel if we kept this direction.

'Right,' he said. 'No snags for a while. You'll be fine as long as you steer straight up this line. Can you follow it on the Decca?'

'Could you give me a compass course? I can do that.'

'I'll do better. Do you see that star there?'

I followed the line of his finger. 'The one to the left of the bright one?'

'You got it. Steer for that. I'll be back in a jiffy,' he said, lifting the mug.

I stood, legs spread, holding the wheel, pressure easing from one foot to the other as the boat rolled in the swell. I was aware that we were being held back. The weight of the great bulk we were dragging across the bed of the Irish Sea saw to that.

The sea was folds of blue so dark they were almost black in the troughs, yet on the crests a vague light danced – water grabbing the starlight and printing it on its own moving surface in a lacework of patterns that assembled and dispersed by the second. As it ran to the horizon, the sea darkened to an intense black. Above that straight line, the sky was a dark velvet covering that housed a thousand pinpricks, each with its own shape and light. Some stars pulsed like hearts, a different colour at every beat. Others held solid – a true yellow that did not flare or fall.

When the moon arrived, all these subtleties were washed away. That fool's light danced on the wave tops, gaudy in gold, leaving everything else to run to black. Only the most boisterous stars competed with it. But as it climbed, it lost its brazenness. It got smaller, too, and took on the colour of white gold. The sky around it had the texture of silk. And there it sat, a large bright fruit in a bowl of blue-black, bigger, but smaller, than everything around it.

Suddenly, it was all bleached by a beam of light so solid it rinsed everything inside the wheelhouse white and raised reflections from dull surfaces. For an instant, I thought it was an explosion, then realised it was constant. Shielding my eyes, I faced it.

A metallic voice blared: 'MFV *Mary Jo*, this is the frigate *Grace O'Malley* of the Irish Navy. Hold your course and speed. We are going to board you.'

Hutch stumbled up on to the deck, squinting. He tried to replace the cover boards to the hatch but the voice stopped him.

Footsteps came racing up from below. Scully and Doyle fell into the wheelhouse.

'What the fuck's going on?' Scully asked, confused, still half asleep.

'We're being boarded.'

'What are you doing on the wheel? Where's Hutch?'

As I pointed to him on the deck, I heard an outboard motor

scream into life some distance off. 'Fuck's sake,' Scully roared, and made for the aft door.

'This is Grimmer. It's got to be,' Doyle said, looking at Hutch's Christ-like form trapped in the white light.

I lowered the window and watched a handful of men scramble on to our deck from a large inflatable dinghy. They were all in uniform, two of them carrying guns. One of the unarmed ones addressed himself to Scully. 'I am Commander William Fitzgerald of the Irish Navy and I have reason to believe that this vessel is harbouring a fugitive. I have full permission to conduct a search.' He produced a piece of paper from inside his jacket.'Which one of you is Kevin O'Sullivan?'

Scully grabbed the piece of paper. 'Me,' he said.

'Am I right to assume that you are presently in control of this vessel?'

Scully handed the man back his paper. 'Who is it you're looking for?'

'Are you in command of this vessel?'

'Yes. Who is it you're looking for?'

'Claire Traynor.' He stared at Scully. 'She's wanted in Britain in connection with crimes against that state.'

'Fuck me backwards!' Scully said. 'What have we got here? A bunch of jumped-up Sea Scouts running around the Irish Sea recruiting prisoners for Her Majesty's gaols. Well, all of youse can go and fuck yourselves.'

'Mr O'Sullivan, I'll advise you now that if you or any of your crew interfere with this search you will be arrested and I will have this boat taken into port where she will be stripped plank by plank.'

'Do what you want, you arse-licking piece of shite.'

The Commander turned towards the frigate and nodded. Suddenly the light was gone. When my eyes got used to the lack of it, I saw that he was looking at me. 'Please turn on your deck lights,' he said.

Scully tore through the aft door and was beside me in seconds. He leant over the control panel and flicked a switch. The deck lit up again, a faint echo of the light it had bathed in minutes before. Then he moved his face close to mine – head-butting distance.'Where is she?'

'I don't know.'

'You're lying to me, Seán.' His breath was hot.

'She's in the hold.'

For a moment his eyes danced. Then, with the movement of a lizard, he was at the chart table.'What's your heading?' he said.

I looked down at the compass: '045.'

He delved into a drawer and pulled out a pair of parallel rules and dividers. 'Speed?' he called.

I checked the gauge. 'A little over three knots. Three point two.'

'Right, alter a touch to port.'

I turned the spokes.

'A touch, I said,' he shouted.

I straightened the wheel.

'Now? What's your heading?'

'040.'

'Come up. Say 038. That should do it. A bit of surface drift . . . tide flooding,' he was muttering, his eyes jumping between the Decca and the chart. 'Now listen,' he said. 'Keep this course and in about ten minutes we'll snag.' As I was watching him, a smile spread across his face. 'Then all fuckin' hell will break loose.'

From behind me came Doyle's voice: 'You're going to deliberately make us come fast?'

'You,' Scully said, meaning Doyle, 'come out on deck with me now. When you can, slip down the hold without being spotted and move her up to the forward bulkhead on the port side. When we come fast, rip down the boards, get her into the anchor locker and put the boards back in place. Any noise you make should be covered by the pandemonium on deck. But you've got to be quick. If we're in luck they'll have already searched the anchor locker and won't go near it again.'

As he was talking, he reached over to the fuse box and removed the fuse marked 'hold'. 'When we strike, Seán, push the throttle all the way forward and all the way astern. Have you got that?'

I nodded.

'Right, come on,' he said to Doyle.

On deck, the navy men were working their way aft from the fo'c's'le, the Commander issuing crisp strings of orders from behind them. Hutch was nowhere to be seen.

The frigate was close enough to see figures on deck. All it would take was one signal from the Commander and they'd be over in force. For the moment, at least, they seemed content with a slow, methodical search.

I concentrated on steering the course Scully had given me. But I was sure my inaccuracies at the wheel would blow his plan. He was expecting me to find the only wreck on the seabed within twenty miles, then tow our nets over it. The compass card kept sliding away either side of the 038 mark. I was overcorrecting and causing a pendulum motion. Seen from the frigate, our wake must have looked like one long repeating S.

My task was not helped by Scully's antics on deck. He countered every order the Commander gave. One of the uniforms was about to make his way into the hold when Scully shouted at him not to. He told the Commander that the lights down there didn't work. When the Commander nodded at the sailor to go ahead, Scully pounced on him with a verbal assault that could have blistered varnish. Everyone looked on. When the steam had leaked from Scully's onslaught, the Commander told the man to go on.

I knew Scully was just playing for time but, as the seconds wore on, I felt sure I had missed the wreck. I redoubled my efforts to nail the compass on 038. Then, with the suddenness of a car crash, I was flung into the wheel as our stern was wrenched backwards. The cables leading down to the net groaned under the strain. The boat careered sideways. There was a roar from the frigate's engines as they were slammed astern to avoid a collision.

I got back to the throttle and rammed it forward, then all the way back. This exaggerated the effect. The boat pitched and bucked as though it was being played with by some mad puppeteer beneath the waves.

On deck, there was chaos. Everyone had been flung forward, fish boxes toppled and two barrels of engine oil tumbled down the deck. Scully was screaming at the Commander: 'I had to leave the apprentice on the wheel while you and your fucking farmers go about your shenanigans. Look! See what's happened! This is going to cost you, you fucking bastards.'

'Shut your bloody mouth.' The Commander was picking himself up, holding his side. 'Get lights on down there.'

'Get your own fucking lights,' Scully said.

Another dinghy was launched from the frigate. It drove in a white sweep to our stern. Four more uniforms jumped on to our deck. Two fed an electrical cable down through the hatch to the hold. The other two grabbed Scully, slammed him against the mast. The Commander walked up to him. 'One more word out of you, one more, and you're under arrest.'

'Fuck you!' Scully said, and shouldered himself out of the grip of the men holding him. He walked aft. He knew that Doyle had either done his work by now or he hadn't.

Lights came up from the hatchway, followed by a man who had fallen into the hold when we'd come fast. They helped him up the ladder and into one of the dinghies. It roared back to the frigate.

On deck, the Commander was reissuing orders. His crew had an urgency to their movements now. They shifted piles of rope, rolled the oil barrels back under the forepeak, shone torches into any space where it might be possible to hide a human. They worked their way aft and went below. In the wheelhouse, they scanned the lockers under the instruments panel, shone a torch in my face, then left. When they'd finished searching the entire boat, the Commander told them to start again. But by now their hearts were no longer in it. They neglected the anchor locker. When they ran out of places to search, the Commander called it off. They got back into their one remaining dinghy and sped back to the frigate, leaving us with three tons of gear wrapped around a wreck on the floor of the H and H.

I came out on deck and stood with Scully, Hutch and Doyle. Once the sailors were aboard the frigate and the dinghy was clear of the water, full power was put on and the great grey bulk disappeared back into the dark.

What happened next happened fast. Hutch turned to walk forward. Scully stepped in front of him, blocking his path. They stared at one another. Then, without taking his eyes off Hutch, and in a movement too quick to register, Scully buried his boot in Hutch's crotch. He buckled, and Scully stood back, took aim and kicked again. This time Hutch took it in the face. He did not move, stayed slumped, his hands on his knees, as though searching the deck for something lost. Scully pulled his gutting knife from his pocket and opened the blade. He walked around to Hutch's side, grabbed a clump of his hair and hauled his head upwards. He pressed the blade into the flesh of Hutch's neck and kept it balanced on the point of pressure needed to make the skin yield. 'Hutch, I've no intention of going away again, not for you, not for anyone. That's the only reason I'm not cutting your fucking throat now.' He withdrew the knife and let go of Hutch's hair. Hutch slumped back to his original position.

Scully turned to me and Doyle. 'Cut the cables,' he said. 'And don't let that bitch anywhere near me.' Then he walked into the wheelhouse.

Neither of us moved. We watched Hutch try to straighten himself. He gave up and staggered to a column of upturned fish boxes where he sat.

Doyle and I dragged a weighty pair of rust-covered wire-cutters from the fo'c's'le. With it, we snapped the cables. Scully watched us from the wheelhouse. As soon as we were free, he pushed the throttle forward and headed for home.

In the galley, I put the kettle on. Doyle passed me, saying he was going to bed. When the tea was made, I brought Scully a mug. He thanked me, then said, with that smile in his voice, 'The lovebirds are up sulking behind the nets. Better bring them a cup. It might be the last romantic evening they'll share for a while.'

I didn't reply. I brought mine and theirs up forward. Scully was right. They were huddled together like swallows in a barn. They took their cups in silence. She had her arm around his shoulders. 'Are you all right, Claire?' I asked.

She smiled and nodded.

'You OK, Hutch?'

When he turned to me, I saw the blood smeared across his mouth and chin. 'Watch that fucking Scully, man. He's a mad fuck. You know he . . .' Silence settled on the sentiment.

I left them together and went aft – the fishing boat's equivalent of a backyard. A place where things are put that are not yet useless. There was a box of rusting shackles, bits of gear no longer used, punctured fenders and scraps of netting. All of it being washed of its oil and deteriorating fast.

Just beyond it was our wake. And when, like now, no gear was down, it spread like a fan across the dark waves. Wave after wave, coated white, then gone.

I thought of Emma between crisp convent sheets, asleep and snug just eighty miles south of where we were heading. Hemispheres away.

We arrived at the harbour mouth just as the sky was lifting in the east. The moon had long gone. Silent figures holding fishing rods stood at the end of the pier. We made a wide sweep inside the harbour, our wake rocking the yachts on their moorings, making pendulums of their varnished masts.

Hutch emerged from the nets and began to coil the forward line. His face was swollen and bruised but he had got rid of the blood. Doyle went aft. Because there was no one about, I leapt ashore to catch our lines. As I was making up the forward line around a bollard, Scully came out on deck. He said something to Hutch. Whatever it was, it left Hutch looking after him. Scully jumped up on to the pier and walked past me without a word.

We sat around the galley table eating fried bread and drinking coffee. Doyle was trying to put some sort of gloss on the night's events for Hutch's sake, but Hutch wasn't having any of it. 'Scully's a cunt, pure and simple, a fucking animal.' The words were quiet and bitter.

Claire wrapped the fingers of both hands around her mug. She was distant. Hutch sighed, then got up, saying he was going to pack a bag. When he'd gone, she spread her arms across the table and covered both Doyle's and my hand with hers. 'Thanks,' she said, then withdrew.

'What do they want you for?' Doyle asked.

'A crime as old as time.'

'Prostitution?'

She shook her head. 'No, murder.'

'They think you murdered someone?'

'A couple of someones.'

For a moment I thought he was going to ask her if she had. He didn't. He sat there staring at her.

I got up when I heard Hutch climbing the steps from below. All he had was packed into a small duffel bag.

'Where are you going?' Doyle asked him.

'Don't know.'

Claire got up. She had no coat, no handbag, nothing. She stood and followed Hutch out to the deck. They stepped up on to the dock, both tall and thin and slightly scraggy, and began to walk. It was then the car doors opened. Plain-clothes men, maybe a dozen, walked up and surrounded them. There was no shouting, no talking. They moved as one to a large black car. Hutch and Claire got into the back, a detective beside each of them. The rest separated into their own cars and together they pulled away. Five in all.

Chapter 10

Bristol, 2008

I opened the door to Kate's smile. She was wearing a white blouse and short denim skirt. As she stepped past me, the air filled with a sweet chemical scent – apple blossom, but delicate. I travelled in its wake down the hall. At the top of the stairs, I stood and watched her go down. All emotion had to be numbed. This was a client, nothing more, nothing less.

She was sitting on the couch by the time I took my seat.

She leant forward and scooped her shaggy hair behind her shoulders. Then she crossed her legs. 'I don't suppose it's possible to smoke?'

'No, sorry.'

'Shame.' She sat back and let her eyes travel around the room. When they met mine, she smiled, as though she had been caught prying. 'Peter and I talked a lot about what happened here the last time, talked a lot about us too. And, well, I think we're going to split up. I'm not a hundred per cent but it seems the logical thing to do.

We're stuck and I don't see any other way.' She was silent, looking about as though she was not quite comfortable with something.

'I think it's helped us, coming here. It's forced us to focus,' she was looking at me again now, 'on who we are, why we're together, you know, all that.' She gave a little laugh. 'Peter's almost always pissed off when we leave here, which is kind of interesting. There's a part of him that he just doesn't want touched, and the weird thing is, I've become a part of that part. Do you know what I mean?'

I was about to say I didn't when she said, 'Our entire relationship is just one big bad habit. For me, for both of us.' She looked at the floor. 'But it's going to be hard to break because he's all I have, all I've ever had, in the way of love.' She lifted her head and smiled. It was joyless and faded slowly. 'He's not like anyone else I know. He gets things done. I mean, he treats everyone like they're commodities but with respect, if that makes sense. That's why he does so well in the music business. But, like, in a way that's the problem. He never stops trading. And I love him, but if I'm going to be with someone, I'd like it to be someone I can relax with. Not someone I feel is constantly assessing and reassessing me against some value system I don't know anything about. This is scary, isn't it?'

'Is it?'

'Yeah, I've talked my way into leaving him, haven't I?

'Have you?'

'You know I have.'

'All that's happened is you're looking at your relationship from a different angle, and you're seeing things you didn't expect to find. Those things don't necessarily mean you've got to hop on the first bus. You can always stay around, see if you can work them out.'

She broke into a smile. 'Can I ask you a personal question?'

'You can ask.'

'Is your relationship . . . your relationships, are they all perfect? I mean, the rest of us just plod along but you guys are trained in this stuff. You must have flawless personal lives.'

I had a sudden urge to laugh and tell her I was terrified of my wife, terrified she'd leave me, terrified she wouldn't. Tell her I had kids I'd forgotten how to talk to. That I lived in fear my clients would discover I was a fraud. I wanted to tell her that my whole life was haunted by doubts so large they'd developed personalities. The word 'flawless' did not apply.

'I can't go into my personal life but I can tell you that no one is immune to being human.'

She smiled. 'You're very diplomatic.'

That was it. The mechanism I had used to see her as a client and me as a professional crumbled. We were two people in a room. She talked and paid me to listen. She did that because she thought I knew things about her and her emotions that she did not. She was wrong.

'You're also quite sexy,' she said, smiling.

I felt as though my insides had drained out of me. I took a breath. 'Kate, we have to stop this. It wasn't a good idea for me to see you on your own in the first place but . . .' I realised I was sitting upright.

'Look, all I said is you're an attractive man. I didn't know it was a hanging offence.'

'Sorry, but we can't do this any more.'

She studied me for a moment. 'You find me attractive too, don't you?'

'Kate, you're a client. This can't continue. There'll be no charge for this session.'

'You are throwing me out?'

'I'm saying that, under the circumstances, there's nothing I can do to help you.'

'You're throwing me out. Pity. I like being down here talking with you.'

'Except this isn't a normal conversation, is it? I'm a counsellor and you're a client. We're here to do a job.'

'And if I don't want to go?'

'Kate, what is this?'

'Oh, nothing. I suppose it's just when I do walk away from here I have to come to terms with the fact that Peter and I are over and I don't really want to face that right now. I'd rather talk to you.' She smiled. 'It's cosy.'

'It's time to go.'

She shrugged. 'OK. Sorry if I offended you.'

'You didn't offend me, you complimented me.'

'It wasn't very appropriate, though, was it?'

I shook my head.

She stood. 'I don't mind paying for the session.'

'You haven't been here long enough to call it a session,' I said, getting up.

'Right. Can I call you, though, you know, if I need to?'

'Kate, you're fine, you don't need me.'

She put her bag over her shoulder and walked to the stairs. There she paused to look at the last photograph in the series running down them. Then she started to climb, but slowly, each picture tugging at her attention. 'Where did you get these?'

'They were taken by a friend of mine in Dublin a long time ago.'

She was examining the one of the woman with the apron leaning out of her shop door. She glanced at me, smiled, then sprang up the rest of the stairs. At the front door, she said, 'Thanks for everything. I'm sorry I was,' she hesitated 'inappropriate.'

'You weren't.'

'Then why am I going?'

'Right, you were. It's complicated.'

She considered this. 'Well, anyway, I'm sure we'll meet again – who knows?'

'Take care of yourself, Kate.'

I closed the door, walked back downstairs and slumped into my chair. I felt weak. The couch still bore the imprint where she had sat. I could have stood, walked over, sat down beside her, run my hands along that hair to her breasts. She'd turn. We'd kiss. Passions would mount.

What was I doing? Emotions, desires that I should be directing towards my wife, were instead pressed into a fantasy about a girl half my age. I wanted to sink my hands into my skull, pull out my core and replace it. Then I'd flick the switch and start again.

Chapter 11

Howth, 1976

Two solid bars of sunlight slanted across the stuffy cabin, hitting the Formica opposite. Beneath them Doyle lay stretched, a naked leg resting alongside a rope of twisted blanket.

In the galley, I put the kettle on, then went up to the wheelhouse to turn on the radio – mostly to get the time. The one o'clock news had just started. The man's voice was talking about arrests in Howth harbour in the early hours of the morning. 'The couple,' he was saying, 'are currently being held under the Prevention of Terrorism Act. The woman is thought to be wanted in connection with a bombing campaign carried out on mainland Britain during the past year. The man is a local fisherman. Both are now helping police with their enquiries.' They went then to a reporter who ran through the details of the campaign Claire was alleged to have been part of. It had concentrated on car bombings but it seemed that the nearest it had got to any bigwigs was some high-ranking civil servant. In all, their activities had killed six people and injured many others. The reporter concluded that this case might well test the new

101

and controversial rulings on extradition. The British government had already requested that the two be brought to England to face trial.

I tuned back into the channels of the VHF and tuned into voices out in the Hs discussing last night's events. One man, with a voice like sandpaper, was saying he had seen three navy ships surrounding the *Mary Jo*. 'They have that Scully now and about time.' The other said that the Irish Navy only had three boats and that one was on the opposite side of the country in Killybegs. 'Aye,' said Sandpaper. 'Well, they must have seconded more for the job because the whole sea was lit up like a city.'

In the middle of the afternoon, a squad car pulled up alongside where we were berthed. Two uniformed gardaí got out and put on their caps. They walked back and forth on the pier, examining us from stem to stern. I watched them from the galley window. Finally, one let out a roar: 'Ahoy, Mary Jo.'

Doyle was at the window in seconds. 'Fuck! Pigs!' he said, then went into the wheelhouse where he slid open a window. I had said nothing to him about what I'd heard on the news. 'Yes, Garda?'

Next thing I heard him say was, 'Oh, yes, come aboard.'

Their black polished brogues looked odd on our wooden deck. But there they stood, their owners telling us to come with them to the station so that statements could be taken and sent by courier to the Castle.

Doyle blabbered non-stop in the car. He'd had no idea who the woman was. If he'd had any idea, there would have been no question of anything other than full cooperation.

Passing an open door in the station, I caught a glimpse of Scully. He was sitting alone by a table, smoking.

I was brought to a room and asked to wait. Outside, I heard Doyle's voice grow faint as he was escorted down the corridor. Then two gardaí came in and took seats. They were both young; one seemed familiar. The other asked questions while the familiar one started writing.

I told them what had happened, in my own words, as they'd suggested, and when I finished there was silence. Both men were looking at me. I could almost see the line in the textbook, 'Observe the suspect.'

'You've come a long way, Farreller, haven't you?'

I looked at him.

'Not remember me, then?'

Suddenly he fell into place. It was maybe eight years ago. He was pinned to the ground by a size-ten boot that had belonged to Paddy Prendergast, the biggest member of our gang. His brother, Shane, was the leader. When Paddy looked over for instructions for what to do with the object squirming beneath him, Shane had told him to piss in his mouth. And that, to our amusement, Paddy had tried to do.

All I could remember was that his name was Walsh. And, now that I was looking at him, I remembered someone telling me he had joined the Gardaí.'You haven't done too bad for yourself, Walsh.'

'Garda Walsh to you, Farreller.'

His colleague was staring at me. I decided it was time to stay quiet. The incident might have left a bad taste.

Behind them, the door flew open and in walked a large round man, whose uniform was having a hard time containing the bulk within it. From his forehead rose an auburn cliff of tight curls. In every other respect his facial features were those of a pig. He had huge pink cheeks, small black eyes and a nose that was nine-tenths nostril. The skin on his face, except where he shaved, was covered with a tight blond down.

He stared at me, then took the notebook from Walsh. He swiped through the pages as he walked around the table, then parked his large posterior on the corner. 'You're looking at five, maybe seven years here, boyo.' His accent was just like Fitz's. I said nothing.

'Aiding and abetting a fugitive, causing grievous bodily harm to a naval officer. It's good. I like it. Do you know why I like it?'

This was a question to which he wanted an answer. The performance he was planning needed input. I didn't give it to him.

'I said, do you know why I like it?'

This time he wasn't going to wait for me to play my role. I had lost my part in the game and for that I would be made to suffer, but later. For the moment, his two young colleagues and I were all he had for an audience.

'I like it because it'll see a flowery little shit like you washed down the toilet and into the sewers where you belong.'

I was used to the tone. It was school. It was parents. It was every bastard who was older and knew better and had the power to inflict pain. The setting, though, was new. The uniforms and the dry pale walls with scuffmarks where no scuffmarks should be. This was the State. Unlike teachers, priests and parents, this was an enemy unfamiliar to me. It cared nothing for morals or re-education. It would simply mete out punishment in a dry, impersonal way that would deny you freedom and have you staring at scuffmarks for years to come.

The big pig man sensed my unease. 'So,' he said, putting a little friendly play into his voice, 'are you going to tell us the truth or do we have to beat it out of you?'

'Look, I've just told these two here. That's it, nothing more, nothing less. It just happened the way it happened.'

'Nothing to do with me, eh?'

'Look,' I said, and sighed. There was nothing else I could think of doing.

'Look nothing. Your comrade-in-arms, Mr Doyle, has told us everything.' He rose from the table. 'You didn't care who or how many she murdered. You hid her from the law. You helped to provide refuge for the most wanted woman in Britain.' He said it as though it was a title to be proud of. I couldn't help smirking.

Instantly the air turned icy. 'Don't laugh at me, boy,' he said in a hurry. 'I wouldn't advise that at all.' He walked behind me. I listened to his footsteps make a slow, wide sweep. 'You're a new breed to me. I know the harbour and, by and large, they're good boys down there. In need of a little curtailment from time to time, yes, but by and large good men. And what a little flowery shit like you is doing in there among them I don't know.' He came into view by my side. 'And what I don't know I don't like.'

He stopped by the side of the table and leant forward, spreading the fingers of both hands on the surface. 'What are you? A hippie, is it? A Communist? Is that it? Or are you from some other high-falutin' cult?' One of his hands suddenly left the table and grabbed my hair. He hauled my head backwards and placed his face directly above mine. 'Now listen, my young buck.' It rained spit. 'If it is decided that charges will be brought against you I will be a very happy man because it means I won't have to see your miserable little face for a long time to come. But even if they're not, and Christ alone knows how those clowns in the Castle go about their business, I never want to have to lay eyes on you again. Do you know why?'

I wasn't sure if I should answer this or not.

He curled the clump of hair he was holding tighter and hauled my head further back. 'Do you know why?'

I shook as much of my head as I could.

'Because you are vermin, a new breed of harbour rat, and it's one I don't care for.' With that he let go. 'Get his details,' he said to the others, and made for the door. There, he turned to me. 'For your sake, I hope I won't be seeing you again.' With that he was gone.

Walsh's colleague got up and said he'd be back in a minute. A silence followed, one for which I felt responsible. I tried to ignore the feeling. The room I was sitting in, and the others like it on this corridor, had one purpose and one purpose only: the extraction of information. These walls would have witnessed many different confessions extracted by many different means. Why shouldn't silence be one of them?

I looked at Walsh, wondering what had made him join the Gardaí. But I couldn't look at him for long. He was sitting there smiling, smug, although where exactly the smile was I couldn't tell. His lips were thin and as straight as the horizon. Where was it, then? The eyes? Perhaps it wasn't on his face but below his skin, darting about beneath the surface like a fish. Or perhaps there was some chemistry that manufactured images in the air that lay between us. If that was the case, was it fair to assume that my face might be launching expressions that only he was aware of?

'How long have you been in the force?' I found myself asking. Christ, if it could put words in your mouth as well as expressions on your face I was well and truly fucked.

Now he was smiling. 'What's it to you, Farreller?'

'Nothing – nothing at all.'

'You think we're beneath you, don't you?'

I clamped my jaw shut, not trusting what I might say.

'Well, I'll tell you one thing. I'm the boss now. I call the shots. And it's just a matter of time before fucking eejits like you end up in here to get dealt with. And make no mistake, deal with you I will.'

When his friend came back the questions started again, but they were of the bland, everyday variety, and I'd answered them all before – name, address, date of birth, etc. When he had what he wanted he got up and told me to wait. He said he had to make copies. This left me and Walsh face to face again but I had lost my appetite for my earlier antics. With elbows on the table, I covered my face with my hands and sighed into my palms. I looked up when I heard his chair creak. He was standing, a hand on the door knob. 'I'll be seeing you, Farreller,' he said, and left.

Then I waited. It might have been an hour. I was leaning back in the chair, legs sprawled, almost asleep when the door opened. 'Here,' Walsh's colleague said, tossing three or four typed pages in front of me. 'Sign that.'

I stared at him.

'It's your statement. Sign it and you can go.'

I signed it.

'But be at one of the two addresses you gave us.'

A light drizzle was falling outside. I was walking downhill towards the pier when I heard my name called from a gateway. I stopped. Scully stepped out on to the pavement.

'Did they just let you out too?' I asked him.

'I was waiting for you.'

'Where's Doyle?'

'They probably had to call a doctor to surgically remove his tongue from O'Hare's arsehole.'

'Is that the one who looks like a pig?'

'Yeah. Listen, we have business to conduct.'

We continued walking. 'What's going to happen now?' I asked.

'As far as the constabulary is concerned, nothing. They have who they want, and they have Hutch as well, if they feel the need for a little bloodletting. But what we have done, old son, is fucked it with the boat. How many boxes did we fill yesterday?'

'I don't know. Eighteen?'

'That'll do.'

We walked on. I wanted to ask him exactly what had happened in the station, to compare notes, but I guessed that, to Scully, the interview he had just left was no big deal.

From the phone box at the end of the pier he called the fish market and scribbled figures on the back of a cigarette packet. When he hung up, he said, 'Right, come on.'

We entered J.T. O'Connell's and found him out the back, hosing down empty fish boxes. He was small and round, with stubby fingers and sharp dark eyes. As soon as he saw us, he started nodding. 'I might have known. What have you got?'

'How much are you paying for cod?' Scully asked. J.T. looked at us for a moment, then walked across the yard and turned off the tap. 'I've got cod coming out my fucking ears.'

'Right,' Scully said, 'we'll be seeing you.'

'For fuck's sake, Scull, don't be so impetuous. You've got boxes of cod up there that are ten times fresher than anything I got here. Of course I'm interested.'

'How much are you paying?'

'Fifty-seven and a half pence.'

'How much is that?'

'Eleven and six.'

'A pound?'

'Of course a pound – what? Do you think I've gone metric?'

Scully was thinking. 'How much do you want?'

'How much have you got?'

'We could have, say, eight boxes here in the next fifteen minutes.'

'Done.'

'Cash?'

'Cash.'

From J.T.'s we went to Brian Moran's. He said he'd take the flatfish and a couple of boxes of cod. By the time we got back to the boat we had sold more than half the fish in the hold. We manhandled them on to the deck and from there on to the quay wall.

'What about that lot?' I said to Scully, nodding at the open hold. He shrugged. 'Let's get paid for these first.'

By the time we'd got our load up the quay to their respective buyers I was in no mood to mention the rest of the fish.

Arms aching, we walked into Findlater's and asked for two pints.

We sat at a table at the back of the public bar. The boy, as he was known, a man about twice my age, brought the pints over and placed one before each of us.

I stared at mine, the brown foam still settling. Almost imperceptibly, a thin mist of condensation covered the glass, fading the reflection of the neon light and dulling the darkness of the liquid within. I wrapped my fingers around it and lifted it. The flavours that flowed through me were many and contrary, smoothness, bitterness and a mellowness that, once swallowed, demanded another mouthful. When I put it down, half of it was gone.

'How much did we make?' I asked Scully.

'Over five hundred quid.'

'How much did I make?'

'We split it.'

'You're going to give me more than two hundred and fifty?'

'I'm not giving you a thing. It's money you earned.'

'What about Hutch? And Doyle?'

'Doyle's share is in the hold, if he has the wit to get it,' Scully said, separating banknotes under the rim of the table. 'The next time you see the other poor bastard he'll be leaking diarrhoea from a much-fucked anal passage.'

I raised my pint again to wash away the image. And my mind swam with arithmetic. With a pint costing twenty-three and a half new pence it came out at just over four pints to the pound. Christ almighty! Two hundred and fifty pounds was a thousand pints, that was ten a day for a hundred days – it would take me to Christmas and beyond. It was mind-boggling.

'Right,' Scully said. 'There's two hundred and fifty-eight pounds and seventy new pence.'

I took the notes. This was unbelievable.

'Look, I'm not telling you what to do with it, but just in case you don't realise what the crack is here, the *Mary Jo* is finished. She'll be impounded now and sold probably. So, that's it. And don't be surprised if our comrades on the pier don't queue up for our services. It's considered the height of bad manners to bring down the law. So, now you know. I'm just telling you this because it might be the last lot of money you'll see for a while.'

I curled the notes into a column and slid them into my front pocket. 'Scully, I've got over two hundred and fifty pounds in my mitts right now. I don't give a bollox what happens,' I said, and laughed. I wanted to shout and scream.

Suddenly a whole new range of products came into view. Stereos, motorbikes, nice clothes. We ordered more pints. The place was beginning to fill.

It was odd because everyone who came in would have heard about what had happened yet only a handful came over to ask Scully about it. The rest, either in early after a good week or laid up due to gear failure, drank and smoked and cast occasional glances in our direction.

The boy was soon too busy to notice the state of our drinks so I was designated gofer. I was waiting at the bar when an elbow pressed into my upper arm and a voice said, 'Sad thing, Seán, to see you consorting with the criminal classes.' It was John Sheehan. He was looking straight ahead, a pound note peeping above the knuckle of his curled index finger.

'Don't believe everything you hear, John.'

'It's not what I'm after hearing, it's what I fuckin' know. Look, Seán, get yourself away from Scully and the like. Come down and see me tomorrow morning. I'm running the *Jasper* now for me sins. We're over on the East Pier for a bit of painting and that. There's a berth but it won't be open for ever. All right?'

With that he moved his bulk into the crowd. John Sheehan was a straight, honest, hard-working man. Everything I supposed Scully was not. Working with Sheehan would mean good wages as regular as clockwork. But I had more than two hundred and fifty pounds in my pocket and windfalls like that would be rare working on a boat run by Sheehan.

When I got back to the table, Scully was talking to a man I had never seen before about New Zealand. The fishing there was the best in the world, and the country itself, Scully said, the most beautiful. As I listened, I wondered where he'd got it all from. He had dark eyes and a face of leather and an expression that said, 'Fuck you!', but here he was in full flight. Passionate about something I had no idea he knew anything about. And maybe he didn't.

I found myself looking around. Everyone was at least ten years older than me and they all wore the strained expressions of people with cares, whereas I had none. My family lived in suburbia, miles away. My girlfriend, if you could call Emma that, was tucked up in a boarding school beyond the Pale. And my school friends would, at this time on a Friday night, be prising coins from their parents' purses with either lies or outright theft. And here was I, sitting on top of the world, with a pint in front of me and a thick wedge of cash curled up in my pocket.

It was time to spread a little cheer among the less fortunate. I went to the phone at the entrance and dialled Cahill's number. His mother answered and told me Declan was not home from school yet. I looked across at the clock. It was five fifteen.

'Are you in a pub, Seán Farrell?'

'Yes, Mrs Cahill. The phone at the end of the pier isn't working.'

'Well, I hope you're not taking a drink.'

'Of course not, Mrs Cahill. I'm still under age.'

'Aye, well, that doesn't stop some of the publicans in this town, I can tell you.'

'Well, you needn't worry about me, Mrs Cahill.'

'Will I tell Declan to phone you at home?'

'No. I'm sure I'll see him later.'

'Well, he has a lot of homework these days. He has his Leaving in June.'

'I know that, Mrs Cahill.'

I put the phone down. Somehow Mrs Cahill and her crackling country voice had taken the shine off my mood. Fuck Cahill! Where was he? That was the trouble: my friends never stayed put. I'd be out at sea for five days at the most, and five weekdays at that, yet listening to them, you'd swear they'd squeezed a lifetime into it.

Back at the table, Scully was in Alaska fishing for crab. He noticed my return and indicated in mid-sentence that his pint was in need of replenishment. I stood and took my place at the bar. 'Two more, please,' I said to the aproned barman.

'Cheer up, it may never happen,' he said, all shiny and clean. I wanted to ask him why he wasted good money spreading Brylcreem across the tiny wisp of hair he still had. It was time to get out of there. 'Cancel those, will you?'

Outside, the rain fell in thin silver folds. I walked uphill and into the fish-and-chip shop. From it, I could see the police station. What had Sheehan said? 'Consorting with the criminal classes.'

Across the road there was a wall that overlooked the harbour. It was a popular place to gather for those who got casual employment from the pier. You could see who was in and who wasn't. If your eyesight was keen enough you could even count the catch being landed. It being late now on a Friday, and wet, the wall was empty. I walked over and looked at the neat rows of boats tied up for the weekend. The *Mary Jo* was parked at the top on the inside. Even from this distance, she was fresh-looking. A new toy in a box of scrap. Out beyond the harbour the sea was running grey with a few breaking white horses.

Some mainsails were flapping from the masts of the yachts at their moorings. On deck, figures dressed in yellow or red slid back and forth. A small blue clinker-built boat ferried the yachtsmen from the harbour wall to their boats. It was on its outward journey now, crammed with men in oilskins. I wondered was my father one of them.

Chapter 12

Bristol, 2008

Some time later, from the bath, I heard the front door open and Lynn come in. I knew it was her from the walk, slow and deliberate, disappearing into the kitchen.

When I came down twenty minutes later she was preparing salads.

'Oh, you're in!' Her voice was bouncy.

'Yes.'

'I bumped into Sarah and asked her and Steve over for a barbecue this evening. They'll be bringing Will. Hope that's OK.'

'Yeah, great.'

'They're just back from California. Steve really took to the surfing.'

'Oh, really?'

'Yes, really.' She looked up from the salad bowl. 'Seán, what is it?'

'How do you mean?'

'You're all distant and . . . Are you pissed off about something?'

'Just tired, maybe.'

'You need a break.'

I plugged in the kettle. 'That's what Geraldine said.'

'Did she? Had a nice conversation with her about it, did you?'

The sound of the kettle coming to life filled in around her sarcasm. A feeling I'd had before came on. I was surrounded by words, colours, textures, but none of it made the connections necessary for it all to be absorbed into life and taken for granted.

'This morning a client asked me if all my relationships were perfect. She thought they would be because I was trained.'

'That must have made you want to laugh.'

'It did, actually.' I smiled.

Lynn did not. 'Well, when people confide in their work colleagues before they talk to their partners, what do they expect?'

The kettle reached its peak, then quietened and clicked.

'Blame it on the modern world. We spend more time with our colleagues than our partners.'

'You've always gone to Geraldine.'

'Are you jealous of her?'

'Don't be so bloody stupid. We live in the same house but we may as well be on two different planets.'

'You're right.'

She walked to the fridge. 'So, are you taking a break?'

'How can I?'

'Well, you've got a nice long weekend on your own coming up. Use it as a dress rehearsal.'

'Dress rehearsal for what?'

'Taking time off. Just do what you want.'

'Yeah. Tea?'

'No. Will you check the shed for fuel and get the barbecue out? I hope it still works.'

As a couple, Sarah and Steve were an odd combination. He was big, broad, tall, black and from North Carolina. She was willowy, white and very English. Steve worked in computer animation. Sarah wrote about food. We'd got to know them when their son Will was in nursery school with Mark and we'd been getting together occasionally ever since.

The Californian sun had turned Sarah's skin brown and Steve's blacker. They sat on our rusting garden furniture talking with great enthusiasm about the sunshine, the food and the wine.

'Look at this,' Steve said, taking a bottle of wine from a plastic bag he had brought. 'I picked up a couple of cases of this stuff in a little vineyard near Sarilla. I tell you, man, you gotta try some.'

'Darling, you know Seán doesn't drink,' Sarah interjected from across the table, her tone scolding.

Steve looked at me, 'Oops,' he said, 'sorry.'

It was a moment of awkwardness I'd seen many times before. 'Don't mind me, Steve, get stuck in.'

Steve laughed. 'Well, "stuck in", Seán, is not the kind of thing you do with a wine like this, but I'll tell you what, I'll give it a try.' With this, he gave a volley of loud laughter.

They were good company. And as candlelight replaced sunlight and the conversation ran its many courses, often simultaneously, I looked at Lynn and thought how beautiful she was. Why couldn't it always be like this, relaxed and calm? When had we got so angry?

I asked them about the social mood in the States and this got us quickly on to politics. Soon Steve and I were off with a type of argumentative banter that we both enjoyed. I noticed that neither Sarah nor Lynn joined in. But it had often struck me that the English did not share the Irish and American taste for argument. When I said as much to Steve, Lynn broke in, 'So you're going to start being an arsehole now, are you?'

'Stereotyping is a dangerous game, Seán my man.' Steve chuckled. 'But I'll tell you one thing, it sure feels good.'

'You're right, it's the refuge of idiots, but – and this is the fuck-up – idiots are not always wrong.'

'You're right there, Seán,' Steve said, 'which just proves the point.' The laughter that erupted now came from deep within him. It forced his eyes to shut and had him holding on to the side of the table, steadying himself.

'It's like a rash,' I said, 'or a virus. Idiocy turns up anywhere. It doesn't take into account education, politics, even IQ. We're all equally prone to it.'

'A rash on the rational,' Steve said, which started him off again, wobbling like a big jelly.

I noticed Sarah and Lynn were standing, clearing plates, collecting glasses. 'What are you doing, Lynn?' I asked.

'It's time the children were in bed.'

I awoke in the curtained light of early morning with a phantom hangover. This sometimes happened when the previous night had been late and full of talk. Lynn's shoulder lay in front of me like a granite boulder worn smooth with centuries of rain and wind. I turned in the bed and peered at my watch. Ten past five. This was unfair. I would now have to chase sleep, recapture it. But sleep was not something that could be caught.

I got up. In the kitchen I found the kettle among the debris and made some tea.

One advantage of working from home was, at times like this, that I could drift down there and, armed with the mug, review the day or week ahead. Today I had my first clients at nine, another couple at eleven, then nothing until three. No, I had an appointment with Philip at one.

I pulled a blank sheet of paper from the printer. On it I wrote 'mid-life crisis'. Was that what I was suffering from? What was a mid-life crisis? It was a term, just one of thousands you pick up and use whenever you need to, its meaning taken for granted. I was forty-nine. Too old for a mid-life crisis unless I lived to be ninety-eight. But, whatever it was, it had nothing to do with arithmetic. I could start by defining how I was feeling – dissatisfied, lonely, frustrated, misunderstood. The road behind was a muddle of memories, and ahead it was narrow and echoey, and at the end of it lay a coffin. Is that what a mid-life crisis was, reaching a point where you catch a glimpse of the shortness and futility of this little strip of a life and panic?

I curled the paper into a ball and tossed it in an arc towards the bin. It missed. Before the first clients came in I would have to pick it up.

At twelve thirty, I was finishing off some notes, aware that time was getting on, when the phone rang. It was Kate Wren.

'Hi!' There was a great beaming smile to it.

'Yes, Kate?'

'Never guess what?'

'What?'

'You know those pictures?'

'What pictures?

'The photographs by your stairs?'

'Yeah.'

'I think my mum took them.'

'What?'

'The one of the old lady, we had that at home.'

I felt as though my body had been drained of blood.

'Are you still there?'

'What was your mother's maiden name?'

'Balstead.'

'Your mother is Emma Balstead?'

'Yeah!'

'Look, Kate, I've got to go now. I'll phone you later.'

'Did you know Mum?'

'Yes, I did.'

'Wow! Imagine!'

'Kate, I've got to go but I'll phone you later about this.'

Chapter 13

Howth, 1976

The Hope Inn was lit by gas. The light came from within glass domes hanging from the ceiling. Inside each was a honeycomb structure of fine mesh that glowed to a yellow so pure it was almost white. The brightness fell across the raw Howth stone, giving the place an impression of warmth. A deep fireplace filled with burning peat added to this. And in front of it, usually, there was a man with a fiddle. He was dressed in tweeds and a cap and sat there horsing out collections of reels and jigs as busloads of tourists filed past on their way to the great hall at the back of the building. He, like everything else in the place, was there for effect.

But it was a place frequented by most of the people I used to share a classroom with, and on a Friday night it was the place to be. As yet, it was a quarter past seven and they'd still be in the process of extracting money from their parents.

I sat at the bar and ordered a pint. Up at the other end, where the mahogany elbowed into a curve, a couple was almost lost in shadow. He had his back to me but I could see her full on. She was leaning forward, smiling, watching him speak. Both wore late-summer coats for a walk in Howth, on the pier or the cliffs.

I found the pint hard to stomach so I ordered a whiskey. I drank it fast, hoping it would clear the fog that was rolling in over what had been my good humour. Down in Findlater's now, it would be black with fuckers roaring for porter, while up here it was just the loving couple and me. It seemed that on a Friday night the pubs of Howth inhaled and exhaled their customers at different times. The further up the hill you got, the later they'd draw breath.

So I sat like some over-eager warrior arriving too early at the front.

I heard the door open but made a conscious effort not to turn around to look. If it was anyone I knew they'd come to the bar. I listened to a cultured voice ask for a pint of Harp and a bitter lemon. More walkers. Behind them the door opened again. When I heard a leather jacket being unzipped I turned. It was Max. He put his helmet on the windowsill and walked to the bar.

'Jaysus, Seán, you're early.'

Max's parents were dead so he had less trouble than most in doing what he wanted.

'I could say the same about you.'

He looked at the stagnant pint in front of me and its neighbour, the empty whiskey glass.

'What'll you have?' I asked him.

The question surprised him. 'A pint, please, very kind.' He looked about. 'Mickey and Dave are on their way. I thought they'd be here by now.'

It was as if bikes flowered between these guys' legs. Two years ago they were sitting at their desks knobble-kneed and terrified, with schoolbags full of neat homework and crustless egg sandwiches. Now they rode around in leather and with purpose. And their talk was of con-rods, piston rings and baffles. The fuckers were fluent in a language that would have been foreign to them six months ago. And their bikes had brought them into contact with a whole new breed of people, a black-nailed, bearded tribe who worked out of leaky garages dealing in spare parts. And these guys, in turn, had opened up whole new social scenes.

When the pint arrived, I ordered another whiskey. We fabricated a conversation in the hope that Mickey and Dave would turn up soon and deliver us. But they must have got lost. The problem was that Max was fresh from a week of classroom discipline while I was full of salt and alcohol. The latter part of my make-up I think he guessed at and decided there wasn't much point investing too much time or talent in the conversation. But I had bought him a drink, a reasonably rare event in the politics of schoolboy friendships, so maybe he felt duty-bound to listen. I mouthed words I thought appropriate. In this way, the subject of how to handle a bike in the wet was established, which led to the tyres and everything south of the forks.

Mickey and Dave came in, relieving us of the one-to-one. Within an hour, the windowsill was packed with helmets. Outside, strips of orange street-light curved across the enamelled petrol tanks while inside their owners drank and talked of cylinder heads and who was doing what to whom on the floors of the free houses around Howth.

No one asked me what I was doing. More than a few commented on the smell – 'I can tell you're still on the boats, Farreller,' followed by a laugh.

Cahill, I was told, hadn't been seen since Wednesday. Word had it that he was shagging some country girl on the south side of the city.

I sat back and watched the islands of torn-up beer mats soak up the spillage. I watched the females, too, the fall of hair past the upturn of a nose, bare arms, soft skin, bracelets, long thin fingers with rings and nail varnish.

When closing time loomed, I knew I was drunker than I had ever been in my schooldays.

I slept on the living-room floor at Liam Duncan's. His parents had a holiday home outside Dublin where they spent three weekends a month. This left Liam in the powerful position of being able to invite people back. Although, in reality, with the exception of certain women, no one was ever actually invited. You turned up at the door and your standing in Liam's favour decided whether or not you'd be allowed in. Even when the place was screaming with Fats Domino, Chuck Berry and the wayward laughter of girls drunk on stolen beer, Liam kept a fairly dry system of assessment going.

He was one of the first characters thrown up by the interest in motorbikes. He was older than us and had little need of our company. Our bikes were small and any attractive girls in our group were spoken for. But Liam was an opportunist. He knew no relationship was as solid as it seemed. And, in an abstract way, he enjoyed this fresh crop of faces showing up at his door. Few people had nothing to offer. He was a poker player fanning out a new hand. His door was always open and, beyond it, chances existed, however slight, of sex in beds with sheets, of drink and music played loud, the long-awaited pleasures of the adult world.

Liam knew me through Cahill. I didn't have a bike and I was much more likely to poach rather than supply anything in the way of women. But he tolerated me. If always with a warning.

His own friends arrived in cars at various times throughout the weekend. Their girlfriends wore jewellery. They mentioned the names of restaurants and clubs with ease and, occasionally, you'd hear them talk of flying to London for a concert.

On this particular night, a barrel had been robbed from one of the pubs in Howth. It lay on Liam's kitchen floor like a blunt silver fish leaking its guts across the tiles. Through a complicated system using a plug spanner and vice-grips, the liquid within could be enticed into a glass hovering beneath the mechanism. It was a messy job, and by the time I got there, the floor looked as if it was an inch deep in piss.

I swilled as many pints of the stuff as I could, then staggered into the front room, scanning the place for somewhere to sleep unnoticed. In the morning, I woke up squinting at the ceiling through the smoked glass of a dining table.

Breakfast in Liam's always involved theft, either rashers and bread from the local shops or direct from Mrs Duncan's larder. The latter had to be done before Liam was up and its relief was short-lived. He always noticed. He'd stand by the bread bin and, in a voice drenched with disappointment, say, 'Ah, for fuck's sake!' Then he'd become silent and leave the room, the rest of us sitting around trying hard not to laugh.

This morning was unusual for three reasons. The first was, I was alone in the room. The second, from the kitchen came the smell of toast without the usual scampering sounds of thievery. And the third was the bulge in my pocket caused by the roll of notes.

Liam looked up when I walked in. 'You stay last night?'

'Yeah.'

'Anyone else?'

'There's no one there now.'

He raised his eyebrows. 'There's bread in the bin if you want toast.'

'Thanks.'

Liam had never offered me anything before. It added to the nervousness I already felt. Here I was, alone with the Great Decider, the man who could make or break your Saturday night. This was my chance to consolidate a friendship, forge a bond strong enough to withstand his darker moods. And all I could offer him was a string of nervous reactions born of a heavyweight hangover.

I couldn't find a bread knife so I used an ordinary one, but I might as well have used a hammer. Inch by inch, I crumbled the loaf to powder.

'So, what have you been up to?' Liam asked, from behind my back.

'You know, fishing and that.'

'I meant are you getting laid, these days?'

'No.'

'What about that blondie one, Emma?'

'She's back at boarding school.'

I could feel his smile behind me. 'Yeah, her and Carol Malcolm and – who was the little one Plasma was chasing?'

'Anna Bradshaw?'

'Yeah, Jesus, that lot were hot to trot.'

'Well, they're all down at St Helen's now. You were sniffing around Carol, weren't you?'

'I took my place in the queue.' He gave a high-pitched laugh. 'Were you riding the blondie one?'

'Of course I was.'

'Well, that was only a few weeks ago.'

'I know but . . .' I abandoned the bread. 'A few weeks is a long time. I'm afraid my virginity might grow back.' I sat down so I blocked Liam's view of the mountain of crumbs I'd left on the cutting board. 'What about you?'

'You know yourself, a bit here, a bit there.'

'You sound like Cahill.'

'According to him, he's riding some stunner on the south side.'

'According to him, he's riding everything on the south side.'

'Maybe he is.'

'Maybe.'

'Anyway,' Liam said, stretching his neck to see what had happened to the bread, 'it's no wonder you're not getting laid, you stink of fish.'

'I thought that meant you were getting laid.'

'Would you mind replacing the bread before my folks get back?'

'Yeah, no problem. I'll go round to the shops.'

Sutton Cross was the usual Saturday-morning mess of parked cars and scurrying humans with brats in tow. I got bread, butter, milk and a newspaper. I hadn't seen a newspaper for months and the thought of being able to go back to Liam's now, with him in a reasonably good mood, sit down and read the thing amid the smells of coffee and toast, had me smiling.

As I turned the corner into the drive I saw Cahill's bike. From the hall I heard the crackle of female laughter. I shot a glance at myself in the mirror. A long pale face framed in a mat of dead curls.

Cahill was sitting with his back to me. His big shiny head matched his leather jacket. Beside him sat a blonde waif with long white legs that stuck out from a red miniskirt, crossed at the knees, then slid into patent-leather boots. She looked up at me and smiled. It was a big, blue-eyed, red-lipped smile, but it was brief. She was paying attention to Cahill.

He turned his head. 'Ah, Farreller, the hard!' he said, then turned back to Liam and continued his tale. 'The copper just stayed there staring at us. Then Susie says, "Listen, it's none of your business."'

'And he didn't do anything?' Liam asked the girl.

'Sure what could he do?' she said, embarrassed but enjoying it.

I put the bread down. 'Toast, anyone?'

Cahill swivelled in his chair. 'So, what have you been up to, Farreller?'

'Fuck all.'

'I heard you came in here gee-eyed last night.' He looked at Liam, who smiled.

'It's possible.'

'Still on the boats?'

'I was till yesterday but I may be resting for a bit. Does anyone want toast?'

'What's the point in replacing the bread if you're just going to eat it?' said Liam, giving air to the accountant within.

'Right, tell you what, I'll take you all to breakfast.'

Liam looked startled. Cahill shook his head. 'I had a slap-up this morning, didn't I, hon?'

The waif smiled. Liam grunted.

Liam's bike was made up from lots of different bikes. It sounded as if a lump of metal had gone astray somewhere in the exhaust – there was a strange rattle every time the engine was revved. He wore a German Second World War helmet he'd had chromed. Now, as we rode along the seafront, images entered the shining dome upside down, travelling along it until they got smaller and then disappeared.

We drove to the centre of the city and parked on the dappled pavement beneath the trees by St Stephen's Green. Liam hauled the bike up on its stand and then, carrying his helmet like a general, walked down Kildare Street to a delicatessen that sparkled with everything fresh. He was brief and businesslike in the execution of the order. Then it came to paying. This I was happy to do. The problem was the sheer volume of notes I had to do it with. Both Liam and the guy serving stared at the wad as I peeled off a fiver and handed it to him.

'Fishing must be good,' Liam said.

'It has its moments.'

We had croissants filled with bacon and melted cheese. It was probably the most expensive breakfast I had ever eaten but it didn't matter. Funds were limitless and the croissants were just some of wealth's smaller fruits.

After it, Liam said he was off to see a man about a piston. I was welcome to join him, he said, but I declined. I'd leave damp garages and overweight greasers for another day. Now it was time to stroll through a city still fresh with sunlight and watch the clip-clop heels and short skirts of the office girls spending their wages.

I caught a glimpse of my reflection in the glass of a vegetable shop on South Anne Street. I looked as if I was wrapped in a webbing of compressed filth. I needed a plan. First, I'd get my hair washed and cut and have a proper shave. Then, in the Seaman's Institute, I could have a bath. If I bought some clothes on the way, I could change afterwards and reappear on the streets a new man.

I went to the barber my father had taken me to when I was a child. I remembered the old man who ran the place. He had evolved into the perfect shape for his trade. Over the years, his spine had arched, leaving his face only inches from the hair he was cutting. His glasses had sliced a deep purple furrow into his nose. All that was left for him to do was raise his arms and snip.

A younger barber looked at me as I entered and indicated I should take a seat. And there he was, the old man, still clipping away over the same leather chair. His own hair had completely gone and his skin had yellowed but he was at his station – the rasp of his breathing the dominant sound in the room.

I sat between two men. Both sniffed the air with genuine curiosity. When they came to the same conclusion, independently, as to the source of the odour, they pushed as far away from me as they could. This was followed by some shared looks and an unspoken decision. Within minutes my head was in the basin. Then the younger man tried to get a comb through my hair. When this was abandoned, I was placed in the chair beneath the old man's breathing.

'I've been away fishing in Alaska,' I said to him.

'I'm surprised they let you on a plane like this.'

That stopped all further conversation. By the time he had finished cutting, his comb could glide through my hair.

The Seaman's Institute was on the quays in a far less fashionable side of town. On the way I trawled for clothes. I bought a denim jacket with lapels like teardrops, black velvet flares, a dark green collarless shirt and a pair of desert boots.

So baggaged, I climbed the steps of the Flying Angel, 'Home for Mariners'. Inside, there was a long corridor of polished floor and varnished woodwork. The door closed behind me, cutting out all sound. Then a hatch rose from a booth at the end and a grey-haired woman was peering at me. 'Yes?'

'Hello, I'd like to take a bath if that's possible.'

'I'm afraid this place is for seamen only.'

'I am a seaman. I'm a fisherman. I work out of Howth.'

She stared. After some moments she said, 'Who do you work with?'

I named the crew.

'Whose boat is it?'

'John Grimmer's.'

'Oh! We know John well here. Mind, we haven't seen him for a while. How is he?'

'Tip-top form, I'd say.'

'And how is that new boat of his working out?'

'The *Mary Jo*? She's a treat, she's got everything.'

'Good. Right. Take Room Six along the first corridor upstairs. You won't be long, will you?'

I took the key and told her I'd be half an hour.

In the bath, a battle went on in every pore. A combination of steaming hot water and soap had to evict some long-standing residents comprising microscopic fish bits compressed by layers of old sweat, sealed in with a rich resin of tobacco smoke. It was a resilient mixture. When my skin had turned bright pink from the scrubbing I stopped and lay there, floating in the soup of my own grime. I hoped this would fool the filth still left into loosening itself and drifting away.

The towel-drying was vigorous and then I spread out the clothes. I had forgotten to buy underwear or socks. It didn't matter. I'd be fine without them.

Out on the street again, I walked directionless. My hair bounced. I was a new pin and the world was at my feet.

After turning over many destinations, none of which ignited a flicker of enthusiasm, I got the bus to Howth. I emerged at the stop at the end of the pier and, as the bus pulled away, I found myself looking at Findlater's.

'You must be in love,' the barman said to me, as I took a stool.

'What do you mean?'

'The haircut and the clobber. There has to be a woman behind that.'

'Well, there isn't – least, not one I can get my hands on.'

'Ah, well, there's always hope.'

The place was the usual storm of voices and glass clatter. Freshly shaven faces, bright-eyed with anticipation, were coating their interiors with stout before heading into town for the weekend. Most of the country boys wore suits complete with cufflinks and cracked leather shoes. The locals looked as they always did, only a little more rested. Most of them I recognised and a number I knew by name, but there was no one there I would normally drink with. Sheehan was with his crew halfway down the bar. Scully was nowhere to be seen.

When I asked the barman for a paper, he looked at me. 'Want to see if you made the headlines?' he said and sauntered into the back bar. He returned with a copy of the *Irish Independent* and handed it to me folded at the headline 'Two Arrested on Howth Pier'.

There were no pictures. It was a long column that ran three-quarters of the way down the side of the front page. Hutch was mentioned but only in passing. The bulk of the thing was a condensed history of the IRA's campaign in Britain. It gave details of the cell Claire Traynor belonged to. They were young radicals recruited from universities where sympathies ran in a republican direction. According to the piece, those cells had proved extremely effective. In nabbing Claire Traynor, they hoped to have blunted that effectiveness considerably.

There was further comment in the editorial. It tackled the dilemma of the IRA's aim, with which the writer, in principle, agreed, and their methods, which he deplored. She had been a student at Edinburgh University where she had organised petitions against the activities of the B Specials. This had brought her to the attention of the IRA, who had persuaded her that there was a far better way to stop the injustices in the North. Once she was trained in the use of arms and explosives, they let her and her team loose on the mainland, supporting them with weaponry and funds. The editorial listed episodes that Traynor was thought to be responsible for. Car-bombing was her speciality.

When I thought of her slumped and shivering in the hold, this was hard to imagine.

'So you didn't come and see me, Seán?'

John Sheehan had appeared beside me.

'No, John, I had to go into town.'

He looked down at the paper. 'That's a right fucking mess. I'll tell you, Scully'll keep low if he knows what's good for him.'

'It had nothing to do with Scully. None of us knew anything about her. Not even Hutch, and he was giving her one.'

'If you believe that you must be a fucking idiot. And if you're asking me to believe it you must think I'm one.'

I said nothing.

'Seán, you haven't done yourself any favours. None at all.'

'Look, John, I swear, none of us knew fuck-all about her.'

He looked at me. 'We're in for a week. Like I told you yesterday, there's a berth but it won't be there after Monday.'

I watched him walk back to his seat. I didn't want to think about work or the social politics of life on the pier. I still had the wedge in my pocket and I wanted access to the freedom it was supposed to buy me.

One thing was for sure: if the world was full of possibilities they'd never come to light in this bar. I swallowed what was left of my pint and was about to go when I saw the door open and Doyle walk in. He was pale and sweaty. When he saw me he stopped. 'Where's my money?

'The fish in the hold are yours.'

'And what fucking good is that to me?'

'Sell them, same as me and Scully . . .'

'And the boat crawling with Special Branch?' He was shouting now.

I fingered the notes in my pocket and peeled off four. When I pulled them out we looked at them. Two tens and two fives, a week's wages.

Doyle grabbed me by the collar of my shirt. 'That's my fucking money, you little cunt.' He was vibrating with rage. 'Don't fucking offer it to me like it's charity.' I knew that any second now I'd feel the force of his forehead crashing into my nose or his knee in my crotch.

'Take it outside, lads.' The barman's voice came up sharp from behind me. 'Outside!'

In the second it distracted him, I pulled backwards. Buttons flew but I was free. I ran. I heard him shouting but he didn't come after me. Outside, I realised I still had the money in my hand. I also realised that the collar of my collarless shirt was torn.

I walked uphill fast. I was angry but I didn't know why. This solid community of rough, sea-tumbled deckhands shot a net, hauled it, gutted the fish, boxed them, steamed home, got paid, got laid, went out and did it all again. Laughter over pints, camaraderie welded by salt, all bound together in the fellowship of the sea. Except that it wasn't. It was just violent and greedy, and no one gave a fuck. The day before yesterday, Hutch was handing me a bag of slops to feed to a woman in the hold, in love, happy. Where was he now? No one gave a fuck. Not even me. Scully was gone too. And Doyle, the cheap, spineless piece of shit, was roaming the bars looking for cash or vengeance.

I stopped at the wall, breathing hard. Down there in the harbour the boats huddled together, shuffling like a collection of shoes without feet.

Chapter 14

Bristol, 2008

I shot through the streets on my bicycle. Sunshine danced on the surface of new leaves and radiated in the yellow lanterns that dropped from the laburnum trees to paint the pink tips of the magnolia in a lustre that was almost obscene. Early summer – the time of year I loved: everything was vibrant, even the traffic on Gloucester Road limping from light to light.

Philip was wearing a dark pin-striped suit, a white shirt and a pink tie.'Morning,' he said.

'Lovely day.'

'Yes, it is. How are you?'

I had just sat down and felt I had better cap what might gush from me. 'Fine,' I said.

Then Philip smiled. I had seen him smile before, within the context of a conversation, but this was unheralded. 'You look well,' he said.

'Thank you, Philip. You look well yourself.'

'I see.' He sat back. 'What is it you want to tell me?'

'Tell you?'

'Yes, Seán, tell me.'

It had been, what, half an hour since Kate's call? I was still beaming and this bastard had picked up on it. The feelings that the call had raised in me were mine. Share them here and they'd be analysed to mulch.

'I got a phone call just now from Kate – Kate Wren?' Why was I doing this? 'It turns out I know her mother.' I waited but he said nothing. 'Kate's mother is Emma Balstead.'

'The girl from your fishing days?'

'Yes. Her.'

He looked from me to his hands, then back to me again. 'There are certain practical considerations that come into play here, as I'm sure you're well aware, but apart from those, how does this make you feel?'

A word popped into my mind. One that I had always felt was too absolute to apply to me.

'Happy,' I said. 'Happy and excited.'

Philip began nodding. 'I see.'

'Oh, for fuck's sake, Philip, has everything got to be dragged out and examined? I mean, is nothing immune from this . . . this searching? And why? What's the purpose of it all? To shed the dirt that experience has left so you can walk around all cool and clever without a morsel of the past clinging to you? There are some parts of my past I want to keep.' I'd surprised even myself with this outburst.

Philip's forehead wrinkled, tightening the dome of his head so the skin shone. 'If you prefer things to remain untouched, why are you coming here?'

'Because things are fucked up.'

'Well, do you want to unfuck them or not? It's entirely up to you.'

It was a question to which there were many answers. The devil you know, the devil you don't know. The phrase rattled through my head like the beat of a train on a track. Yes, yes, I wanted better relationships in my life. Or I wanted to rid myself of whatever stopped me forming real relationships. I had lain in the mud of my infant past with therapists galore but it was access to myself that I hadn't yet got. My whole personality was a fabrication designed to change its shape and form so it would fit wherever it found itself. It was no wonder Lynn found it impossible to have a relationship with me. I was a fake. And what would happen if I found the real me? Would I like it? Would it like me? It was just so much fucking easier to stay where I was. But if I did, my life would continue to wither and I'd end up alone, transmitting whatever version of myself I thought was required.

When the session was over, I cycled back to the house a little less aware of the joys of the season.

Mark was excited about his cricket tour. Karen, too, was excited but in a very cool, pre-teen way. Lynn had a crispness about her. Footsteps on the stairs raced faster, doors slammed louder and requests were everywhere.

'Dad, I'll need a new club tie,' Mark said at breakfast.

'What's wrong with the one you have?'

'It's too small.'

'How can a tie be too small?'

'It is!'

Karen's approach was different. 'Dad, you name it and I'll do it, the garden, my bedroom, everything will be spotless after I get back if I can just have a couple of things.'

'What do you need?'

'Mum knows.'

'It's too complicated for me?'

'It's just not stuff you know anything about.' Her smile was strained with impatience. 'All I need is a couple of hundred pounds.'

'You've got to tell me what it's for.'

'Mum knows.'

'Right, I'll talk to Mum.'

Karen slunk away, angry at her inability to extract cash from me. When Lynn came into the kitchen, I asked her what Karen needed a couple of hundred pounds for. That smile crossed her face, the one that said, 'You haven't a clue, have you?'

'What are you talking about?' she said.

'Karen says she needs things for Cornwall, a couple of hundred pounds' worth of things.'

'It's news to me.'

'She said you knew all about it.'

'I said if there was anything special she needed she should ask you.'

'She presented it to me like it was a done deal.'

'Look, Seán, I'm busy. If you don't want to give the child any money then don't. It's up to you.'

'What? I didn't say that.'

'I'll sort it out.'

'Lynn, will you stop this?'

'Stop what exactly?'

'Stop doing this thing.'

'Oh, for Christ's sake, your daughter's going away with a friend for a weekend and she'd like a few new things, that's all. But if you're too tight to put your hand in your pocket, don't worry about it. I'll do it.'

'That's not the point.'

'Oh, is it not?'

*

I bought a map of Canada, a place I knew almost nothing about. A continuous mountain range ran down the centre slightly to the left. I saw a small tent between the trees, silhouetted by a lake glimmering in the full moon. Coyotes howling and the high sky chilling with the onset of autumn, or fall, as the Canadians call it.

I smiled, thinking I had just made my own internal advert for the Canadian Rockies. But a question plagued me: would a temporary change of geographical position make any difference? Geraldine thought it would and she was always right. Maybe time alone was what I needed. It would change the perspective. And maybe all those questions that had poured out of me at Philip's would disappear – no longer relevant.

But something else was going on. Since Kate's call, I was aware of excitement. The gods of coincidence had flicked me a card that was pure, simple and sweet, the Emma Balstead card. The question was, how to play it? Straight away, the boys in the advertising agency went to work. Offerings all began with her image. She was still beautiful, more so in fact because the intervening decades had chiselled character into the perfection of her face. They then took us on the romantic route, hand in hand, crunching the leaves of an autumn forest (these advertising boys seemed stuck in one season). The sexual route where Emma and I lay smiling and exhausted, nothing but a twisted sheet coiled about our drying limbs.

But all of this was a fleck of sparkling glitter laid down in the midst of a cold dull season. Emma, my Christmas. And what was wrong with that? People needed something to help them through winter, so perhaps they needed a little something to help them through life. Alcohol for some, heroin for others, gambling, golf and a thousand other supports to pass the time between cradle and grave. Why should Emma Balstead not be one for me? Because she was a person with a life of her own and I was a person who was supposed to have a life of my own? And if I stopped trying to leach off other people's lives maybe my own would become fulfilled and I wouldn't have to. But if I was going to do something positive I had to make a definite decision to do it and not just leave myself in neutral to be shunted into whatever was in front of me.

OK, here it was: as far as Emma Balstead was concerned, I would call Kate back, thank her for the information, tell her to wish her mother well from me, then put the phone down. That done, I would remove the fantasy, and the role I had allowed it play, from my life. That way, I might begin discovering who I was.

Chapter 15

Howth, 1976

I left the wall, walked through the village and then uphill towards the Summit. Halfway there I heard the high-pitched whine of bikes coming from behind me. I was about to turn to see who it was when they whizzed past. Cahill was at the front with Susie on the back. Two more bikes followed. They leant into the bend ahead and were gone.

As I neared the Summit Inn, I saw the bikes parked in a cluster by the road. Sitting around a long wooden table outside the pub were their owners.

'Jaysus, would you look at the cut of that!' Cahill said, when he saw me.

I said my hellos and sat. Apart from Cahill and Susie, there were three others at the table. One was a tall thin strip called Plasma, so named because of the amount of blood transfusions he had had after his many bike accidents. The other was his friend, Joey, a rodent-like art student who never said much. And the third was a lank, gormless collection of spots known as Dudley.

'I'm amazed you can walk after the state you were in last night,' Plasma said.

'Were you in Liam's?'

'Was I in Liam's? For fuck's sake, man, I was talking to you for a fucking hour.'

This was met with general laughter.

'Speaking of drink, does anyone want one?'

'If those are new clothes, you're not looking after them very well,' Susie said. She and Cahill were draped around one another – her bare thigh lay over his legs.

He laughed loudly. 'Farreller can't look after anything very well.'

I stood. 'I really didn't think I'd have to ask twice.'

This stirred them. It was pints all round, except for Susie: she wanted a crème de banane with soda. Asking the old man for the pints was fine, but when I asked for Susie's concoction he just looked at me. For a moment I thought he was going to ask my age. 'I'll see if we have it,' was all he said. With that he walked to the far end of the bar and bent forward as though he had decided instead to vomit. He stayed in that position long enough for me to think he was suffering some kind of seizure. Then he straightened, holding a bottle.

I brought the drinks out on a tray. Susie's cocktail was sampled by all. Plasma winced and pretended to spit. Joey tasted it, then immediately rinsed his mouth with the pint. By the time it got back to Susie it was almost empty so I went to get another. At the bar I decided to get us all one. On the final pour into the last glass the barman threw the empty bottle into the bin.

The taste was complicated, sweet but with a harsh sting. It gave us a taste for the exotic. And Susie seemed knowledgeable on the subject. She described Brandy Alexanders, Stingers and a variety of rum cocktails. The thought of going back to the old man and asking for five banana daiquiris was more than I was willing to do. But the Stingers sounded viable. Plasma volunteered and emerged ten minutes later, to everyone's delight, with a tray of green cocktails. The instant I tasted mine I was in love – peppermint and brandy fighting one another to lay down layer after layer of competing flavours.

I sipped and smiled. This was freedom, sitting on top of the hill, friends, laughter, a view of the coast that stretched into the blue. Just beyond the point where it disappeared there was a building I had never seen, a place that housed two or three hundred young ladies, one of whom was Emma. What was she doing now – in her dark room, studying, lying on her bed watching the fluff fall though the sunbeams?

The rattle of Liam's bike broke through the conversation. He drove right up to the table. Max pulled in behind him. They placed their feet on the ground and their helmets on their tanks. Both surveyed the table. 'Bit of a party, is it, lads?' Liam asked.

'The trawlerman's gone mad buying cocktails,' Plasma told him.

'Why don't you join us?' I asked them.

'Don't mind if we do.'

When they were settled with their Stingers, Liam turned to me. 'I was just on the blower to Carol.'

'Yeah?'

'Apparently you wrote to Blondie and told her you'd be down to take her out one of these nights.'

'Liam, it was part of a letter, a rant, poetic licence and all that.'

'How old do you have to be to get one of those?' Joey smirked.

'Well, it seems the poor girl has her heart set on it now.'

Suddenly life seemed rich. I could jump on a train. I'd be there in two hours. Then another thought struck me.'Anyone fancy a blast?' I said to the table. 'I got the cash – we could just fill the tanks and go.'

'Go where?' Dudley asked.

'Down to St Helen's in Wexford and liberate a couple of the inmates.'

Cahill laughed, again too loudly. Liam said, in a serious tone,

'I'm running in a new piston so I'd have to take it easy. I can't take anyone on the back.'

'That's OK,' I said. 'I can go with Max. Between us we have enough bikes.'

'You must be fuckin' mad, Farreller, if you think me and Susie are freezin' our arses off all the way to Wexford just so as you can get your hole,' Cahill said.

'I'm game,' Max said.

'Well, if you're paying, I'm definitely game,' Plasma said.

'In that case, we'd better have one for the road,' said Liam, smiling.

Half an hour later, leaving Cahill and Susie with a table load of empties, we climbed aboard the bikes and engines blared.

I went with Max, Joey with Plasma. Liam and Dudley were on their own bikes. We pulled into Liam's house so he could phone Carol and tell her we were on our way. When he came out, he was carrying a leather jacket. He threw it at me. 'Be warmer than that poncy thing you're wearing.'

I put it on over the denim one, pulled up the zip, turned up the collar and we were away.

It wasn't Hollywood – no orange sunset igniting chrome and the roads were too familiar – but it was freedom. Above us a large sky was darkening; beneath us black asphalt sped under our wheels, engines sang and the leather jacket remained solid against the wind.

We skirted the base of the Wicklow Mountains, which rose above us like great dark waves. If I ever saw their like at sea I'd count my life in seconds. But here they were frozen. And above them the first scattering of stars twinkled.

When we left the mountains behind, the roads became long, straight and dull, darkness robbing them of features. The excitement of bike travel gave way to monotony. By the time we reached Wexford I was huddled behind Max, cold and stiff.

Liam took charge of directions. The school was eight or so miles south of the town. With the help of some locals we found the right road but St Helen's evaded us. It wasn't until we were heading back up the same stretch of road for the third time that a headlight picked out a large tarnished brass sign that read, 'St Helen's Catholic School for Girls'.

The plan had been to pull up at the gate, beep once and wait. As soon as the last of the engines was silenced, Carol's voice came down from the trees: 'For fuck's sake do you want the whole school down here?' Her face floated like a mask in the leaves. 'Push the bikes to the lane.' She indicated that that was somewhere up the road.

We did, then gathered in front of this dark passage and waited. I was nervous. Now that the effect of those sugary cocktails had worn off, I realised that this was not how I had pictured the reunion between Emma and me. I'm not sure what I had pictured but, whatever it was, it was not this.

Out of the darkness they appeared. Carol was in front, picking her way through the vegetation. Behind her was Emma, although all I could see of her was her hair. There was another girl beside her, smaller and dark. They stumbled through the undergrowth and out on to the road. Carol walked towards Liam. Emma and the other girl stood as if they were posing for a photograph.

I walked up to Emma. 'Hi,' she said, smiling.

'Hi.'

'I like the new look.'

I nodded.

'Are you going to just stand there or are you going to give me a kiss?'

We embraced. I was aware of her hair in my face and then her lips kissing mine. There were sounds all around, all distracting. Carol was saying, 'Come on, you two, let's get out of here.'

We separated. I couldn't tell what she was thinking. Everyone was mounted on bikes, Carol with Liam, the other girl with Dudley.

'Can you take three, Max?' I asked.

He wasn't happy about it but he nodded. We climbed on, Emma in the middle. I put my arms around her, interlocking my fingers. The scent of lemon came from her hair. She was saying something but the wind took it away.

During a quick conversation between Carol and Emma at the first set of traffic lights in Wexford town, a destination was decided. We were going to the Nest. It turned out to be a bland-looking place, squashed between a grocery and a factory entrance. We pulled the bikes up in a line outside it.

'I've got to change before we go in,' Carol said, indicating a bag she was carrying over her shoulder.

'So have I,' said the other girl.

'This is Alice,' Carol said.

'You'll have to take me as I am,' Emma said. She was wearing jeans and a denim jacket.

'Where are you going to change?' Liam asked.

'In there,' Carol said, pointing to the doorway of the shop.

'Just shelter them, chaps,' Emma said. 'We'll be inside.'

It was packed. 'It's one of the only pubs in Wexford that isn't bothered about age,' Emma said. Any of the clientele that looked legally old enough to drink were in their nineties, the rest wore long hair, bell bottoms, full-length skirts and Afghan coats.

We found a seat at the back.

'Well, I suppose I'd better get you a drink,' I said.

She was staring at me. 'The haircut makes you look quite . . . different.'

'You preferred the scraggy-sheep style?'

144

'No, it's good. It's good to see you.'

'Your letters are amazing.'

'Yours too!'

Suddenly we both laughed.

'I'm nervous,' I said.

'Me too.'

'Look, I'll get us a drink, OK?'

'Mine's a vodka and tonic. Thanks.'

As I was walking to the bar the others came in. Alice was wearing a yellow shirt and wide red trousers. Carol had on the shortest skirt I'd ever seen.

'Down the back,' I called to them, and continued to the bar.

When I got there, Plasma came up beside me. 'Get us a pint of Harp, man, will you? Jesus, this was a fucking terrible idea.' Behind him I watched the others move like a herd into the haze.

'What's wrong with you?'

'Just get us a fucking pint. Jesus Christ!'

'Calm down, for fuck's sake. You can't drive all the way to Wexford just to turn around and drive back.'

We ferried drinks to the table and found we had no place to sit. They had all squeezed into what little space there was. I perched on the arm of a wooden chair occupied by Max, Plasma towering behind me. Emma was diagonally opposite.

Carol and Alice had put on make-up. It made them look older. I couldn't tell if Emma was wearing any or not. The three were sitting in a group, talking fast. Dudley was attempting to keep up – possibly streamlining himself for an assault on Alice. The rest of us sat; two hours of wind and raw road had robbed us of all earlier enthusiasm. The pints in front of us looked cold and tasted foreign.

I kept catching Emma's eye. We'd smile but it was hard to bridge the distance with words. Eventually, Carol engineered movement so we could sit together. In a way, this was worse. I couldn't think of a thing to say. She was looking at Alice and Carol, who were joking with Dudley and Liam. I began to tell her about the situation on the boat but it was too long and complicated for a crowded bar.

'Why does it say that on your T-shirt, Joey?' she asked. He was on the other side of the table from us. It was black and scrawled across it in white was 'Long time no sea'. He turned around and on the back was the skeleton of a fish.

Emma laughed. 'That's very clever. Did you do it?'

'It's part of my arts degree.'

'I'll get some drinks,' I said.

Emma put her hand on my knee to force me to sit down. 'Let someone else get them. Relax, we don't have to talk. It's just great you guys are here.'

'Emma, we've driven all this way and you've risked your necks to get out . . .'

'I know. Look, it's great to see you, it really is. Where did you get the jacket?'

She was referring to the denim one with the teardrop lapels. Liam's was on the floor at my feet. 'What do you think? I got it today.'

'Looks like it came out of an Oxfam shop.'

I didn't know what an Oxfam shop was but I presumed, from her tone, that it was not the place to shop if you wanted to look good. 'I was in a hurry,' I said.

She laughed at this. 'If you're going to the bar get me a large one.'

As the drinks seeped into us, the conversation reignited. I watched Emma's face move as she talked: her eyes danced, her smile flashed and she continually brushed curls from her face. I was aware of myself withdrawing. In my imagination it had been so different. Because of the intimacy of her letters I had begun to think of us not as people who interact with others but as something separate, something floating, two wisps of smoke that had curled around each other and were now one. But instead we sat there as awkward as strangers.

By closing time, Dudley had his arm around Alice and she had no objection to it being there. Plasma was slouched at the bar trading his wisdom with some of the pub's older customers. Carol and Liam were kissing and fondling where they sat. Emma, Max, Joey and I were chatting – well, maybe they were, I was doing more listening and, in fact, not even that. Joey was being entertaining, as he sometimes could be, with a series of sarcastic observations about the locals. He had Max and Emma in stitches.

When we were bundled outside by the bar staff's cries, I steered Emma into the doorway where Carol and Alice had changed.

'Will I go?'

'If you want to.'

'I don't.'

'Then why say it?'

There we were, inches apart and unable to clear the little space that remained. Emma stared at me for a moment and then at the ground. 'Seán, what we had was lovely and nothing's changed, but it was brief. And it's hard for both of us to pick up where we left off. Do you know what I mean?'

Her words were a relief. 'I do. Listen, it's me, I'm all fucked up – I'm sorry, I'll stop being a prat.'

'You're not a prat but you can be a bit of a ninny sometimes.'

'What the fuck's a ninny?'

She looked at me and laughed. Her eyes were silent and clear. 'If we just stop trying so hard, what we had might come back.'

Then we kissed. It was soft, gentle and delicate. When it was over, we hugged, and for the first time since I'd arrived I felt at ease.

Around us the pavement was clotted with groups of people, their laughter bouncing off the walls of the nearby houses. Carol, who had been talking to a group of locals, shouted something to Plasma about where to go next. I caught a glimpse of Liam trading attentions with Alice, while Dudley sat glumly on his bike behind them. Joey and Max were lost among the noise and the silhouettes.

'I don't know what all the fuss is about,' Emma said. 'We'll end up going to the boat club.'

'Is it far?

'About a mile.'

'Right, let's go.'

We began to walk.

'Did you ever play hopscotch?'

'Where I come from, men don't play hopscotch.'

'Well, you should.' She sprang one-footed from the ground, hopped and jumped through a set of imaginary squares, turned in the air and landed with two feet on the pavement. I tried it and fell in a heap.

'Christ, you're appalling. Look, here's an easier one, chasing.' With that she was off down the street. I ran after her but wasn't catching up. I cheated at the corners by grabbing them with an open hand and catapulting myself down the next street. When I got close enough, I broke into a sprint and launched at her with a rugby tackle. We crashed to the ground and lay there panting.

Above us a window slid open. 'What the bloody hell's going on out there?' When the only reply they got was laughter, the voice said, 'Here, I'm calling the police.'

Emma struggled to her feet. 'Now the police are after us. See ya.'

'Wait for me.' We ran to the end of the road and around a corner where we leant against a wall to get our breath.

'See, Mr Serious? Being a kid can be fun.'

A tangle of replies caught in my throat. I swallowed to send them back and said that, yes, it was, with her.

We walked on. She talked about the trouble she was in at school. But listening to her, I realised that, for her, school was not the battle it had been for me. She played the game but did it on her terms. When that led to trouble she'd use lies and pretence to try to get away with it. Getting away with it seemed to be what mattered. Whereas I had met it head on and had done battle. A mad strategy because I could never win. All that happened was endless beatings and, in the end, expulsion.

We were strolling by the seafront. But the sea was a long way out. Between us and it, the ribs of rotting hulls stuck out of the mud like the remains of the monsters from a child's nightmare.

'How come you go to a Catholic school in Ireland?'

'It's all my mum's idea.'

'Is she Irish?'

'No! But she's a Catholic and she wanted her darling to be brought up in an environment of strict Catholicism. If she had any idea what really went on she'd have a heart attack. Serve her right, the bitch.'

There was a deep-felt streak of bitterness in the words. 'Is she really a bitch?'

'Yeah, she is. A bitch and a hypocrite.'

'Jesus, that sounds bad.'

'She owns boutiques in London and Manchester and she treats the people who work for her like shit. She lives off their labour but won't pay them a decent wage. But every Sunday without fail she's down on her knees, tongue out, receiving the body of fucking Christ. She makes me want to vomit.'

I looked out past her to the thin strip of water catching moonlight and the swollen mud around it. I wanted to say something to lift Emma away from the bitterness but I could think of nothing.

But suddenly she stopped and gazed into the distance. 'Last year,' she said, 'Dad nearly died . . .' She clasped her lower lip between her teeth. 'He didn't want me coming back here but she wouldn't entertain anything else.'

'I don't think my mother would ever dare disagree with my old man.'

'Mine are separated so Dad doesn't get much of a say.'

'You live with her?'

'Yeah, when I'm not down in this hellhole. Although I don't know which is worse.'

The moonlight was shining on her skin. 'Why don't you come back with me?' I said.

She picked up a stone and flung it. It sat into its path of flight and dropped in a slow arc towards the water, landing so far out we almost missed the splash.

'Fuck!' I said.

'See? I'm a champion.'

I found a stone.

'Come back with you?'

'Yeah, come back to Dublin.' I threw it. It landed with a slurp in the mud fifty feet away.

'You really are appalling. What would we do?'

'In Dublin? We'd rent a flat and tell them all to go fuck themselves. Parents, teachers, nuns, the police, drunken arsehole skippers, anyone. We'll raise a flag – it'll be our declaration of independence. It'll say, "Anyone who thinks they have power over us, anyone who thinks they can tell us what to do can just fuck off!"'

'That would be fantastic.'

'Well, let's do it, then.'

She was smiling at me. 'OK.'

'Are you serious?'

'Yes, I am.'

'Emma, this is fantastic – it's brilliant. You'd really do it?'

'Yeah!'

'What about the nuns, and your mother?'

'We'll just raise the flag.'

I was laughing now. 'Listen, there's an old trawler on the East Pier. We can stay there till we get organised. I've got a shitload of money. Emma, this is really fantastic.'

'Don't get Mr Serious back.'

'No, no, he's gone.'

We kissed but there were too many things jumping around in my head for it to linger. I smiled at her, took her hand and we climbed up towards the street-lamps and the road.

Emma said, 'We're walking through the palm trees on a moonlit stretch of the Ivory Coast on our way to the Officers' Ball. You have just proposed and I'm all a-flutter with a sweet little song in my head.'

'What's the song?'

She stopped and smiled and began to sway her hips, smooth and slow, then she pouted and sang, 'It ain't the meat, it's the motion,' then broke into laughter. Finally, when she could, she said, 'You should have seen your face!'

Plasma and Joey were at the bar while the rest of them sat around plates of luncheon meat laid out on circular tables at the end of the long room. The boat club was packed. Up by the stage, couples lurched to Rod Stewart singing 'Maggie May'. We joined Plasma and Joey.

Plasma wasn't happy. 'Look, man, we're in fucking Wexford, it's midnight and we're all gee-eyed. What the fuck's going to happen?'

I gave him a ten-pound note and told him to buy a drink for everyone. For a moment he was speechless, which, for Plasma, was saying something.

Emma and I danced, then joined the others at the table. Plasma had followed instructions – the table was a sea of pints and shorts. Max was slumped in his chair. His eyes were closed, the pint he was holding perched at a dangerous angle. When I tried to remove it, his grip tightened and his eyes slid open. 'Not so fast, Spanner Boy,' he said, and let his eyes fall shut again.

The girls got up in a group, saying they were going to the loo, leaving Liam, Dudley, me and Max at the table. 'I'll tell you one thing,' Liam said, 'he's not getting up on a bike tonight.'

The question as to where we would stay was lurking. But I didn't want to think about it. Emma and I were going to live together from now on. This was the equivalent of a marriage. Emma was probably in there telling them about it now. This was huge and it was exciting, but it was also scary. I would have to be more careful now: I had someone to look after, and someone to look after me. This was going to be good.

White neon spat, flashed and droned into solid life, revealing tabletops awash with food scraps, cigarette butts and spilled beer that had dried dark and hard into the Formica. There was a migration of couples from the floor. Among them was Plasma. He had his arm around the shoulders of a woman in a red frock who was at least five years older than him. Joey was in tow with her friend.

'This is Joan,' he announced. 'She's got somewhere we can stay.'

She was reversing out of his grip, mumbling something about it only being a caravan. Plasma laughed and spoke into her ear. Emma, Carol and Alice returned. None of them looked happy.

Emma sat beside me and asked for a cigarette. I had never seen her smoke before. 'What's the matter?' I asked.

'Alice wants us to go back now, all of us.'

'What about Carol?'

'She wants to stay out till dawn.'

'And you?'

She looked at me. 'I'm with you.'

Outside, Plasma got busy arranging who went where. He seemed to be a master at getting people to move in the direction that suited him while letting them believe it was they who had made the decision. The girls had gathered into a group again and I could see it was Alice who was conducting the conversation, talking fast and pointing at Emma. Dudley made the mistake of sidling up to them and putting his arm around her. She shrugged him off like a fly.

I was standing beside Max, having to put out my arm every now and then to steady him, when Emma came up to us. 'You OK?' I asked. She didn't reply, just held her lower lip with her front teeth.

Plasma called, 'You three walk out towards the beach. Someone will be back for you. Wait a second.' He hurried over and, in hushed tones, said, 'Listen, if we play our cards right we'll all have a place to crash. Just walk out along that road there.' He pointed into the blackness. 'Liam or Dudley or some-fucking-body will come back and get you. It's only a mile. You'll see it, a field full of caravans. Joan's is at the back, furthest corner from the gate.'

'How do you know all of this?' I asked.

He pointed to his nose, tapped it, and winked.

We found the road; it was dark and straight. We wedged Max between us to stop him floating into the hedges. He was obedient, but slow. He kept wanting to stop and admire the heavens.

I was becoming sober and beginning to feel very tired. I wanted so much to crawl into a bed, snuggle into a pillow and look at Emma lying beside me. But I knew there was almost no hope of that happening. The best we could hope for was a space on some floor.

The bikes sped past us hooting; Liam shouted something about coming back to get us soon. The road began to weave and turn but showed no signs of producing a caravan park. The lights from cars came up behind, illuminated our shoulders and hair, swept by. Then, from ahead, came a single light. I could tell as it approached that it was Liam. He made a U-turn behind us and stopped by Emma. 'Who wants to come with me?'

We steered Max on to the passenger seat and there, face against Liam's back, he said, 'See you, Spanner Boy.'

Liam tipped his shining helmet. 'See you at the party.'

'Wait a minute, how far is it?'

'A mile or so.' He smiled and shot off.

'A long fucking mile!' I mumbled.

We walked on.

'What's with Spanner Boy?' Emma asked.

'Don't know, haven't a clue.'

'Are you angry?'

'No, just tired.'

'You're beginning to think this whole thing is mad?'

'No, I'm just tired. But soon we'll have our own flat and in it will be a bed.'

'A big double bed.'

'Yes.'

'And a cat.'

'I hate cats.'

'You're a monster, then.'

'See how desperate you are? You're running away with a man who hates cats.'

She was quiet for a while. Then she said, 'I am desperate. But I'm not running away because I'm desperate. I'm running away to be with you.'

'I'm glad,' I said.

We were alone on a road beneath stars that jumped in and out between rags of clouds being driven across the sky by a wind I couldn't feel. 'What'll happen tomorrow, at school?' I asked

'They'll freak,' she said, and laughed. 'They'll haul Carol up, and Alice too, interrogate and strike. First stop will be to the printer to get the posters made.'

'You'll be famous all over Wexford.'

'Not me, ninny, you. "Seán Farrell, Wanted in Sixteen Counties for Schoolgirl Rustling".'

'How much reward?'

'Five hundred, tops.'

'Not a lot, is it?'

'We'll have to do banks, take hostages, that sort of thing.'

'Become mindless criminals hiding out above the tree line.'

'No! We'll be basking in the sun on the stern of our yacht off some tax-free haven like the Cayman Islands.'

'You see, that's the difference between you and me. You've got style and imagination. I've got nothing but a brain covered with fish scales and a vision that can't see beyond the H and H.'

'Whatever that is.'

'It's a square patch of waves in the middle of the Irish Sea.'

'Sounds delightful. Is it tax-free?'

'It's everything-free.'

'Well, that's perfect, then.'

The hedge gave way to a low wall over which we could see white oblongs parked in rows, their black windows as silent as sockets in a skull. Over the gate, further up, was a sign, saying, 'Glenhaven Caravan Park'. We followed a cinder pathway towards the back of the field. Noise came to us on the breeze from the far corner.

We passed Dudley and Alice. She was sitting on his bike. He was standing, the front wheel between his legs.

'You guys OK?' I asked.

Dudley said, 'If youse two are stayin' in there, youse better do it standin' up.' At this he gave a bellow.

'I'm going back as soon as Carol's ready,' Alice said. 'Are you coming?'

'No,' Emma said.

Inside the caravan, Joey was spread across the bed with his new friend. Max was slumped in a corner, asleep. Joan was sitting on a stool in the galley area, an elbow on the counter, looking at Plasma, who was spouting a variety of reasons why he and she should 'have at it'. His fingers were clasped about the neck of a bottle of Jack Daniel's. Carol and Liam were standing by the door. They might have been waiting for a train.

Emma looked at me. 'What now?'

'I don't know, but it's a shame to think of all those empty caravans scattered about and us with nowhere to stay.'

'It would give them something to put on the posters.'

'It would be a start.'

I suggested what I had in mind to Liam and he nodded. 'Right,' he said, 'let's go.'

He went to his bike, lifted the seat and took two screwdrivers from a small suede wrap. We crept through the aisles of caravans. It seemed obvious to me that, except perhaps for a few at the top where there were cars, they were empty. But Liam was cautious. When he eventually chose one, he knocked at the door and waited, like a postman. When no one came, he slid the bigger of his two screwdrivers into the weatherproofed slit of the door and levered it open by about a quarter of an inch. He inserted the smaller one where the lock was and the door popped open, wobbling on its hinges. Then he moved a couple of feet down the caravan and stood dead still.

I peered inside. It was empty and dark, about the same size as the one we'd just left. I stepped in. There was even a blanket on the bed. Liam was behind me. 'This is OK,' I said.

'Come on, let's get the women,' he said.

When we got there, Alice, Carol and Emma were talking outside. Carol looked at Liam and shook her head. Emma turned to me and smiled. 'So, what pumpkin have you turned into our marital bed?

'Emma!' Alice said. 'You know what's going to happen in the

morning if you're not there. You don't give a shit, do you?'

Emma slid her arm around my waist. 'Shall we go?' she said.

I could see Alice was on the point of tears.

'You'd better drive us back,' Carol said to Liam.

Emma and I walked away.

'Alice is upset,' I said.

'She'll get over it.'

'You're a hard woman.'

'Oh, for fuck's sake, I just want out,' she snapped.

'Look, Emma, you're fine, it'll be OK.'

She was silent until we reached the caravan. I climbed in and she followed. She sniffed the air. 'Well, things can only improve.'

'Don't count on it.'

'Seán, sorry about just now. I'm tired.'

'Well, it is a quarter past two.'

'God, in less than five hours the bedlam will start.'

What I thought was bedding turned out to be the thinnest woollen covering ever manufactured. We took off our shoes and climbed under it.

We kissed. It was strange kissing horizontally. I was afraid my saliva would leak out of the seal of our lips. Also, my arm was wedged under me. I tried to move so I could lift it and put it around her. The movement broke the kiss. 'Sorry,' I said, and lay down again, stroking her hair.

'Seán, do you mind if we just cuddle?'

'That's fine. Are you cold?'

'No, this is nice.'

And so we lay there under the paper-thin blanket, legs and arms wrapped around one another. I felt her curls on my cheek. My heart pounded, a cannon in battle, smoke drifting without urgency from the rim. My thoughts jumped about like children on a trampoline. I heard the bikes start up and listened as they trailed into silence.

I squeezed Emma to see if she was really there. I was in bed with her. I was an adult. She and I, almost asleep, like hundreds and thousands of couples everywhere. Ahead lay life, hard times, drudgery, laughter over the rim of a pint. I saw the bow of a trawler rise in a swell, bursting a wave, an explosion of white that froze in the air and fell, the gunwales awash and me gripping the wheel, my crew below, resting in their bunks, a bulkhead between them and a hold full of olive-green cod making pillows in the ice.

The door burst open. A tall figure carrying a bottle stumbled through it. 'Farreller, I want a blow-job from your wife.' It was Plasma. He fell over the step and crashed on to the floor. 'Fuck it!' he said, from beneath us.

Emma peered over my shoulder. 'Is he all right?'

'Plasma? No.'

Another figure appeared. I could tell by the hair it was Liam. 'Apologies, apologies, apologies,' he sang. 'I presume by now the consummation has taken place. I can only hope it was . . .' In his search for a word, his feet found Plasma. 'Get up, ye fucking guttersnipe,' he said.

'I'm going nowhere till I get a blow-job.'

'Fine,' Liam said, and stepped over him. He made his way to a narrow couch at the far end of the caravan and disappeared into the shadows.

I got up and closed the door. When I got back, Emma was shivering. I put my arms around her and rubbed her back. 'Turn around,' I said. She did and sat into me. I nestled her breast in my hand. It was a perfect fit. The mouse nose of her nipple nudged into the skin of my palm. An erection sprang to life. It was hard and hot and sent orders of its own as to what should happen next. Emma's breath trailed away. She used the air around her without a sound. Unlike Plasma, who lay feet from us making a slobbering feast of it, or Liam with his methodical, mechanical snores.

Chapter 16

Bristol, 2008

Peter answered when I called.

'Peter, hi, this is Seán Farrell. I'm looking for Kate.'

I heard the thud as the receiver went down, then her name being called in the distance.

'Hi,' she said, clear and out of the blue. 'Now is not a great time. Can we meet?'

'Meet?

'Yeah, meet up.'

'OK. Where, when?'

'Do you know Woodes on Park Street? It's a coffee shop.'

'Yeah.'

'Eleven tomorrow?'

'Let me have a look.' She had thrown me. I was supposed to be telling her to wish her mother the best from me. Instead, I was leafing through the pages of my diary. Tomorrow was a busy day but, oddly, there was room around eleven. 'Right, that's fine,' I said.

'See you then,' she whispered, in a hurry, and the phone went down.

Maybe Peter and she were in the middle of a row. She knew what I was calling about and had just presumed I'd want to meet up. So why hadn't I interrupted her presumption and done what I'd intended? Why hadn't I?

I didn't have to look far to find the answer. Inside me now an emotion danced, making everything seem frivolous, as if it was the last day before the holidays.

That night I helped Mark with his packing and even managed to talk to Karen about what she needed for her trip. It all boiled down to the fact that she did not have the right backpack to go away with. She had about three that would do, but none carried the right trademark. From the pages of a catalogue she showed me the one she wanted. It cost what it would take the average person in Britain two days to earn. My daughter had been taken over. Her entire self-worth, it seemed, depended on her being in possession of certain items with particular brand names. She hadn't been brainwashed, she'd been brain-bleached.

I had to be at least partially responsible for this state of affairs. I asked Lynn about it when she finally sat down.

'Don't tell me this is the first time you realised it?'

'Lynn, I don't shop with them, I don't buy their stuff. I guess I've just presumed they're as capable of seeing through marketing as anyone else.'

'Pretty stupid.'

'So it's fine by you that our daughter is a complete puppet to these corporations? They say, "You need it," and she runs out and buys it.'

'Oh, get off the bloody stage, for God's sake.'

'Lynn?'

'Listening to Karen, or the kids at school, going on about what they need isn't an awful lot different from listening to you go on about your expensive office furniture or Steve and his bloody wine. We're consumers, they're consumers. They're just a little more obsessed.'

'They're being manipulated by some very sophisticated machinery.'

'So what are you going to do – dismantle it?'

I came down the next morning to find the hallway full of bags. Mark had removed the shoes from the cupboard under the stairs searching for his trainers. When he couldn't find them, he abandoned the heap.

'You can't just leave this mess.'

'Dad! I only have a few minutes.'

'Clear it up!'

He flung the shoes back.

Karen stormed past without a word. When I got to the kitchen she was sitting by the table, crying. Lynn was hunkered down in front of her, telling her everything was going to be fine.

'How can it be?' she was saying. 'I may as well not go.'

Lynn shot me a look.

'Is there a problem?' I asked.

Lynn stood up and sighed. 'Just pack what you need, love.'

Karen fled from the room.

'Things are a little sensitive around here this morning,' I said.

'Yes,' she said. 'Anyway, you won't have to deal with it much longer. Karen is going off straight after school, I'm dropping Mark at the cricket club at five, then I'm off.'

'You're not coming back to the house between now and then?'

'Hardly. I'll be lucky to get away from the school by four.'

'I see.'

'So your weekend starts now. Any idea what you'll do?'

'I was thinking of going to Canada.'

'What? This weekend?'

'No! Some time in the future. You know, for a break.'

'Nice! We'll discuss it when I get back.'

There was the last-minute flurry, all funnelling towards the eight-thirty bottleneck when door slams were followed by more door slams and forgotten kisses were sought and received. Then silence.

The view from the basement window was still. Thin shoots curved outwards from bushes heavy with early-summer growth. Small birds, in their relentless squabbles, sent shivers though the leaves of the hedges. Overhead trees stood tall and silent, observing all.

I lowered myself into my chair and took out the notes on the couple who were due at nine. I read through every familiar word in an attempt to force myself to focus. It didn't work. I was excited about meeting Kate, about what might lead from it. All earlier resolutions had evaporated. And I was aware that I had mentioned nothing of this to Lynn. I had, in effect, lied to her. When she had asked me directly in the kitchen what I intended to do, I had used Canada to wrong-foot her. I was being devious. I was about to walk willingly into a situation that might put at risk everything I had and I was excited about it. I was a man with a death wish being led to the gallows.

At nine o'clock, the doorbell rang, and for the next hour I focused solely on the couple in front of me. When they left, I tidied the kitchen, watered the plants, then walked to Woodes on Park Street.

Kate was sitting outside, wearing a battered leather jacket. She was holding up a folded newspaper in one hand while chewing the tip of a pen she held in the other.

'Hi,' I said.

'Oh!' she said, dropping the paper on to the table. 'Hi.' She moved her chair, giving me access to the empty one beside her. I sat. 'Sorry. I'm terrible, I get completely mesmerised by these things.' She pointed to the newspaper. It was open at a sudoku puzzle.

'Would you like a coffee?' I asked.

'Sure, they'll bring it out. There's a waiter.'

'OK.'

'So, what about that, then?' she said.

Emma's eyes had been blue, I was nearly sure of it. Kate's were brown but, apart from that, there were resemblances everywhere. Why hadn't I noticed this before?

'You're looking at me weird,' Kate said.

'Sorry, I was just noticing.'

'What?' She seemed alarmed.

'How much like your mother you are.'

'Oh, I thought I had that chocolate stuff around my mouth – the stuff they sprinkle on the cappuccino.'

'No, your mouth's fine.'

'Oh, good. Sorry, now I'm being weird. This is a bit strange for me.'

'For me too.'

She seemed to relax. 'Right, I suppose it must be. How well did you two, I mean you and Mum . . . I couldn't get anything out of her but she definitely remembers you.'

'So you've told her?'

'Of course!'

'Right. I'm flattered she remembers me but I'm not surprised.'

'So it must have been big?'

'Did you tell her I was your marriage-guidance counsellor?'

'Oh, yeah! She thought that was hilarious.'

'I bet she did.'

'She's coming down.'

'She's coming down? What do you mean she's coming down? Down where?'

'Here, Bristol, today. Don't worry, this was all planned weeks ago. You're not being hoodwinked or bushwhacked or whatever the word is.'

'Why is she coming to Bristol?' My fingers were tingling and my stomach had just filled with air.

'Would it surprise you that she'd come to see her only daughter?'

'No, not at all.'

'I'm messing. She's editing a documentary.'

'I see.'

'I did tell you Mum makes documentaries, didn't I?'

'Possibly.'

'You mean you don't listen to every word?'

'I do, actually, but they get stored in different departments.'

A waiter appeared and I ordered.

'Are you going to tell me?' Kate said.

'Tell you what?'

'What the bloody hell went on between you and my mother.'

'It was a long time ago.'

She was quiet for a moment. Then she looked at me. 'Before Dad? I mean, it was before Dad?'

'God, yes. She was at school.'

Her eyes widened. 'Wait a minute, you're not the guy she got kicked out over?' She stared at me. 'You are, aren't you?'

'I don't know. What did your mum say?'

She sat back on the chair. 'There was this story about Mum running off with some madman she'd met when she was at school in Ireland.' Suddenly she straightened. 'Of course it was you, it has to have been. So you're the madman?'

'I don't really fit that description, though, do I?'

'But are you the guy she ran away with?'

'Kate, I'm not the person you should be talking to about this.'

'Well, either you are or you're not.'

'I can't just step out of your mother's past and fill in a load of detail that she might not want you to know about. Besides, it was all a long time ago, so nothing I told you would be reliable anyway.'

164

'Are you always so boringly cautious?'

'Look, we were both very young so it left an impression, but my impression and your mother's might be two very different things.'

Kate drank her coffee. She seemed thoughtful. 'Would you like to meet up with her again?'

The question caused chaos in my head. 'Yes,' I said, plucking the word from the riot.

Kate didn't say anything.

'When will she be here, in Bristol?'

'She normally doesn't leave Manchester until after the rush hour.'

'Does she stay with you?'

'No, at a hotel in Clifton. She visits us when she's here but she likes her independence does Mum.'

'How are you and Peter doing?'

'OK. We're together. Giving it another try. But never mind about that. I want to know about you and my mum.'

I laughed. 'Kate, my hands are tied.'

'Oh, go on, you're not bound by some weird-ass counsellor's oath here.'

'If I was you, I'd want to know every detail. But I can't tell you. I can't even tell you my impression of it. You've got to ask your mum.'

'You know, when Pete and I first went to you, I thought, Wow, this is a really cool guy; he's old, but not old. But I was wrong. You are old.' She stood up. 'Mum stays at the Rodney Hotel. I'm sure the number's in the book.'

'Kate, are you all right?'

'Me? Fine. Gotta go, that's all.'

Chapter 17

Wexford,1976

Cold had seeped into my bones. When I put my arm around Emma, there was a deep pain in my shoulder. She stirred. I squeezed her tight. She shivered into my back.

When I opened my eyes again it was daylight. Why did they call it 'broad'? Because the sun had the width of day to travel across?

Plasma was sleeping where he'd fallen. Liam was stretched on the narrow couch, one of his legs making a fire escape from his body to the ground. Emma's hand reached out behind her and landed between my legs. From her breathing, it sounded as though she was still asleep. An involuntary slow thrust of pelvis had me shoving my penis into her open palm. My erection felt like a hot stub encased in my trousers. I slid my hand to her breast and began to massage it. Her breathing changed.

I lay there almost afraid to breathe. My erection was one screaming demander in something I wanted to be tender, soft, delicate. Her fingers were almost touching it, separated only by a layer of velvet and a brass zip. It wanted to be freed, to be the centre of attention, to grind into her with a recklessness and explode in a torrent of fluid heat.

But her fingers lay almost still. Her breathing was slipping back into the regular routine. I turned on my back and sighed. Emma turned too. 'You OK?' she said. I tried to think of an answer but she took my attention away. Her fingers were on the move, slowly, with a destination of their own in mind. They trailed across my stomach, across my crotch, then down along my thigh. Please, God, no! Go back! The fingers stopped, curled and began to retrace their path. Then her other hand appeared. It went to the top button of my trousers. The zip made a slow smooth sound as she undid it. Her fingers sank into the gap and curled around the column of flesh, then, slowly, they began to pump. With every movement, cells splintered and a dangerously sweet pressure built. When it could no longer contain itself it burst up and out – the physical manifestation of every desire I had.

'Jesus Christ, Emma,' I said, a line of sweat receding from my forehead. She smiled and cuddled into me. And I was back surfing through images that were vague and plotless. Thoughts floated. Finally becoming too thin to make sense, they dispersed like liquid cobwebs.

Later I became aware of warmth on my feet. A patch of sunlight landed at the end of the bed and became a terminal for floating dust. Liam was sitting on the couch he had slept on. When he saw I was awake he said, 'We'd better get out of here.'

'What time is it?' I asked.

'Half nine.'

Emma's blue eyes, round and clear, were staring at me.

'Are you ready for your new life now?' I asked.

'I feel awful,' she said.

'About school?'

'No! Hungover.'

'We'll have a walk on the beach.'

'Yeah, while we keep the police busy chatting on the clifftop,' said the huddle of leather and bones on the floor beneath us.

One by one we got up. Liam went down to the caravan to see if Joey and Max were still there. Plasma dragged himself off the floor, took a seat and shivered. 'Christ almighty, big mistake coming down here – never again. Any cigarettes, anyone?'

I tried to close the door behind us when we left but it wouldn't shut.

The morning was cold and bright. Blue rollers crashed on to the beach below us in explosions of white that were chased back into the sea by hordes of dancing pebbles. Gulls hung in the air, only their heads moving.

Down at the other caravan, Joey was still in bed. So were Joan and her friend. Max was walking about the galley area in search of a kettle. 'Morning, all,' he said, as though greeting us in his own home.

'Jesus fucking Christ, what do youse all want?' said Joan, from the bed.

'Come on, Joey, it's time to fuck off,' Plasma said.

There was no movement from Joey.

'Where's Dudley?' I asked.

'He drove back last night,' Liam said.

'You're joking!'

'No, after we dropped the girls back he just kept going up the Dublin road.'

'Mad bastard.'

'Is there some place we could get a cup of tea?' Max asked.

'Not in here,' Joan shouted. Max took this as his cue to leave. We followed.

Emma and I walked to the cliff edge. I looked down at a stretch of white sand below us and wondered what it might be like to have a land yacht. Haul in the mainsail and rip across the smooth surface, dried kelp crackling under the wheels.

Behind us, Liam's bike rumbled into life. We turned and watched him, with Max on the back, wobble up the path. I presumed they were off to get Max's. Plasma was sitting on his bike with his helmet on. He was waiting for Joey. After a moment, he drove up to the door of Joan's caravan and shouted for him.

Joey appeared in his underpants, holding the rest of his clothes. He dressed in the doorway, hopping about on one foot. From there he leapt on to the back of the bike and they drove down to us.

'We're going to see if those guys need help,' Plasma said. 'We'll be back in a minute.'

'Whatever you say,' Emma said to him, with a smile. Plasma didn't smile back. He turned the bike and disappeared up the path.

'Why would they need help?' Emma asked.

'They don't. It's Plasma – he just wants to be on the move.'

Emma sat on the ground and huddled. 'I'm freezing.'

I put Liam's jacket over her and sat beside her. 'Cheer up. You'll soon be warm.'

'I want to be hot.'

I lay on my back. 'What are you complaining about? You're on Ireland's riviera.'

She rolled over on to me. 'How come you're so chirpy?'

'Oh, you know, young and in love.'

'Oh, fuck off!'

'It's true.'

'You mean you got to splash your wild oats about this morning.'

'Is that what wild oats are? Jesus, I think I'll give porridge a miss.'

'I'm going to suck your blood till I'm warm,' she said, putting her mouth on my neck.

I pushed her on to her back and held her on the ground. I placed my face directly over hers and threatened her with a long string of saliva. She screeched and twisted, trying to get her head out of the way. 'No, you don't. One good push and you're over the edge.'

She threw me aside and, for a moment, we lay in silence, looking up into the blue, caught by the sounds of the waves pounding on the shore below us.

'What do you think will be happening in school right now?' I said.

'Christ, I hope Carol remembered to take off her make-up.' Emma propped herself up on an elbow. 'Sister Agnes is away. And the other thing is, it's Sunday, so after mass there's benediction.'

'Which means?'

'I won't be missed till roll-call after breakfast, which will be in about an hour's time.'

The bikes appeared. Max's was minus its headlight and front indicators. Someone had kicked them in. He didn't seem too worried about it. When he echoed his earlier desire for tea, I climbed on the back with him and Emma got on behind Liam. She zipped up the jacket and smiled at me. 'You're right, I am getting warmer.'

The town of Wexford was crisp with church bells and people in their Sunday best heeding the call. We cruised, looking for a café, but nothing, except a few newsagents, was open. During a quick conversation at red lights it was decided to head for Dublin. There was bound to be a café on the way. Emma looked relieved.

Three hours later, after a brief stop in Arklow for breakfast, we pulled into Liam's drive and dismounted. I had become frozen into position crouched behind Max. The denim jacket was useless against the cold and the wind. Emma, on the other hand, was snug in Liam's leather. She came up to me as I was trying to rub some life back into my limbs. 'You poor boy,' she said, with a smile in her voice. 'Are you very cold?'

'Don't, Emma, I'm not in the mood.'

'Look, Seán, sooner or later you've got to learn you can't expect to be on the cutting edge of fashion and keep warm.' This caused huge amusement all round.

Inside we sprawled on the corduroy sofas, listening to Chuck Berry, gathering our senses. Liam came from the kitchen with a large pot of coffee and mugs on a tray. This was historic. We sat up as he placed it on the glass table. It brought an air of artificial politeness to the proceedings. When Joey thanked him I couldn't work out if he was taking the piss or not.

'After this, guys, you've got to split. My folks get back at four and I want to clean the place up. The kitchen's a shambles.'

We drank the coffee and left. Outside, there was talk of where to go. But through the indecision it became clear that everyone had had enough and wanted to slide under the cover of home for a few hours. We were offered lifts but, not sure where we'd go, we didn't accept any.

The bikes left. Liam closed his door. Emma and I took each other's hand and walked down the drive. Howth was less than two miles up the road and that was the direction we went. The sky was now grey, that particular type of grey that only a Sunday can produce, solid, steely, Monday-is-coming grey.

We walked along the main road and I began to look at people as they passed in their cars. They just sat there, staring through their windscreens, waiting for their destination to appear. Which it would, if they didn't take any wrong turns, break down or crash. And to them we were like any young couple, fresh from their individual homes, out for a Sunday-afternoon stroll. I wished they were right. There again, maybe they were. It was Sunday afternoon and we were strolling. The long stroll to nowhere.

And it dawned on me then that everybody presumes everybody else's life is hunky-dory and that theirs is the only one that's a mess. I mean, there I was holding hands with Emma. We'd be just a speck of insignificant detail to the occupants of the passing cars. And if they did clock us, the emotion the sight was likely to evoke, in men anyway, was envy. 'Christ, lucky swine, what I'd give for a half an hour with her.' Or they didn't clock us because they themselves were up to their tonsils in skulduggery. This one'd just killed his wife, that one her husband. This one had the body in the boot. That one'd just hatched the plan. This one'd been told they had cancer, that one that their child had. Each metal mould that housed a human had any one of a million thoughts or emotions going around in it. And every one that housed two had at least four times that number.

When I told Emma what I was thinking, she was silent. Then she said, 'You can't always live outside your own life.'

'What do you mean?'

'Outside, as though you're not part of yourself. You know, you're looking at these people and yourself with equal distance.'

'No, I'm seeing us the way they'd see us, just for a minute.'

'But they're in their lives, living them. We're in ours.'

'But I don't know what mine is,' I said.

'Well . . . that's OK.'

'It's not. It feels like I'm sliding around the outside of mine all the time. Things happen – I don't make them happen, they just do.'

'No, you make decisions.'

'Like what?'

'Well, like quitting school and going fishing.'

'I didn't quit, they threw me out. And I went fishing to piss my old man off.'

She smiled a little. 'You take pissing people off pretty seriously, then.'

I didn't know what to say. 'It's hard to explain,' I said.

'And now, you and I, it's not a Sunday after-lunch stroll, is it?

'I wish it was.'

'Why? Are you sorry I'm here?'

'No! It's just that I'd love to have just eaten lunch.'

She laughed and swung my arm.

'The Belmont Hotel does lunches,' I said.

'Shall we?'

'Fucking right.'

The dining room smelt of steamed vegetables. The waiters wore black suits and dicky bows and moved with speed through the tables, taking and delivering orders. No one raised an eyebrow when we entered. A waiter met us and brought us to a table by the window, the harbour behind the folds of the net curtains. He placed menus before us and disappeared.

'This is great,' Emma said.

Another waiter appeared. 'Will you be having a drink?'

'We'll see the wine list,' Emma said.

'Wine list?'

'Yes,' she said, insistent but smiling. I watched him hesitate for a moment. Then he said, 'OK, then.'

I exhaled as soon as he was out of earshot.

'What's the matter?' she asked.

'It must be the accent. He wouldn't be bringing us the wine list if you talked like every other fucker.'

'It's different in hotels. I have dinner with my dad in London all the time and the waiters never question it.'

'Yeah, but he's a full-grown man, sophisticated . . . He probably wears a pin-striped suit.'

'He does, actually,' she said, and laughed. Then she went quiet. 'I miss him.'

'Now, that's something I could never say about my own father.'

'Really? Don't you love him?'

This was embarrassing. 'The guy's a shit, a hypocrite and a liar and I hate him.'

'Seán, really, is that the truth?

'Yes.'

'But how can he be?'

'He is, trust me.' I could see she was looking at me all curious and disbelieving. I wanted to shake free of the conversation. But Emma was still staring at me. 'Look, he hangs out up in the yacht club – you can go and meet him if you want. I'm sure he's there now, buying drink for people who make more money in a month than he will in his life. He does it to impress them and then, when their backs are turned, he'll be sniffing around their wives.'

'Gosh! What does your mum do?'

'Valium, mostly. Honestly, my family's not something you want to be around.'

'So why go to all that trouble to piss him off?'

'You mean the fishing?'

'Yeah!'

I wanted badly to change the subject, so I said that, really, I'd always wanted to be a fisherman. I rattled on about how we were the last of the great hunters. I was glad when a waiter came and took the wine order, and another to find what we wanted to eat. I was bullshitting and Emma knew it. 'At least fishing will give us enough to get set up,' I said, when the waiter was gone.

She raised an empty glass. 'Well, here's to my great hunter.'

Now I was embarrassed. 'Well, here's to the hunted,' I said, raising mine, not knowing what the fuck I was talking about.

She smiled as though I'd said something profound.

The waiter appeared again, this time carrying a bottle of white wine. He showed Emma the label. She read it and nodded at him. He poured a little into her glass. She picked it up, passed it under her nose, then nodded again. He smiled and put the bottle into a silver bucket of ice in the centre of the table. I was stunned by the intimacy of the ritual they had performed. 'Impressed?' Emma asked, when he was gone.

I shrugged. 'Not really. We do that sort of thing all the time on the boats, only with tea.'

She poured me a glass. The taste was sharp and left a host of crisp sensations that flushed themselves away leaving me wanting more. 'Nice,' I said.

'Should be at the price.'

Then the food arrived. Emma had ordered hake. It might have been the very fish Scully and I had sold on Friday. I had a steak.

'Oh, you can't believe what it's like to eat real food again,' Emma said.

'Don't they feed you well?'

'They feed us slops. Then, three weeks before the end of term, they force-feed us pasta so we look like we've been eating properly when we get home. Nuns, I tell you, pure scum.'

'That's terrible.'

'Well, it can't be a lot better out on those boats.'

I began to talk about life aboard. Maybe it was the way she listened, in so far as she did listen, or maybe it was the wine, or the oddness of the circumstances – whatever it was, the words just spilled out. As I spoke, I felt the back of my neck tighten. I was telling her this and telling her that and making it all a little funnier or harder or more ridiculous than it actually was. But all the time I couldn't ignore that it was my life I was talking about, and I wished it was someone else's. It wasn't the work, or the smells, or the filth, it was just all so much without any tenderness. It was strange to be aware, in the back of your mind, that there was a concept like tenderness, jumping up and down to make itself heard. It was because we were here in the soft Sunday-afternoon murmur, so far from it all.

When I thought the feeling was leaking into my voice, taking the polish off the humour, I tapered off with a few irrelevancies and a large slug of wine.

'Seán, you can't do that for ever.'

'The world is a big place, Emma. Fuck schools and boats and the bastards who run them. We'll go away travelling. We'll hitch to Morocco.'

'What are we going to do now?'

The wine was making a puppet of my tongue. 'We'll get a room here for a couple of weeks and then be gone.'

'They'll never believe in a million years we're married.'

'They served us wine.'

'That's something else entirely.'

'See the pier – the one on the right, see it?'

She peered through the net curtains and angled her head. 'What am I supposed to be looking at?'

'Two boats.'

'There's boats everywhere.'

'Well, there's two down the end of that pier. We're going to stay on one of them and I've been offered a job on the other. So, first thing tomorrow, I'll see the skipper and then we'll head into town, go to one of those student rental agencies and get a place. They'll ask no questions.'

'So we'll live in the city?'

'Yeah, in one of those leafy Georgian parts with lots of bricks and railings. We'll both have umbrellas and black bicycles. It'll be brilliant.'

'Seán, it would, except you'll be away all the time.'

'Not all the time. There's the weekends.'

'And what'll I do during the week?'

'Shop, coffee in Bewley's, have a whirlwind romance with Dublin, and when we get a little money together we'll take off.'

'Where?'

'The Cayman Islands.'

'What about the other place, the place where you fish?'

'The H and H?'

'Yeah.'

'We're definitely not going there.'

'But you promised!'

'No, we'll stay far away from anywhere with a H in it.'

'Seán, this would all be so fabulous if you didn't have to work.'

'Welcome to life with the proletariat. We're dirty and loud but we're honest.'

'You condescending little shit.' Her eyes were shining.

When the empty plates and glasses were taken away, we let our fingers link. Our fellow Sunday swallowers had gone, out through the cream-coloured doors and off. We sat.

'Let's go for a walk, a proper Sunday after-lunch stroll,' Emma said.

'I'd much rather slide with you between the sheets of one of the beds upstairs.'

'Come on, dreamer,' she said.

Outside, she snuggled into me. 'Listen,' she said, 'no matter what happens, this is a million times better than school.'

We walked without direction. Up the hill past the Lighthouse pub and around the corner where the doors of the Hope Inn stood closed for the duration of the long Sunday holy hour. We took a short-cut through the community-centre car park, which led us on to the cliff walk. It was a four-, maybe five-mile path, skirting the peninsula, too far for us in our present state. Besides, it would drop us in Sutton. No one, except the people who lived there, would choose Sutton as a destination. But we were strolling arm in arm and, for the moment, neither destination nor time mattered.

Once on the clifftop we were exposed to a sharp north-easterly wind. To the right of us, the hill swept upwards in a tangle of gorse, ferns and rock. To the left, a few feet away, was the cliff edge. The path we were on was just wide enough for two. Fulmars glided in arcs, vanishing and reappearing under the rim of the cliff. Kittiwakes perched like ornaments on its ledges. With a slow, regular monotony, waves shed their volume among the rocks at its base. There was something calming about the sound of their destruction, as if the elements were breathing.

To the west, the sun slipped out from under a bank of low grey cloud allowing the light to run horizontally across its underbelly, touching its lumps and bumps in gold. The surface of the sea turned from grey to a milky green that stretched all the way out to the horizon. The black and white stripes of the Kish lighthouse, ten miles away, stood bold in the sun. The navigation buoys glistened. A blackbird's song burst up from a bush and, for a moment, it might have been an evening in early summer. Emma looked at me and smiled. It was the perfect smile. I wanted to stop and hold her face, watch the light as it hit the edges of her curls. I squeezed her hand instead. 'What is it?' she asked.

'Nothing, I'm happy.'

'Me too.'

This sunburst did not last long. It was as though the sky had got suddenly tired of sunbeams screaming through it, and an almost imperceptible darkening began.

As we walked, the hill to our right changed from scrub and brambles to hard, solid rock. It looked as though it had just burst out of the ground and, proud of the achievement, wanted nothing more than to be admired. Straight in front of us the path dipped and a tiny meadow of short grass spread out towards the cliff edge.

Emma let go of my hand and walked on to it. She stood inches from the edge and folded her arms. The updraught sent her curls skywards.'Look at that expanse,' she said, staring at the miles of sea. 'It's like a slab of steel you could walk across.'

'If you did you'd get to Wales.'

'My uncle has a house in Wales,' she said, a hand retrieving a curl. 'Do you know what would be wonderful?

'What?' I said.

'To be able to fly. Wouldn't that be just amazing?' She stepped closer to the edge, stretched out her arms and hovered. 'Come on, let's fly.'

I went to the edge. Cold air hit my chest and ran up into my face opening my nostrils, sending my hair astray. I cupped my hands and let the wind lift my arms. I felt as if I was floating over the vast expanse in front of me.

'Dive!' she shouted. 'Dive!'

She was hovering like a bird of prey, the wind rippling her clothes. 'Swoop down and bank. Go on! Swoop, then straighten. Level now. That's right. Now climb. Come on, Seán, climb!'

I closed my eyes. The wind roared in my ears.

'Are you climbing?' she shouted.

'Yes.'

'Are you high?'

'Yes.'

'Above the cliffs?'

'Nearly.'

'Right, now swoop – swoop and glide out. You're over the wave tops. Drop. Go on, drop. Lower. The cliffs are behind us – drop till you can smell the breaking crests. Use the air pockets. Skip over a wave. Go on. Into the next trough. Flap if you want to. Out, over the sea. Over the H and H, and the H and G, through all the Hs. It doesn't matter, we're free, we're flying.'

She stopped. Grass fluttered at her feet, her arms fell to her side. She turned back to the path. 'Come on,' she said.

'Wait a minute – I'm still out in the Hs somewhere.'

'No, you're not. You're on a clifftop in Howth. Come on.'

I let my hands drop and followed her. She left the path and began to climb a track that led to the summit. It was steep, narrow and gravelly. At times, where a cluster of red rock interrupted it, it disappeared altogether. Then it would reappear further up.

At the top, a belt of gold light stretched across the western horizon. In front of it stood the city, every minute detail clear against the brilliance. Above the gold was grey, solid, compressed cloud, shoved up to make room for this gaudy display. Everything around us reflected the light, every spindled spike on every gorse branch, gold on one side, dark green on the other. No one would ever come to rotate them so they'd get done on the other side, like sausages.

Immediately in front of us there was a circular sweep of parked cars. Most of them were occupied. Sunday-paper readers, too old, too warm, to wander about in this autumn air. From the car park a road led straight downhill until it met the main road. At the crossroads stood the Summit Inn.

The curtain of gold was now a ribbon, its intensity fading rapidly as dusk and overhead clouds pushed it beneath the horizon. This allowed the neon outside the pub a vividness and strength it did not deserve.

'I suppose, Trainee, you think you've earned yourself a drink?' It was the first time Emma had spoken since we'd left the cliff.

'Trainee?'

'Trainee pilot.'

'I see. Was I a bad flyer?'

'I wouldn't say that, just a bit slow getting airborne.'

'Sorry.'

'Not your fault. It's your cargo, too heavy.'

We entered through a small door at the side. The same old man from yesterday was behind the bar. Emma slipped into a seat with her back to him. I didn't want to have to deal with being ejected now. I wanted just to sit and let my emotions catch up with me. At the moment my heart was still somewhere out on the cliffs, perched like a kittiwake, all solemn and coy.

'What's it going to be today?' There was contempt in his voice.

'A pint of stout and a glass of lager, please.'

'Is she of age?'

'Yeah!'

He let out a little laugh, a pig snort of an affair. 'For a kindergarten, maybe,' he said, and walked away.

I stood there, not knowing if this had been a dismissal or just a wisecrack. I watched him travel the length of the bar. He put the towel he was carrying on a shelf of glasses, then parked himself on a stool and stared at the television in the far corner.

I followed him. 'Excuse me, the pint and the glass of lager?'

His head made the slightest of movements in my direction but his eyes didn't leave the screen. 'Would you ever fuck off before you get me arrested?'

'It's the first place we'll do over when we're up and running,' Emma said. We were outside, walking downhill.

'Yeah, we'll smear shit all around the place.'

'No point, no one would notice.'

'Come on, we'll get a pint down the village. And then some sleep. Things will be better in the morning.'

All about us now was the essence of Sunday. It was a feeling that leaked into everything you looked at. Into the cars, the buildings, even the sky.

The cars were easy: almost every one of them was full, and everyone in them was gawking at everything they could. And because the place was a peninsula they couldn't sit there pretending they were on their way to somewhere else. This was their destination. And their job, once they got here, was to cram as much crap as they could into their vision.

The buildings we passed reflected what was going on inside them. And on Sundays that was fuck-all. So they stood there, brick upon brick, not looking in, not looking out, waiting for the day to subside.

The sky knew nothing of Sunday. In fact, some of it, somewhere, was probably already in Monday, or still in Saturday. But in the same way that it gave its colour to the sea, it poured the dullness and the boredom of its twilight on to everything that surrounded us. So everything looked faded. But yet, even in this dullness and fatigue, you could feel the dread of tomorrow – Monday. And although I no longer had to go into school with a bagful of undone homework, I could not get rid of the anxiety of Sunday. There was the religious aspect too. A piousness that walked about in dry-cleaned clothes and wore hats with pins in them. It filed into churches that hummed with a thousand movements – personal needs being attended to in a confined space: coughs, rasping breaths, moustache-smoothing, neck-scratching, rasher-digesting. And beyond the field of shoulders, the antics on the altar. Boys in lacy dresses surrounded a man wearing a green cloth sandwich board advertising a golden cross. High-pitched bells that rang in solemn moments were followed by the sounds of oceans of phlegm being dragged from lung to larynx. Feedback from the microphone in the pulpit was followed by dusty Latin droned through tall speakers strapped to ancient columns. The entire thing compressed a week of boredom into an hour and buried it so deep inside you that for the rest of the day you sat around yawning with the television on and the smell of steamed vegetables wafting all over the house. And some bastard got crucified for this?

The road dropped below the grey-slated roofs of the village. Then, in front of the church, it flattened and separated into three. One led into a warren of streets of one-storey cottages, another continued down to the harbour, and the third narrowed and rambled up towards an ancient graveyard, passing the Hope Inn and a few shops in need of paint.

Lights had come on but the streets were quiet. We walked past the church and up the road to the pub.

Once through the door, we were hit by a wall of heat and noise. In the far corner a collection of musicians were hammering out traditional tunes with banjos, guitars, fiddles and pipes. Around them were gathered the faithful, egging the music on as if it were a runner in the last stages of a marathon. The place was packed and the clientele seemed happy to roar above the music. This did not look like a place that had opened two hours before: this was the result of a lunchtime lock-in.

We elbowed our way to the bar, rested and took stock. Doyle was wedged into the opposite corner. He had a collection of pints in front of him and was surrounded by fishermen, some of whom I knew. As yet he hadn't seen me. I was too tired to worry about him.

Since the cliffs, Emma had been quiet. I got the feeling that she had set some sort of a test for me there that I had failed. She wasn't so much withdrawing from me as reassessing me. It was a mad thought, I knew, but my mind was dragging its anchor, making its way towards the rocky shallows.

I didn't care that the barman had a full view of us. When he saw me, I hurled an order at him. He nodded. A few minutes later we had our drinks and left the bar to find a place to perch.

I saw Susie sitting under the window. She was all legs and bunched-up shoulders, a stream of smoke flowing upwards from her parted lips. Then a hand slapped my back. It was Cahill, heavy-lidded, a smile stamped on to his lower face. 'You missed the crack, I'm telling you.'

'Yeah, looks like it,' I said. Then he saw who I was with.

'For fuck's sake, would you look what the cat dragged in?'

'Hi, Declan,' Emma said, squeezing my hand.

'We're just inhaling these,' I said, 'and then heading.'

'Well, the least you can do is come and have a drink with us. Susie's over there.'

She was staring at us.

We squeezed in beside her, on to a bench seat under the window. She was to my left, Emma to my right, and Cahill next to Emma. He bent forward at the waist, made introductions and started telling us of the afternoon we had missed. Susie lit another cigarette.

'You like Irish music, Susie?' I asked.

'It's the pits, if you must know.' She turned towards me, arching her back, draping an arm over the back of my seat. 'So, this is the one you went all the way to Wexford for?' I looked at her crossed thighs, her thin frame, her breasts, which were pushed forward by her stance. I nodded.

'Hope it was worth it.'

I felt for Emma's hand, then took a gulp from my pint. I didn't want us to be sitting there with Cahill and Susie. There was something sour in the air between them. Emma got to her feet. 'I'm going to the loo,' she said.

'Me too,' Susie said, getting up. Emma walked into the crowd without acknowledging that she was being accompanied.

'What's going on with you two?' I asked Cahill.

'Never mind her,' he said. 'Time for pastures new, old boy.'

'Like that, is it?'

'Look, Farreller, I could have any fucking woman I want. Last week I was in town and I picked up this Swedish one.' He rubbed his eye. 'No, she was Finnish, or one of those Scandahooligans, anyway. I swear, you wouldn't believe the fucking carry-on. Went like the clappers she did. I dumped her and then I met up with these two

Portuguese ones in a café. Fuck me, my dick'll be worn away if I don't fucking watch it.'

He was looking at me, blinking, smiling, wanting me to smile too, smile and admire. But I couldn't. 'At least, Farreller, I don't have to go all the way to Wexford to get me hole.'

When I didn't say anything, he said, 'You know, son, you'd want to cop on to yourself. A lot of people have you written off as a drunk. You don't realise that. And it's like you're getting a bit hard to defend, if you get my meaning.'

'Really?'

He raised his eyebrows. 'You were gee-eyed on Friday in Liam's, then you go playing Mr Big Shot up the Summit yesterday. All I'm saying . . .'

'Look, Deco, as far as I remember it, it was your girlfriend who started the fancy drinks.'

'She thinks you're a pisshead.'

'Yeah?'

'You're getting to be a bit of a big-headed twat. And I'm telling you, you're heading for a fucking tumble.'

'I'm going for a piss and then me and Emma are going to leave, right? I'll see you tomorrow, or whenever.'

Cahill turned away as though he was looking for a sentence he'd left on the windowsill. Emma emerged from the crowd.

'You all right?' I asked her.

'Just tired.'

I stood. 'I'll be back in a second, then we'll split.'

'Don't be long,' she whispered, 'or I'll end up clocking that cow.'

'Don't do that.'

I was standing watching the white tiles, urine flowing in an arc to the trough, when the door opened. I knew by the shuffle that the place had just filled.

'So, you think you can run away from me, eh?' It was Doyle. My testicles tightened. I was no Scotsman.

I turned, pulling up my flies as I did. Urine went everywhere.

'Are you going to let him piss all over you, Doyler?' a voice said, and laughter erupted.

'Look, whatever this is about, we can talk,' I said.

'Oh, yeah? This is the only talking I'm doing.' He threw his head forward. I ducked. His forehead came to a stop inches from the tiles. This had his friends in knots of laughter. Doyle was now furious and I was cornered. 'I'm going to rip you apart.'

'Look, we can talk about this – for fuck's sake there's no need—' I didn't even see him move. I was aware only of sliding downwards into the trough, one side of my face numb. I halted the slide but knew there was little point in straightening up. He was standing above me, his fist recoiling. Behind him, they were expecting me to lash out. That was what was supposed to happen. That was what would have happened if I had been anyone else. All I wanted to do was sink into a bed somewhere and let the world continue without me.

'Come on, get up,' Doyle roared.

'Do you want me to get up?' a voice said from the back. It was Scully's. Everyone turned.

Someone muttered that this had fuck-all to do with them. The room emptied. I pushed myself up the wall and saw Scully's dark eyes trained on Doyle. 'Outside.' He said it softly. 'Now.'

Doyle's rage had just found a new focus. 'I've been looking forward to this,' he said, and stormed past Scully.

'After I deal with him I want a word,' Scully said to me.

I went into a cubicle and sat on the toilet. My face was throbbing. I put my head into my hands. I wanted to slither into the water in the bowl and swim through to the sewers, down among the brickwork, the dark and the echoes. A twirl of my tail to put on speed when it was needed and a dive when cover was necessary.

But I couldn't sit and fantasise about a life in the sewers when there was a real one waiting for me outside.

I got up and looked at myself in the mirror. The side that had received the blow was reddening. It looked as if it might be swelling too. I splashed water over it and tried to clean the piss stains from my trousers. Lucky they were black.

Emma had a close-up view of my face when I sat down. I swallowed some of the pint and realised she was staring at me. 'What happened?' she asked.

'Come up to the bar with me,' I said.

'This place is a nightmare,' Emma said, when we had squeezed our way into a corner. 'What the hell happened to your face?'

I told her. And I told her that now, outside, as we spoke, Scully was dismembering Doyle on my behalf.

'The little wiry guy?'

'You met him?'

'He came up to Declan and asked him if he'd seen you.'

'Well, he found me.'

'Just as well he did. You look like you were hit with a brick.'

My insides felt as if they had turned to jelly and my fingers were trembling.

'I can see I'm going to have to import my own friends if we live around here,' Emma said.

'It's not usually like this.'

'Who is she?' Emma nodded towards Susie.

'Cahill's girlfriend, or was, anyway.'

I caught sight of Scully peering at us from the door. Someone was talking to him. He nodded at them, then walked towards us.

'He's here. I'll be back in a minute,' I said.

'Well, I'm not going back to the Bore and Cow over there.'

'I won't be long.'

Scully eyed Emma as he approached. I had never seen him take notice of a woman before. I decided I'd better introduce them. 'This is Emma,' I said. 'Emma, this is Scully. We work on the same boat – or at least we used to.'

Scully was staring at her but it was hard to read his expression. 'Where did you blow in from?' he asked.

Emma looked from him to me, then back at him. 'I'm on a weekend break from school,' she said, and tried to smile. He kept staring.

'Scully, if you want to talk, let's talk,' I said, and headed past him to the door.

There was no sign of Doyle outside. I was looking on the pavement, at the walls, for something, entrails, anything. But Scully had probably performed a thorough clean-up service when he'd finished his work.

We walked to a low stone wall that overlooked the ancient graveyard and the ruins of the abbey. Beyond, in the distance, I could make out the lights on the East Pier. I folded my arms and rested them on the wall. Scully, who had taken his place beside me, was looking back at the pub.

'When did Miss Blighty show?'

'Emma?'

He didn't answer.

'I liberated her from her convent in Wexford last night.'

Again he was silent.

'Why do you ask?'

'You're a fuckin' idiot, Farreller,' he said. 'Do you really think they'll let one of their charges slip out the back door and away?'

'They don't know where she is.'

'And how long do you think it'll take them to figure it out?'

'I don't know. Look, Scull, I appreciate what you did for me in there, I really do, but I'm tired and I don't need hassle.'

A smile spread across his face. 'Well, for a man what's avoiding hassle you have a strange fucking way of going about it.'

'I don't care. We just need to get a night's sleep and we'll sort everything out in the morning.'

'Good plan that, Seán. And tell me this, where do you two intend to spend the night?'

'On the old steel trawler. Anyway, what's it to you?'

'Fuck all. It's fuck all to do with me.'

'Look, Scull, every bastard who's been able to has fucked me about from day one. Now I can tell them all to fuck off. We both can.'

'Well, the very best of luck to you, but something tells me you don't know the meaning of being fucked about, least not yet.' He stepped on to the road. 'I'll be seeing you.'

I watched him walk away. 'What did you want to talk to me about?'

His slight form disappeared down the hill. I turned back to the lights of the harbour, and the numbness of my face seeped into the rest of me.

The wind had got up. It sent leaves and litter scurrying in tight circles. I could just about make out the shape of the hull where we'd stay. It looked old, out of commission. If it had been a human it would have been sitting beside its hospital bed, waiting for a nurse to come and change its catheter, its pyjamas rumpled and stained. But it wasn't a human, it was a boat. And I had to do something to stop this mood growing inside me. I had a beautiful woman waiting for me, a place to go, money in my pocket. What was the problem? Everything. There wasn't a single element in my life that wasn't wet with problems.

I heard footsteps coming up behind. 'What's the matter?' Emma asked.

I turned back to the harbour. She leant on the wall, mimicking my stance. 'Doubts are dancing?' she said.

'The wind's dancing.'

'Talk to me, Seán, what's going on?'

'Emma, I don't know what to say to you, to anybody, to myself, even. You know, you and me walking on the cliffs, we're fine, no one there except the birds, but as soon as we come into contact with people, look what happens. It's crazy and I think it's going to get worse.'

'Well, well, Mr Glum.'

'Emma, I'm serious.'

'Well, don't be.' The wind played with her curls. 'Where's the H and H?'

'Somewhere out there beyond the black.'

'No people, right?'

'No.'

'Let's go.'

'I can't swim.'

'You don't have to – we'll float all the way underwater.'

We looked at one another. 'But first there's an exercise we have to do,' she said. She leant forward and we kissed. I had to struggle with the numbness to find a comfortable fit but when I did the kiss was long, slow and passionate. And, finally, when we broke, her cheeks glistened in the orange street-light.

'Come on,' I said. 'Let's go and get some sleep.'

The East Pier is a much different affair from its counterpart on the other side of the harbour. It seems to take its time about its excursion out into the sea. Perhaps that's because halfway down it there is an elbow that, in effect, creates the harbour. Also, it's split-level, so you can stroll along with a granite wall protecting you from the Irish Sea on one side while on the other you can watch the yachts swinging safely on their moorings. It is also much quieter. Except for one or two boats tied up for repair or in semi-permanent retirement, it's empty.

The boat we were heading for was owned by a shipyard that had once used it to tow hulls up from Portugal. When its days were over, it was tied up just beyond the elbow and had stayed there ever since, decaying slowly as the seasons passed over it. The few of us who knew it was accessible used it often. It was the ideal place to go when you wanted somewhere to lie low.

As we approached, it appeared like a round lump of black, listing slightly to port. A gangplank came from its middle and dropped at a sharp angle down to the harbour.

As soon as our feet began to climb it, echoes erupted from within the hull. I took Emma's hand and, at the top, told her to wait by an oval door. Then I walked up the deck, climbed through the window and into the blackness. The smell in here was of dead air and mould. I felt my way along the interior walls to the door and let Emma in. I bolted it behind her, then led her to the galley. There, a small table was littered with candle stubs, empty beer bottles and cartoon hills of melted wax. I closed the porthole covers before I lit a stub.

Emma's eyes were black in the candlelight and her skin glowed. The tears had gone. 'Is it safe here?' she whispered.

'As houses.'

'It's spooky.'

Behind her, long, flickering shadows raced around corners into the silence and the darkness below.

I picked up a candle. 'Come on, I'll show you to your quarters.'

She put a hand on my elbow and allowed me to guide her towards a flight of metal steps. Slabs of black moved across the orange walls as we descended. There was a cabin just before the main crew's quarters. It was where the skipper had slept when these walls had resounded with the noise of English fishermen out in the North Sea.

The cabin was tiny with one single berth at knee level. On it was a quilt so sodden with damp it was heavy. Emma didn't seem to notice. We climbed in and lay in one another's arms.

Chapter 18

Bristol, 2008

There was a noise, a periodic, persistent bleep. My sleeping brain transformed it into droplets of molten steel falling into sand, each leaving a mark where it landed. The gap between each bleep was almost long enough to allow me to slide back into a deep sleep, but their persistence finally brought me to the surface. That was when I realised it was my phone – the battery needed to be charged. I'd either have to get up and switch it off or plug it into the charger. I looked at my watch. Seven thirty! This was supposed to be a day to lie in. I reached out to the bedside table, found it and switched it off.

Then I lay there. Beside the phone was a piece of paper with the number of the Rodney Hotel. Once I'd had it in my hand, Emma had suddenly become real. I thought of her now, lying in a bed less than two miles from me. Was she awake? I wondered. Was she alone? I'd forgotten to ask.

I turned in the bed. It was none of my business whether she was alone or not. She and I had nothing to do with one another. We'd had a fling, and that was a long, long time ago, a mad juvenile dash to adulthood that had ended in disaster. Apart from that nothing connected us.

But she was lying there and I was lying here and beside me was an sequence of numbers that could connect us. And it was up to me to activate them.

I turned again. I had a feeling in my stomach that I hadn't had since adolescence. It was a mixture of excitement and fear. I didn't want to think about picking up the phone and pressing those numbers. And yet the thought of not doing so was unimaginable. I was a mature man. She'd be a mature woman. We'd both had whole lives since we'd last seen one another, lives that included all the sorrows and sadnesses, the joys and dramas, the decades of slog that every life has. And all those experiences leave coatings on a character, change a person, twist, blend them into something unrecognisable from the people they were thirty years before.

So I was going to pick up the phone and expect to get through to the tall, blonde girl I had last seen in Wicklow Police Station three decades ago? She was as gone as yesterday was gone. Maybe that was what this was all about: me wanting to nip back into my past and steal something. And what would I do then? Try to build my present around it? Perhaps if that wasn't so miserable my past might not be so attractive. But my present wasn't miserable. There were miserable bits but whose life hasn't got those, like pips in fruit? Plenty about my life was worthwhile.

Christ, this was ridiculous, lying here, tossing and turning over a woman I hadn't seen for thirty years. But this wasn't about her – how could it be? I could almost see Philip smiling here, egging me on. 'So what is it about, then, Seán?'

'Fuck off, Philip, you stay out of my daydreams and I'll stay out of yours.'

I got up. Today was a day free of commitments. I could do exactly as I liked. I could ride out along the cycle path to Bath. That would be a twenty-two-mile round trip and would certainly blow the cobwebs away. Or I could drag out the easel and have a try at a picture, something simple, a still life. I could read, I could even write. I could tidy the house, paint the back window frames, weed the garden. I could do anything I wanted, but I knew none of it would distract me from the one thing I was trying to ignore: picking up the phone and speaking to Emma.

OK, this was what I'd do. This evening, say about six thirty, I'd phone her. I'd say hello, wish her well, then put down the phone and away she could sail, back over the horizon and into the past.

That was it. That was what I'd do and that would be the end of it. Then I could use this event, if you could even call it that, as something to spur me on to tackle the real problems in my life, the ones that had me entertaining notions of Emma as an escape route.

I went downstairs, made coffee, cut bread and put it in the toaster, then sat down. It was useless. I could pick up the phone or not, it didn't matter, and it didn't matter what I said or when I did it. My life was at a crossroads, one which Emma Balstead had not created. I had put myself there. Choose one way and everything I saw around me – the kids' invitations stuck to the fridge, their drawings on the kitchen wall, the crumpled clothes by the top of the stairs, all of it, all the signs of a family life being lived out – would disappear. Take the other route and life would continue in its monotony, frustration and predictability.

I went back upstairs and got the number, then walked down to the basement to use the phone there.

'Rodney Hotel, can I help you?' said a crisp female voice.

It suddenly dawned on me that I didn't know what surname Emma might be under. I tried to think of Kate's but I couldn't.

'Do you have an Emma Balstead staying with you?'

There was hesitation. 'No, I'm sorry, there is no one of that name here.'

What was Kate's surname? It was a blank in my head.

'Right, thank you.' Then it hit me. 'Wren.' I said, 'Emma Wren?'

'Yes, Emma Wren is staying here. Would you like to leave a message?'

'Could I be put through?'

'No. Mrs Wren is not here at the moment.'

'Could you tell her Seán Farrell called?' I spelt the last name and left my number. Then I put down the phone, realising I had left the home number. Should I call them back and leave my mobile? No, I'd done enough. She could contact me if she wanted to. I went out to the garden shed, dragged out the mower and half an hour later had a striped lawn.

Chapter 19

Howth, 1976

A network of rust stains ran like a road map over the ceiling. On the wall there was a chart of the North Sea, 'The Wash to Rotterdam'. It also showed sections of the English Channel and the Dutch coastline. Wedged into the frame was a photograph of two men. They were on a beach, standing, one with his hand on the other's shoulder. Their legs were skinny and their swimming trunks were black. It reminded me of photographs I'd seen of my father and his friends when he was younger. The price they'd pay for stepping beyond the border and into the land of colour and three dimensions was to grow fat, old and cranky.

There was a writing desk under the porthole. A red pencil lay on it. The paint had broken around toothmarks at the top. The same teeth had dented the metal band that had held the rubber. Now it resembled the crown of a monarch who had been involved in a road-traffic accident.

When I looked back at Emma, her eyes were open. 'Hi, sailor,' I said. 'How are you?'

'OK. I was just trying to work out who I was and where I was and who I was with.'

'That's a lot to work out first thing in the morning.'

'Well, a girl needs to get these things straight.'

Our damp crib had warmed. I reached my hand across and found Emma's naked belly. She had taken off her clothes during the night.

'You didn't sleep very well, did you?'

She slid into my arms. We were alone and cosy and she was naked. She brushed hair from my face. 'You grind your teeth, Seán, did you know that?'

'Sorry.'

She kissed me on the lips. 'I forgive you. Take a peep out of the window, see what kind of a day it is.'

'It's not a window, it's a porthole. If we're going to live on a boat you'd better get to know what these things are called.'

'Are we going to live on a boat?'

'I don't know. Not this one for sure.'

'Good.'

'Don't you like it?'

'It's scary and it stinks.'

I slid my hand along the furrow of her back, then down over the upper curve of her buttocks.

'This is nice,' she said.

I didn't know how to reply to that. I was hot beneath the blanket, encased in my clothes. I sat up and took off my shirt.

'Have a look out,' she said.

I got out of bed and swung the plate away from the porthole. Suddenly our interior brightened. I had to stretch over the writing desk to get a view. Even then I couldn't see much. The porthole must have been just above the waterline. I could see that it was windy: there were small waves inside the harbour. From between the hulls of the moored yachts I caught a glimpse of the West Pier. It seemed the whole fleet had stayed in today.

'Well?' Emma asked.

'It's a bleak, windy day, perfect to hole up here.'

'Better get back, then.'

I was just about to jump in beside her when she said, 'Is that all you're going to take off?'

I smiled, wriggled out of my trousers and slipped in beside her. I felt giddy, as if I wanted to laugh, but I thought I'd better not. 'Are you OK?' I asked her. She leant forward and kissed me. It was slow and delicate and she ran her tongue across my lips and squeezed my thigh with her fingers. I almost exploded. She was delivering too much sensation and everywhere I touched I'd find her skin. When she stopped kissing me she moved her lips down my neck. Then she looked up at me as though something vital had just crossed her mind. 'Have you ever done it before?' she asked.

'Yes,' I said. My voice was croaky. I put my arm around her shoulders. 'Have you?' I asked.

She shook her head.

'Would you like to?'

She was silent and still, then said, 'Yes.'

I put my hand on her thigh, in exactly the same place where hers was on mine. But her hand was still now. I tried to leave mine there too, all cool and nonchalant. But I couldn't control it. My fingers spread and moved upwards. Her skin had the texture of a petal. I found her breast and played with her nipple. It hardened between my fingers. Emma's breath quickened but she didn't move. The hand on my thigh was frozen.

'Are you sure you're OK?' I asked.

'Nervous,' she said, and laughed.

'That's OK. Me too. Look, we can just hug.'

'You think I'm a terrible tease?'

'No!'

'You do.'

My penis was aching for attention, its desire so absolute it took over the thinking part of my brain. Words flooded into a position where, normally, they would be taken up and spoken, but these words, I realised, could only be of use to the erection. I didn't speak them. Instead, I found my hand guiding hers to it. The erection's dominance over me was physical as well as mental. She wrapped her fingers around it and began a slow, almost imperceptible movement. I sighed. My physical need was so utter, so simple, its demands so clear, it could not be ignored. The movement stopped.

'Keep going, please, Emma,' I said.

'You know,' she said, 'they do it with their mouths too.'

A blizzard of thoughts wiped away my ability to speak. I could not trust myself to say a word. Anything might tip the balance away from the thought she'd just had. Including silence.

'Have you ever done that?' I asked.

'No. Carol says she has.'

'What did she say it was like?'

'Polishing brass.'

'What?'

'That's what she said.'

An image came into my mind – of my grandmother sitting at the kitchen table with a cloth, a load of cutlery and a tin of Brasso. I expelled it.

'Do you want to try it?' I asked. Now my voice was high-pitched.

'I'm not sure I'd know what to do.'

My heart pounded. The part of my brain that my penis had taken over wasn't very good at forward planning. It leapt about like a dancer who had just stepped on a nail. Plucking words out of this mess was just not possible.

Emma knelt and pulled the blankets away, leaving my penis

surrounded by nothing but air. She looked at it and then she looked at me. She watched me as her hand, which was on my knee, began to travel up the inside of my thigh. The sensation was of water flowing. Her long fingers cradled my scrotum and her other hand appeared, wrapped itself around the base of my erection and the slow massaging began again. Finally she took her eyes from mine and lowered herself until I felt a nipple trace across the skin just below my stomach and her mouth come down over one of my nipples. She left it wet and hard and started to kiss down my body.

Your lips are on the move, Emma, they're kissing their way to my navel. A penny for your thoughts – polishing brass, how could that be? I might soon find out. The hand massaging me slows. I've never had a blow job, I've never polished brass. Your lips are almost there. You climb between my legs. You look at me and before I can imagine what you might be thinking you sink your mouth over me. Sensations both strong and delicate flood me. You raise your mouth, then sink it again. You curl your tongue around my penis. With every plunge you send sensations so rich they transform themselves into syrup. You stop. You look up at me. 'Is this all right?' you ask. I nod – it's all I can do. You sink your lips lower and as you do I know I can't contain this.

A metallic boom comes from the upper deck. It is followed by another. You lift your head and look at me. My insides scream. There is another. I don't care where or what they are. Just don't stop, Emma.

I focus on your blue eyes, your fingers wrapped around the base of my penis still. Concern on your face. Then the door up there pounds again, its echoes resounding down the metal stairwell. My heart is racing.

'What's that?'

You look frightened.

It sounds again.

'I don't know. I'd better see.' I disentangle myself. Get up and pick up my clothes from the floor. I get my trousers on, but the erection won't fade. 'It'll be all right,' I say. I put my shirt on and open the door of our cabin. You look at me from the bunk. 'I'll be back in a minute.' I turn and clamber up the metal steps.

I unbolted the oval door and swung it open to see Scully's pinched face.'Is Blighty still with you?'

'Yeah.'

'Well, youse two better scarper, and fucking quick. 'He stepped past me and walked up into the wheelhouse. I followed, zipping up my fly. 'There,' he said, looking straight ahead. I walked around from behind him. All I could see was the boats on the West Pier. Then, between the avenues of bows and sterns, I caught sight of a flashing blue light on the roof of a black Cortina. Then another. That one was facing back down the pier, pointing at Findlater's.

'There're three squad cars as well as Special Branch.'

'Why? What's going on?'

Scully fixed me with a look and I knew what was going on. I felt as if I was being sucked into my own interior, leaving only the shell of me standing there. 'They're looking for Emma?'

'It's the sheer weight of your intelligence I marvel at,' Scully said, still with that look.

'Oh, fuck off! What are we going to do?'

'I told you. Get out of here, quick.'

'How? We can't go down the pier – they'll see us.'

Scully was looking ahead. 'Take Sheehan's boat. If they see it leave they'll just think, There goes another poor bastard forced to make a living in appalling conditions.'

The *Jasper* was tied to the pier just ahead of us. It was small and tidy and there was no one aboard.

'What time is it?' I asked.

''Bout eight.'

'Sheehan will be down any minute. Scully, do us a favour, will you, and start up the engine while I get Emma?'

'I've risked all I'm going to coming down here. You're on your own. I told you last night to offload that bitch but you wouldn't fucking listen to me, would you?'

'Scully, please, I've no notion how to start that thing. I can drive the boat out, no problem, but I need an engine. It'll only take a second. Please, Scully.'

'And you'd do that to your old mate Sheehan?'

'Oh, for fuck's sake, don't play games with me. Either do it or don't do it.'

'Right, I'll start the engine and that's it. Keep Blighty out of my sight and wait till I'm well clear before you let go the lines. Do you understand?'

'Thanks, Scully. I really appreciate this.'

'Tell it to me bollox.'

I raced back down to the cabin. Emma was staring wide-eyed from the nest of blankets. I told her about the police.

'Shit! Shit!' She spat the word.

'So, here's the plan. There's a boat in front of us. I know the guy who owns it, and we're going to borrow it.'

'To go where?'

'Anywhere. But we have to hurry. They could be over here any second.'

She got off the bed. 'Sorry about the blow job,' she said.

'Don't be. It was fantastic.'

'When the next one ends you'll have a smile on your face, I promise.'

'I can't wait.'

'Go on, I'll see you in a minute.'

When I got aboard the *Jasper* I looped the mooring lines around the bollards, then brought them back to the boat where I tied them off. That way I could release them from the deck. I had just finished doing the aft one when the engine burst into life and a cloud of grey smoke erupted from the stern. I looked aft. Emma was coming down the gangplank. I waved her on. Then Scully appeared on deck. He went to the stern and peered over the side, perhaps to see if cooling water was coming out with the exhaust. When he looked up, he froze. Two squad cars were racing up the pier. They were almost at the elbow.

'Get aboard!' he shouted at Emma. 'Quick, jump!'

He ran back to the wheelhouse, shouting at me to let go of the lines.

'Better get in and out of sight,' I said to Emma, running forward to release the line. I went aft and did the same. The police cars had stopped at the gangplank of the old trawler. The doors flew open and out they charged, clattering up the metal ramp.

I went into the wheelhouse to tell Scully we were clear. He grabbed me and stuck me behind the wheel. Then he crouched low. The wind was blowing us away from the wall so I pushed the throttle forward and pointed the *Jasper* towards the mouth of the harbour. I caught a glimpse of a police car parked at the end of the West Pier. I would have examined it for longer but the roar of a wave grabbed my attention. The seas were big. I tried to turn the boat into them once we were clear of the harbour mouth wall but there was no time. A wall of solid water was bearing down on us. It caught us broadside and threw us on to our side. The engine howled as the propeller rose out of the water. There was an explosion of noise from the galley. But she righted herself.

'Turn into them,' Scully shouted. 'Turn into them and throttle back.'

I swung the wheel around and immediately we were climbing up the face of the next wave. The bow came clear of the crest and, finding itself in mid-air, hesitated, then plunged downwards until it smacked into the wave's trough with a wood-splintering crack. And just in front of us was the next.

We rode up the face of it, fell off the top and crashed again into the trough. The only way I could support myself in the falls was by holding on to the spokes of the wheel.

'It'll get better once we clear the Nose,' Scully shouted, from the corner where he had braced himself, legs spread.

Where Emma had got to I didn't know. I thought of shouting to her but the crashing and banging would have drowned my voice.

The seas were piling in from the north-east. The air was a mist of flying spray. Every time we crashed into a trough we took on a load of water, which rushed aft as the boat climbed the next wave, thundering into the wheelhouse, rinsing the windows, so for a few seconds you could see out.

Battling these waves meant we weren't getting anywhere. We still hadn't even cleared the elbow of the East Pier. Until we did we'd have to stay on this course.

Scully was peering through the side windows.

'What do you think?' I shouted over to him.

'What do I think? Don't fucking ask me. Jesus Christ, I can't believe I've been so stupid.'

I knew better than to ask him to elaborate. He grabbed the wheel from me. 'Just get out of my fucking sight. I need time to think.'

I stood aside. His face was grey. I decided to find Emma.

In the galley, the contents of every drawer and cupboard had emptied themselves on to the floor and formed a massive rubbish heap of metal and cloth that rolled from one end of the galley to the other. By the stove, there was a square hole. A ladder dropped from it, leading down to the sleeping quarters on the left and the engine room forward on the right. I climbed down it and saw that the table in the sleeping quarters had come away from its moorings and crashed, splintering the cupboard at the back of the cabin. Locker doors opened and shut, like a line of over-wound cuckoo clocks.

Emma was in a corner. She was sitting with one leg on the floor and the other stretched out along the seat. Her back was against the forward bulkhead. It was about as safe a place as you would find. She was pale. I stood over her clutching a brass rail. 'It'll get better in a couple of minutes. Are you all right?'

We took another plunge. From down here the engine's scream was deafening when the propeller came clear. Then, suddenly, there was silence. The engine had stopped. But after a brief moment, it burst back into life and, with a sickening sense of dread, I realised what had caused the stoppage. The silt in the diesel tanks had been disturbed so the engine was drawing dirty fuel into the lines. It was only a matter of time before they clogged up completely and the engine stopped. Out here, without an engine, we were dead.

'I hit my head,' Emma said. Her tone was listless.

I tried to crouch beside her but lost my grip and found myself flung with the rest of the debris to the end of the cabin. I clambered free as soon as the boat levelled. 'I'm going to get him to turn back,' I said to Emma, and made for the door. 'Just hang on.'

Scully's knuckles were white and his face was grim.

'Scully, we can't do this. We'll be on the rocks in minutes. We've got to turn back. I'll take the blame. You'll be fine, I promise.'

What I saw next I couldn't believe. He left the wheel and walked towards me. In his eyes was the unmistakable desire to destroy me. Behind him the wheel spun like a top and the boat fell sideways on to the oncoming wave. I could see it bearing down on us through the side window. It hit before he reached me. The *Jasper* was thrown on to her side and the wave broke over us, obliterating all light. I found myself lying against something solid, then freezing water pouring in all around me. Suddenly there was light. We had righted. Scully scrambled for the wheel and pushed the throttle forward to get up enough speed to straighten her into the next wave. We wouldn't survive another of those.

'I don't know who's more fucking stupid, me or you!' Scully roared. We were both wet to the skin.

'Scully, if we go back, I'll take the blame for everything,' I said again.

'Say another word and I'll kill you both.' I realised we were in much more danger from what was inside the boat than outside. 'Think, for fuck's sake,' he was saying. 'Half the Special Branch were there this morning. They don't do that for some runaway schoolgirl.'

We had just begun to drop down the side of another wave. I braced myself. This one was steep. We plunged downwards so vertically it looked like we'd go straight through the bottom. As we hit, the bow buried itself beneath blue water and then, against all reason, fought its way to the surface, scooping with it tons of water that ripped down the deck and crashed into the wheelhouse.

'Who is she?' he roared.

'She's my girlfriend.'

'Fuck with me again and I'll kill you.'

'Emma Balstead.'

At least the seas were keeping him anchored to the wheel.

'What's her father?'

'Her father?'

'Yeah, what's he do?'

Instinct told me to say nothing. 'I don't know.'

Just then the engine shuddered and stopped. We stared at one another, listening, waiting. The boat's momentum leaked away almost immediately. In front of us I watched a mountainous sea building. Scully spun the wheel. There was no response. Out of the side window I saw the dark cliff face of the Nose.

'Take it,' he said, leaving the wheel. 'Where is she?'

'Below.'

He headed straight past me. 'Keep her into the seas. If she takes another one broadside we're finished.'

I grabbed the wheel and turned it so we could greet this wall of water towering in front of us. The spokes spun through my fingers. There was no response. On it came. As we climbed I could hear the roar of the breaking crest. When it hit, we were pushed backwards and sideways, water boiling all about us. As we lay dazed in its wake, I heard the sounds that were no longer drowned by the engine – the rage of the wind whipping through the rigging, the dull, voluminous roar of the huge seas breaking all around us and, from behind, the low rumble of thunder as they crashed into the rock face.

Everything was happening at a slower pace now. We popped over the crest of the next wave and, as we slid down the other side, I could feel the boat picking up a little momentum. Enough to give us the tiniest steerage. With this gift, I tried to point away from the cliffs. I figured that the surface area of the hull and the wheelhouse might act like a sail if I kept it at an angle to the wind. From that, we might get some forward motion. Every inch now was precious. But as soon as I tried to swing the bow up towards the next oncoming wave, the wind caught it and pushed it away. Up this moving wall of water we'd go to get hit at the top by the crest. This would push us back, throwing us on to our side and then break over us. When we righted we'd be sitting in another trough, the next wave seething overhead, the rocks closer. When I looked at the cliffs now I could make out the guillemots and kittiwakes sheltering in the crooks and ledges.

Panic seized me. I left the wheel, ran to the hatchway and screamed down the ladder to Scully that I couldn't hold it, we'd be on the rocks in minutes.

'Calm down,' he shouted back. Then, in a different tone, he said, 'Push when I pull. Hold it there. Yeah, like that.'

'Emma?' I called.

'What?' she shouted back. They were working together, bleeding the diesel lines. I almost laughed – Scully and a woman working together in the engine room of a boat that was just seconds away from becoming matchwood.

We tumbled again. Water poured through the galley door. It swept me and everything else into one corner and back again as we righted. It poured down the hatchway.

'Keep her steady, for fuck's sake,' Scully howled. 'We'd be there now if you'd just keep her steady.'

I got back to the wheelhouse. The sight I saw through the window was wrong – pure black and dark green cliff, every ledge carpeted in white. We were no more than two wave lengths away from it. I gripped the wheel and swung it wildly. Nothing. I felt the boat being lifted and, with horror, felt us begin to surf. We were moving fast towards the solid rock in front of us. The wave, travelling faster than we were, passed underneath and crashed in a confusion of white against the cliff face. The birds on the ledges were alarmed now by our approach. The next wave would do it. I couldn't move. I couldn't think. Then I saw a wave in front, coming at us. It was the backwash, a muted version of the one that had just crashed on to the rocks, wobbling back out to sea. It was timid, smaller than anything else around it, but it had momentum enough to nudge us away from the cliff.

Then, from behind, I felt the next wave lift our stern. This would be the one. But just as we began to surge forward, the engine spluttered, coughed and burst into life.

The wave was fully under us now and we were surfing. I spun the wheel all the way over and pushed the throttle forward. The boat sheared sideways and fell into the trough on the other side of the wave, leaving it to roar to its doom.

Within seconds, Scully was beside me. He looked back at the cliff. 'Fucking hell,' he said. Emma arrived at the doorway. I didn't say anything to either of them. There was a wave in front of us to deal with.

Then the sun came out. It was weird and unwanted. It made the sea bright green and the wave tops sparkle with a shade of white they save for detergent commercials. But we were getting away from the cliffs and I was learning to control her better so there wasn't quite as much rolling and tumbling. We were making progress.

After about half an hour, Scully said, 'I think we can turn now.'

'What do you mean?' I asked.

He was leaning against the side window. 'Alter course, about seventy degrees to starboard.'

I shot a quick look behind. The cliffs now were no more than part of the landscape. I breathed in and turned the wheel. Now we'd be taking the waves on the other side of the boat. It was still the same game. Throttling back and increasing the revs in the troughs, trying to progress as much as you could without danger. No one spoke. I was becoming aware that I was cold and hungry.

The sun kept jumping in and out from behind the ragged clouds. I preferred it in low light, everything muted, no distractions.

'Alter more now,' Scully said. 'Head south.'

I did as he asked. Now the big seas were coming in from behind us, lifting the stern so that the whole boat tilted, its bow looking down into the troughs. But it didn't slide into them. Before that happened the wave would come up under our middle and you could watch the bow rise. Then it took us on a scorching surf that lasted for many seconds before it dropped us back into the trough behind. And the whole process would start again. It was exhilarating. And it was steadier. Like this, we were taking no water over the sides.

Howth was passing fast on our right, Dublin Bay opening out in front.

'I'm going to see if this cunt Sheehan has the makings of a cuppa tea,' Scully said. It was hard to read his face. Whatever else happened, whatever he decided to do, he had saved our lives so it didn't seem likely that he'd go on a killing spree now. But this was Scully, so all bets were off.

Emma cleared out of his way and settled herself in a seat behind me. 'It's really quite beautiful,' she said.

I supposed in an isolated way it was. But it was an element of our situation that I couldn't fully appreciate just then. 'How's your head?' I asked.

'My head? Fine. How's yours?'

'Fucked.'

She didn't reply.

'We must be mad,' I said.

'Still, it beats double geography on Monday mornings.'

'Yeah, well, in that case it's all been worth it.'

She started laughing and, despite myself, I did too.

'Do youse take sugar? There's no milk.'

'Two for me,' I said.

'None for me, thanks,' Emma said.

Scully disappeared.

'What happened down there?'

'He said he needed me to hold a spanner on a bolt while he turned the bottom of it. Once it was loose, he pumped a little button until diesel came out, then he tightened it up. He did four like that. Then he pressed another button and the engine started.'

'Amazing.'

'It was more awkward than anything, actually.'

'Without her we'd be impaled on the rocks by now,' Scully said, carrying the three mugs.

'I just did what you told me.'

'Fucking pity more didn't,' he said, handing me the tea.

I couldn't hold the wheel and the cup at the same time so I wedged it by the compass. Both my arms ached. Scully didn't offer to take over. He was happy nearby the chart table, leaning against the side window.

The steering was still demanding. As we'd sink back into the trough, the boat had a tendency to slide away to port so there was a danger of dropping sideways on to the oncoming wave. Something like that now would shatter the sense of well-being that had established itself since we had begun to go with the seas.

'So, Emma,' Scully said, 'how come the Special Branch get out of their beds on a Monday morning to go looking for you?'

'The what?'

'The Special Branch, police involved with state security,' I said.

'I know what the Special Branch are,' she said. 'It's probably because of Dad.'

Scully looked from her to me. I didn't say anything. I was concentrating.

'What does your da do?'

'Military attaché to the British Army.'

The mug slipped in his hand. 'He's what?'

'Military attaché to the British Army.'

'What's your surname?'

'Balstead.'

Scully had gone pale. 'You're Reginald Balstead's daughter?'

She nodded. He put the mug on the flat surface in front of him. Immediately, it rolled and crashed on to the floor. He raised his hands to his head as if he was surrendering, then turned his back to us. In a slow, deliberate move, he smashed the wooden panel between the windows with his fist. Then he turned to me, pointing a finger, his hand vibrating. 'You . . . you . . .' His breathing had gone shallow. 'You fucking moron!' The finger folded into his fist. His entire body shook and his eyes penetrated me.

Suddenly he turned back to the windows and spread his hands on the panels above them. Through the window, in the distance, I noticed small regular explosions of white at the bow of some boat trying to fight its way out of Dublin Bay. 'I just don't fucking believe what's happening here,' he said, turning back to stare at me with the same intensity, but now, somehow, he seemed more in control. He came towards me, every movement slow and deliberate. He took hold of my collar, pulling my face to his. 'You can count the hours remaining of your miserable little life on the fingers of one hand, you fucking wanker.' A part of me was aware that the stern was lifting, that I should be counteracting this with the wheel, but I didn't move. Every detail of his face mesmerised me, his wet lips, his cracked and stained lower teeth, the broken blood vessels spidering his cheeks, the eyes that were looking into mine with calm hatred. We were sideways on to the wave now. Scully didn't seem to care.

He let go just as the boat was about to be hit by the crest. As soon as he did, I spun the wheel as hard as I could and got the hull around so the stern took the brunt of the breaking wave. It knocked us sideways and we took on a load of water, this time racing upwards from the stern. But I was able to get back in control and have us facing away from the next.

He turned and gazed out of the window. Emma was behind me on her seat. One wave after another slipped under us without anyone saying a word. Then Scully said, 'He's back.' He was referring to the boat I'd seen earlier. I could make out the grey of its superstructure – it was a corvette, most probably the same one that had searched us. Scully turned to face me. 'What I can't believe is what a fucking moron you are.' He was using the flat, matter-of-fact voice, the forerunner to violence.

I knew I had to be careful but I also had to know what was going on. 'Look, Scully, can you just tell me what—'

'Balstead – the name didn't ring any bells?'

I shrugged.

He stared at me without expression, then turned to Emma. 'When was your father's car blown up?'

'Last November,' she said.

'He wasn't killed?'

'No,' Emma said.

'The driver was seriously injured and the bodyguard was killed?'

'Yes.'

'Any idea who might have done that?'

This was to me. I wished he'd just get on and do whatever he was going to do – the build-up thing was more than I could handle. 'No, Scully, I've no fucking idea.' I swung the wheel to put our stern into the oncoming wave. I could make out the numbers on the corvette's bow clearly now.

'Claire Traynor,' he said.

'What?'

'You heard me.'

'Claire Traynor – Hutch's Claire? Are you saying that Claire tried to kill Emma's old man?'

'Yes.'

I didn't know what to do with this information. I wanted to talk to Emma, say something, but I couldn't think what.

She got up and stood in the far corner opposite Scully, where she could see my face. 'You knew the person who tried to kill Dad?' she asked.

'Well, if what Scully's saying is right, yeah!'

Now she, too, was staring at me.

'Look, Emma, I don't know anything. This is all news to me.' I turned to Scully. 'Will you just explain it?'

Scully's eyes narrowed. 'Claire Traynor?'

'Yes.'

'Was arrested.'

'Yes, Scully, I was there. I read all about her in the paper.'

'Well, then, you shoulda known one of her targets was your girlfriend's father.' His tone was flat again.

'You're joking!'

'Yeah, I am. This whole fucking thing's a joke. The Special Branch on the pier this morning, our friends in the corvette there, me standing here, we're all having a fucking laugh. What the fuck do you think?'

I was silent.

Emma returned to her seat. I swung around to see her. She perched there, pale, not looking at me.

I turned back to Scully. 'What do you mean exactly?' As soon as the words were out of my mouth I regretted them.

'Jesus fucking Christ, Seán, work it out! The day after Claire gets arrested, Emma Balstead disappears from her boarding school with a fuckwit from the boat Claire was using to hide out on. They think this is political.' He was pointing in the direction of the corvette. 'They think she's been kidnapped, that she'll be used as a hostage for Claire's release.'

The inside of my head was rushing around trying to find places where his words might fit.

Scully continued, 'And because I'm here they'll have me down as the fucking ringleader. And the reason I'm here is you.'

'I didn't know any of this,' I said.

'Shut up!' he shouted. 'Shut your fucking mouth.' Then he made a noise. It was almost a laugh but it wasn't: it was something dry that twisted up from his insides making a sound like a trapped animal. He was in a situation where he might kill me just to vent his anger and leave himself no worse off.

He turned back to the window.

Would he kill Emma too? The two of us should be able to overpower him. I turned quickly to her. This time she looked back at me. Her face was drained.

Scully began pacing between me and Emma. I kept expecting to feel a bang on the back of my skull, a split second of pain, then nothing. But he didn't seem to be aware of either of us. He had covered his mouth with his hand, his middle finger tapping his cheek. Then, with that sudden movement of his, he dropped to his knees and rooted through a locker under the chart table. If it was a weapon he was after he had his choice floating around the galley floor.

He pulled out a chart and spread it out over the flat area on top of the locker, then began looking around. 'Has Sheehan got Decca?' he said.

Sheehan had nothing.

'Doesn't matter, we'll do this the old-fashioned way.' His tone had a touch of lightness now. Whatever had gone through his mind, his mood had changed.

The corvette seemed to be holding off to let us pass.

'What about him?' I asked Scully.

He glanced at the ship. 'Fuck him.' He turned to Emma. 'Get me a plastic bag from the galley, will you, one without holes?'

Behind me I heard her get up. He was hardly going to put our bodies in plastic bags, then slip them over the side in full view of the Irish Navy, was he?

I wondered if Emma would think of picking up a knife.

'Make more easting. I want to be outside the bank.'

Emma came back and handed Scully a black plastic bag. 'I found this too,' she said. I swung around to see. She was holding two slices of white bread, both decorated with discs of green mould.

'Don't tell me you're going to eat that shite!' Scully said.

'We have it like this at school all the time.'

'Hear that?' he said to me. 'You pay a grand a year and all your kid'll get to eat is mouldy bread!'

'Yeah,' I said, trying to fit in with his shift in mood.

The corvette came up behind us and lay off our stern. It was nice to see that she was having a hard time too, maybe even worse than us: her long, narrow lines and sharp bows meant she didn't have anything like our buoyancy. But on her bridge you could guarantee they weren't discussing the merits of stale bread.

Scully's attention went back to the chart, his stubby forefinger running up and down a section where a lot of depth contours converged. That must be the bank he'd mentioned. The finger kept stopping and tapping at a point halfway down it.

The sun had come out again and the seas seemed to have eased. Up ahead I saw navigation buoys. Beyond them was breaking water. The nearest land to this was five or six miles off to our right – the Wicklow Mountains. I could see the foothills, in all their shades of green, rise clear from the flat foreshore. I mentioned the buoys to Scully.

'Right,' he said, peering at them. 'You need to alter ten, fifteen degrees to port.'

This would take us outside them too. The new direction was not a lot different from the old one but it did mean the waves were coming down at us from an angle that made the steering harder work. My arms were now heavy with aches. When the buoys were abeam, Scully told me to go back on the original course, almost due south.

The bank was over to our right now. I watched the waves as they neared it. They'd rise in height before disintegrating into a foaming blizzard of white. It was a wild, raging mess and it went as far south as the eye could see.

Scully raised his head from the chart. 'What time is it?' he asked.

'Ten past eleven,' Emma said. She was the only one of us with a watch.

'Right,' he said, still focused on the chart. 'We left on the high tide, about eight.' I didn't know if he was talking to us or himself.

'So low water'll be two, give or take.' He suddenly looked up. 'This might work.'

'What might work?' I asked.

He didn't say anything for a moment. He was staring over at the breaking seas. 'Something that just might save your miserable fuckin' hide.'

'Yeah?' I said.

'And if it doesn't, it'll drown it.' His laughter now was recognisable as such.

I didn't say anything.

'A few years ago, I fished these banks – channels fucking everywhere. But there's one goes all the way through, and at this stage of the tide there might be just enough water for us.'

'Leaving our friend here outside?'

'Top of the fucking class.'

'Yeah, but that's a sandbank, isn't it?' I said.

He didn't answer.

'I mean, doesn't sand move?'

'It does,' he said.

'So that channel might not be there now.'

'Well, if it is and we get through it, we're laughing. If it isn't, or we don't, we're dead. And if you've got a better plan I'd love to fucking hear it.'

I looked out at the bank again, the rage and the chaos. It was suicide. But at least it didn't involve our death at his hands. There was a certain relief in that.

'What do you think the corvette will do when we go through?'

'The bank is forty-odd miles long and the channel we're looking for is just about smack in the middle so she'll stay heading south if she has any sense. Going north about would mean doing battle with these fuckers. But if she goes south, she'll have them behind her and then be in sheltered water when she turns north. She'll blast up the inside of it, doing thirty-five knots.'

'So what are we going to do after we get through?'

'If we're still floating, you'll drive this thing as close to the beach as you can and then I'm going swimming.'

A strange series of emotions hit me, relief that he was going but anger too. He had a rat-like instinct that could get him through a situation like this. With him gone, we didn't stand a chance.

'I'm going to tell you one thing now and I want you to listen,' he said.

We both looked at him. 'If we get through and I get away, youse two can do what youse fucking want. If youse get ashore you'll get caught. And after you're caught you'll be interrogated. Both of you, separately. And if either of you mentions me I'll kill you. It's that simple.' He'd been looking at me as he spoke. 'Did you hear that?' he asked.

'Yes,' I said.

'Did you hear it?' he asked Emma.

'Yes.'

'Make no mistake about this.'

'Scully, we get the point.'

'I'm very glad to fucking hear it – if I go down because of this, I'll find you. I don't care how long it takes, I'll find you. And when I do I'll kill you.'

'Scully, I promise you, if we get caught neither of us will mention you. You have my word.'

'It's not if, it's when.'

'Why did you help us this morning?' Emma asked.

'I'd no fucking choice.'

'No – I mean, why did you come down to the boat to warn us?'

'Let's just say it was an error of judgement.'

'Well, thanks,' Emma said.

218

'You mightn't be so grateful when you're trying to set up home on the Arklow fucking bank,' he said, and laughed.

With the following wind and seas, the land was shooting past. Bray had gone by and Wicklow Head was coming clear. Scully began to take bearings off it. He had to stoop low, drawing a line with his eye from the headland through the centre of the compass. I had to move out of his way to let him do this, which in turn made the steering awkward and caused us to pitch. This, of course, didn't help him. But he kept calm and, using Emma as a time-keeper, took a series of running fixes off Wicklow Head. He plotted them on the chart with a pencil Emma had found in the galley. I could see our progress by the line of dots he was leaving on it. I could see, too, where the channel was indicated. We were approaching it fast.

'Slow her down, right down,' he said.

He was looking at the bank now, studying it intently.

'Right,' he said. 'Let's do it.'

'What do you want me to do?'

'Turn the fucking wheel and head for the surf.'

I did as he said. Now we rolled. The contents of the galley were up and running again. It was all noise and fury, the sense of calm gone. Scully, gripping the side of the chart table, peered through the window. 'What's our friend doing?' he roared above the din.

'I don't know. Stopped, I think,' Emma told him.

'Not coming after us?'

'Doesn't look like it.'

'Chicken fuckers.'

What was in front of us had every instinct in me wanting to turn and run. The shallowing seabed tripped the waves that came roaring in, causing them to tumble into sheets of white that the wind whipped skyward, obliterating everything. It was impossible to tell what was sea and what was sky.

Scully came over and pushed me off the wheel. 'See you on the other side,' he said. I stepped back and found myself shoulder to shoulder with Emma. The waves curled in behind, picking us up by the stern and sweeping us at high speed into this wall of white. Scully was singing some bawdy, raucous tune, something to give him comfort, but it couldn't compete with the sounds outside. There, the deep-throated roar of tumbling water was one long bass note with the high-pitched screeching of the wind on top.

Each time I felt the stern lifting, solid fear arose in me. Every wave now might be the one that had us surfing into the bank. If that happened, the following wave would turn us on our side, and two waves later we'd be splinters.

I felt another lift us. It must have been big because it shot us forward so fast our hull vibrated. Each side of us I saw a mixture of sand and foam. Suddenly the wave turned to bubbles and I felt us drop. There was a thump. My weight compressed into the floor. Everything shuddered. Just as I braced myself for whatever happened next, another wave was lifting us. But it had none of the height and power of its predecessors. Ahead there was no longer mist, just a stretch of rippled water and, two miles off, the shore. We all looked back. We were leaving the bank. It was behind us.

'Now that's what I call deliverance,' Scully said. 'Here, take the wheel.'

I held the spokes in my hand but my fingers were weak. I was feeling as though we'd just walked through a wall.

Behind us, the Arklow bank was acting like a breakwater. There were waves in here and they were being scurried along at force by this wind, but they had no past: they were babies.

'What happened?' Emma said. She was still staring at the mist behind us.

'We were carried right over the fucking thing,' Scully told her. 'Someone up there loves us – or one of us anyway.' He was laughing again. 'And those fuckers are now totally mystified. Where's that plastic bag?'

He was stripping off. I had never seen how lean he was. Muscle, sinew and ribcage, a tight, efficient package. 'To the shore and don't spare the horses.'

I drove straight for it. I was angry now, I didn't know why. I wanted him gone. We had no chance without him and he didn't care. But, then again, why should he? He had helped us and got himself trapped because of it. Now, because of a little good fortune, he could get himself free. But Emma and I didn't have that chance. We never would. Not now.

When I'd got as close as I dared, I turned the boat around so the stern was facing the shore. Then I put the throttle in neutral.

Scully picked up his bag of clothes, tied it at the top and walked out to the aft deck. Emma and I watched him from the door at the back of the wheelhouse. He stepped up on to the gunwale. 'Remember what I said.'

The wind was blowing us sideways on to the land, closer to the shore than I wanted to be. I was just about to get back to the wheelhouse when he said, 'Wicklow Harbour's just up there beyond the headland. Get in, tie up, stay calm. Then walk away. They'll get you but give them a run for their money.'

'Give you enough time to get away,' Emma said.

Scully smiled. 'You should listen to her,' he said, threw the bag into the water and jumped after it.

I got to the throttle and pushed it forward, leaving behind the shingled shoreline and its swaying reedbeds.

Emma came in and stood beside me.

'You OK?' I asked.

She shrugged. 'I don't know what I am. I'm numb.'

'Emma, I had no idea about Claire being who she was.'

White spray pelted the windows. The waves in here were nothing like the ones on the far side of the bank, but the wind was strong enough to give their spray some punch.

'Sometimes I feel like I don't know who anyone is,' she said.

'How do you mean?'

'Well, just that. I don't know who anyone is. You know, I'm talking with someone and they seem nice, and the next minute you realise they'd be happy to blow you to kingdom come because you were born in a country that sent its soldiers over to theirs hundreds of years ago.'

'Not everyone's like that.'

'That's exactly what I'm saying. How do you know? How can you tell? I mean Scully, he's one of them. He has to be. Otherwise the girl wouldn't have been on your boat, would she? And if he is, the rest of them probably were too. So where does that leave you?'

'Emma, I don't believe this.'

'I'm just saying, all this business leaves you not knowing who's who or what's what. I can't even trust my own feelings.'

'You can trust me, you know you can.'

Tears were welling in her eyes. 'I know I can. At least I think I know I can. Oh, Seán, everything's such a bloody mess.'

I held the wheel with one hand and put the other arm over her shoulders. 'Let's do what the mad bastard said we should, get in, tie up, walk away.'

Emma broke away. 'What was she like?'

'Who?'

'The woman who tried to kill Dad.'

'I didn't get to know her that well. I'd say she was lonely.' I told her about bringing her food in the hold and about the *Mary Jo* getting boarded and about the arrests.

'And that was the day before you came down to see me?'

'Yeah. Jesus! It's all just so fucking mad.'

'What are we going to do?'

'We'll sort something out as soon as we get in.'

'But Scully was right. The police think you've kidnapped me.'

'We'll just have to tell them I didn't, it wasn't like that.'

'Seán, listen to me. One thing we're not going to do is go to the police.'

'But why? They'll have talked to Carol, to Plasma, Joey, everyone. They'll have searched my room at home, found your letters. They'll know by now exactly what this is all about.'

'The police don't work like that. I know.'

'Emma, they'll realise we're just two people in love trying to rid themselves of the rest of the world.'

'Are we?' she asked. 'In love?' Her hair fell like curled string to her shoulders and her eyes were wide with a combination of anguish and innocence.

'Of course we are.'

She broke into a smile. 'Right, then, come on, we'd better get ourselves out of this.'

Wicklow Head was looming closer. It dawned on me that I would now have to dock this boat. I had never docked a boat before.

'Any ideas?' she asked.

'Sorry?'

'You know, ideas, as to how we give them all the slip.'

'Oh, right, sorry. Well, we'll get in, tie up, then walk straight up the main street, buy new clothes and catch a train to Dublin. We can work things out from there.'

'You're not very good at this, are you?'

'What do you mean?'

'If I was to go into a clothes shop at this time on a Monday morning, dripping wet, with an English accent and a handful of cash, they'd be on to the police in seconds.'

'Do you think?'

'Yes, I do, and you're going to have to as well or we'll both be behind bars before teatime.'

'Right, OK. New me. Totally cool. Mr Smooth Guy, pleased to meet you.'

'Besides, I don't think Dublin's our best move.'

'Why? Where else is there?'

'There's Rosslare and the ferry to Le Havre, then the train to Paris. I know some people in Paris.'

'Paris. Wow! That'll be amazing.'

'How much money have you got?'

I fumbled in my pocket for the wad. It felt like it was losing weight. I handed it to her.

'That navy boat, they'll radio the shore to say they lost us. I mean, they'll figure out what we did, going through the gap and everything, won't they?' Emma asked.

'Yeah, I suppose they will. Which means we might have a reception committee waiting for us when we get in.'

'If there is, we just turn around and go.'

'Yeah, but if it's anything like it was for Hutch they'll wait till we're tied up, and then as soon as we step ashore they'll pounce.'

Emma counted the cash.

'But,' I continued, 'they'll have to guess what harbour we'll head for. They're not going to have every port on the east coast packed with police!'

'We've got a hundred and eighty-one pounds here. That'll be loads.'

'Paris?'

'Fucking right!'

'I'll paint pictures.'

'I'll work as a dancer.'

'That's a bit iffy.'

'A cocktail waitress, then.'

'We'll live in an attic.'

'No, an apartment with a flower garden on the roof.'

'OK, this is brilliant. All we have to do is get in, tie up and walk away.'

Chapter 20

Bristol, 2008

I left the house and walked down Gloucester Road. It was one of the few roads I knew in Bristol that had kept its individuality. Most of the rest had swapped their character for the lifeless livery of the chain stores. I leafed through racks of leather jackets in a second-hand store, and passed an hour searching among the shelves of an old book shop. Then I had a coffee and walked into the centre and along the docks. A signwriter painting the name on the side of a barge caught my attention. He had placed a stick against the hull and rested his wrist on it as he painted. It gave him the ability to manoeuvre his brush over the letters, getting the twists and curves he wanted. Maybe that's what I needed, a signwriter's stick. There was a name for those sticks. There must be. It was the sort of question you'd hear on a TV quiz. I could ask in an art shop. I'd pass two on the way home.

It was late afternoon when I got back. I went straight downstairs and looked at the indicator light on the answer machine. It was blinking '1'. I pressed play.

'Seán, I should have asked you yesterday. There's a ton of stuff that needs washing. Could you put a load or two in, it would really help me out. Also, there's pork chops in the fridge that should be used by today. Hope you're enjoying yourself!'

I sat and played the message again. She sounded cheerful. No, it was more than that: there was a lightness to her voice I hadn't heard for a long time. Jesus, what were we coming to? She was happy because she wasn't here, and I was disappointed that the voice on the tape was hers and not Emma's.

Back in the kitchen I washed up. I then went to the laundry basket, fished out garments of similar colour and texture, and fed them into the machine. Now I had to figure out how the thing worked. Icons that looked like the punchline to some hieroglyphic joke surrounded a large circular button. There didn't seem to be an on/off switch. This, of course, underlined all that Lynn had said about my lack of interest in domestic matters. I went looking for the instruction book. There was nothing either in my memory or in the mess of the drawers I opened that gave me any indication as to where the thing might be.

I strolled into the hall. The local free newspaper was lying by the front door. I picked it up and went into the TV room. Wimbledon was on. I kicked off my shoes and decided I'd lose myself in the endeavours and precision of others.

When the phone rang, I was lost in the match. 'Hello.'

There was a moment's silence.

'Seán?'

The voice was female, but low, husky. Emma's? I reached for the remote and turned down the sound. 'Yes.'

'Seán, this is Emma – Emma Balstead. You left your number at the hotel.'

'Emma! My God!' An avalanche of thoughts and words tumbled, interwove, then disappeared, leaving me blank.

'Kate told me and I . . . Is it really you – Seán Farrell from Howth?'

I laughed. 'It's really me. How are you?'

'But you're a relationship counsellor?' She sounded amused but doubtful.

'It could be worse,' I said.

'This is so bizarre! Kate told me and I thought, no, it has to be a different Seán Farrell, it couldn't be you.'

'Well, it is. But what about you? A film director.'

'Yeah, well, at least I'm consistent.'

'What are the chances of meeting up?' The words flowed out of me as if they had an agenda of their own.

'Today – this evening?'

'Yeah.'

'I've been working all day on an editing machine so my head's a bit fried. I mightn't be great company.'

'Emma, it's fine – we can always do it another time.'

'We're just tidying up some details here but I'd love to see you. It'd be great.'

'OK. Where will we meet?'

'Oh, God, I don't know that many places – do you know the Wills Building? It's a big tall tower thing at the top of Park Street.'

'Yeah, I know it.'

'Well, let's meet there. Say seven?'

'OK.'

She laughed again. 'You sound like you but I don't think I'll actually believe it until I see you.'

'You probably won't recognise me.'

'Why? Are you bald and fat now?'

'I'll wear a red carnation just in case.'

'This is just the oddest . . .'

228

'I know, but, look, don't worry – if I turn out to be revolting you can always make an excuse.'

'I'm sure you're as lovely and charming as ever.'

'Maybe you do have the wrong Seán Farrell.'

She laughed. 'Just don't be late.'

Chapter 21

Wicklow, 1976

As we got close to the headland, I asked Emma to steer and went out on deck to prepare the lines. Almost everything that had been there when we'd left Howth had been washed overboard. The few things that remained were collected in a jumble aft. In among the dangle I found enough rope for lines.

I fed them through the fairleads and coiled them so they'd be ready to throw. This whole docking business had to go without a hitch. The headland was drawing closer. I could see the leading edge of the south pier of Wicklow Harbour. It was dark against the land but a small red beacon at the end was flashing. I watched it until I got a clear view of the entrance. It seemed straightforward enough. Then I went inside.

'Did I do all right?' Emma asked.

'Yeah, sorry, you did so well I didn't notice.'

'Right. We can always work on your compliment skills when we're in Paris.'

'What?'

'It doesn't matter. What do you want me to do?'

'Give me the wheel and stand by.'

We watched as the mouth of Wicklow Harbour opened up. It revealed a quay wall packed with fishing-boats. They were all smaller than the ones in Howth. There didn't appear to be anyone on them. In fact, the whole harbour looked deserted. Crews were probably still in their bunks or ashore.

I slowed the Jasper right down. I was looking for an empty space by the wall. Hitting a wall would not cause as much commotion as hitting a boat. But there wasn't any space. My heart began to race. I had a sudden and strong urge to have a shit. I had to squeeze myself and wait for a tight internal pain to pass. Emma was standing there like a tourist on a harbour cruise.

'There aren't many cars about,' she said.

In my anxiety about docking, I had forgotten to look for police cars. I just had to pick a spot and get in. Cruising around the harbour as we were would only draw attention to us. Up closer to the top, by the entrance, there were two boats about our size. It was as good a place as any.

'OK, Emma, I'm going to drive up to those two and try to bring our bow in line with theirs. So, before we get there you go out on deck and pass me that rope coiled up at the bow.'

'Pass you the rope? Why? Where will you be?'

'When we're closer, I'm going to jump on to the other boat. Then you pass me the line, I'll tie it up, go back aft and you pass me the rope that's there.'

'You've never done this before, have you?'

'What do you mean?'

'You're nervous – your voice is all deep and authoritative.'

'Oh, for fuck's sake, Emma, it doesn't matter what my voice is like. Do you think you can do that?'

'Of course.'

'That doesn't fill me with confidence.'

'Well, it should,' she said, and left the wheelhouse.

I could feel my mood slip and I didn't want it to. I had to concentrate. This had to be smooth.

We were edging closer to the two boats. I pulled the throttle back and we ghosted through the water. At close quarters like this, distances were difficult to judge. I might have been a few feet from the other boat, but there again it might have been closer. I heard a crack, followed by a splinter. I rammed the throttle into reverse. The *Jasper* shuddered, vibrating violently, then started backwards at speed. Emma came rushing in from the deck.'What are you doing?' she asked.

'We hit it – we hit the bow!'

'We were miles from it!'

'Were we?'

'Yes, about eight feet.'

'OK, sorry. Let's try again.'

Emma looked at me as though she was about to say something but then she went back to the bow. There, she picked up the coil of rope and rested one foot on the gunwale. Her hair hung in tight curls around her face and her wet clothes hung from her in folds but she looked like a model posing for a photograph. She waved me on. I let the other boat's bow disappear under ours. When she held up her hand, I gave the throttle a slight blast astern, just enough to stop the forward motion. Then I went out and walked halfway up the deck where it would be easy to jump the gap between the two boats. But even as I watched it, the gap was widening. The wind was pushing us away. I leapt, landed on the deck of the other boat, then scrambled to the bow. It was uncomfortable watching Emma standing alone on the *Jasper*'s deck. She was drifting away fast now. I cursed, I hadn't even thought about windage. 'Throw the line!' I shouted.

She, too, watched the widening gap.

'Throw the line, Emma!'

She hurled it. It tangled like a bird's nest in the air and fell well short of my hand. Emma was hauling it back on board even before it hit the water. The *Jasper* was now gaining momentum, her bow swinging away faster than the stern. Emma coiled rapidly, then separated the coil into two parts. She looked up at me and flung the line into the air. It unravelled as it flew. I leant out as far as I could. The rope missed my hand but I heard it land with a thump on the deck behind me. I raced for it, fed it through the fairlead and made it up on a cleat.

I looked aft. Emma was already going back there. But the stern was now being blown away into the harbour. She gathered as much of the line as she could and carried it up to the middle of the deck where she would have more room. There she coiled the line and hurled it into the air. It was the perfect throw. I caught it and ran aft pulling in the slack as I went. At the stern, I hauled on the line. I had to pull against the wind. It was a slow process and my hands were burning by the time the two boats were together. I tied off the mooring line and went to do the same with the forward one. When I had finished, the boats lay alongside one another as if they'd been resting together all their working lives.

'Where did you learn to coil and throw like that?'

'It helps when you spend your summers on the Solent with a father who's as bad at docking as you are.'

'I'm not bad at docking. It was the wind.'

'Funny – that's exactly what he says.'

I had to smile. 'Come on, let's get out of here.'

'What about the engine?'

'Oh, Christ! I don't know how to turn it off.'

'Follow me.'

We stepped over the mess on the galley floor and went down the ladder. I peered into the crew's quarters. It was like a collection of wood amassed for a bonfire. There wasn't a locker door left hanging.

The engine room was hot. Emma had gone in ahead of me. She stretched around the back of the engine and twisted a small valve on a pipe leading from the fuel tank. The engine ran on for several seconds, then spluttered and stopped. The silence was intense. I stood in the doorway suddenly feeling very tired. Emma took my hand. 'Come on,' she said.

'You're a genius.'

Back on deck we came face to face with a small round man in his fifties. He was standing on the deck of the boat we'd just tied up to. He was watching us without expression.

'Blowy old morning,' I said to him.

'It is that,' he said.

'All right if we tie up for a while?'

'Well, you're here now so you best stay put. I wouldn't like to see another performance like that.'

'Yeah, thanks.'

We stepped on to his boat. He was looking at Emma, his face giving away nothing. 'Where have you just come in from?' he asked.

'Arklow,' I said, then added, 'We were making for Howth but it's too bad out there.'

'You're not the skipper of this one,' he said.

I couldn't decide if that was a question or a statement. The fishing community was small, he may well know John Sheehan.'No,' I said, 'my brother is.'

We climbed from his deck to the next boat, then up on to the harbour wall. From there I looked down at him and nodded. He turned and walked back into his wheelhouse.

'There's a couple of cars at the end of the pier,' Emma said.

'Nothing we can do about them now.'

'Look, Seán, whatever happens, I want you to know it's been fantastic, every minute of it.'

Her words lifted the feeling of doom that had descended on me since we arrived in the harbour. I smiled at her. This was living. Maybe there would be a horrible price to pay but it didn't matter. It had been worth it.

'Tomorrow morning we'll be eating croissants in a Paris café,' I said.

She was smiling. 'Pain au chocolat for me.'

The cars were empty. In fact, the whole town seemed empty. In the main street the shops were open but there was no one in any of them. One or two people passed us, bent and holding on to their hats, but their stance might have had as much to do with age as the weather. Anyone in this town under fifty was still in bed.

A sign squeaking in the wind told us that coffee and tea were to be had in Foley's Café. But you couldn't see much through the misted window beneath it. Whatever else was in there, there had to be a toilet. I badly needed to go.

The place was thick with smoke and the smell of grease, everyone hunched over cups, talking, smoking and old. We walked to an empty table at the back. I excused myself and asked the woman behind the counter where I'd find the toilet. She looked me up and down and indicated a door at the far side of the counter. It was a narrow room with yellow lino, a pink toilet and washbasin and beige walls. A colour scheme designed to make you vomit. I emptied my bowels urgently and a rancid odour filled the cubicle.

I examined myself in the mirror. My eye was bruised, not quite black but swollen and purplish. My hair was pasted to my skull. I washed my hands and scooped water on to my face. It tasted of salt. Then I looked again in the mirror. 'Don't worry, son, this time tomorrow it's Paris, home of the brave, land of the free.' No, that was

America. It didn't matter. We'd make it to the Promised Land. We'd got this far.

Outside I caught a glimpse of Emma among the customers. She, too, was wet and worn.

'Do you speak French?' I asked, when I'd sat down.

'Seán, don't look now but behind you there's a guy reading the paper and a minute ago I caught a headline on the front page. It said, "Kidnapped." There was a picture. I couldn't make it out. I only saw it for a second.'

'That has to be a coincidence.'

'Seán, please!'

'Did you order?'

'No. I think we should just get out of here.'

'Emma, let's just have something to eat and plan how we're going to get down to Rosslare. Where's the guy with the paper?' I said, turning. I saw him straight away: he was studying form on the racing pages. He glanced up at me for a second but that was all. I had a quick check. There weren't any other paper-readers in the place. They were all too busy inhaling smoke and talking. Emma wasn't happy.

'You want us to leave?' I said.

'I wish we were somewhere we could relax.'

'Well, that'll be on the ferry tonight. Meanwhile, let's get some breakfast.'

She didn't reply. The woman from behind the counter came out and approached with her pad. I ordered bacon, eggs, sausages, toast and tea for us both.

I thought I'd better focus on our escape, something that would give Emma hope. 'The train to Rosslare stops here in Wicklow.'

'Seán, if that article's about us they'll be watching the ports, won't they? And the trains.'

'Well, we'll hitch.'

She was staring at me, pleading in her eyes. 'They knew where we were an hour ago, right? So they'll work out where we are now. We should just go.'

I could smell the bacon. But there was that look in Emma's eyes.

'We can buy a car, drive to Rosslare.'

'Seán, buying a car is not like buying a packet of cigarettes.' She was angry now.

'We'll steal one, then.'

'I can't drive.'

'Neither can I.'

Suddenly she was smiling. 'You're fucking useless,' she said, too loudly. Several nearby customers stopped and looked at us. Several for too long.

'Right,' she said, 'we'll eat, then get the train, and if they haul us off, they do.'

'I can't think of a better plan.'

'It's not a plan, it's a suicide pact.'

'Look, some food will have us up and running again.'

She was just about to speak when her eyes caught something behind me. She turned pale. I swung round. Nothing had changed. Then I saw it. It was Emma. A big picture underneath the one-word headline: 'Kidnapped'. Her hair was shorter; she was younger. You could see the V of her school jumper. The man folded the paper so that half the front page was facing out. Anyone who looked would see it.

'What are we going to do?' she said. She was like a ghost, only her lips moving.

'Oh, Jesus Christ!' was all I could say. 'We have to go to the police.'

'No! Never! Never.'

'Emma, they'll be everywhere now.'

'I'm not going to the police.'

237

The woman arrived, holding two plates. They were white and shiny and the food glistened.

'That'll be thirty-eight new pence.'

I gave her a fifty-pence piece and told her to keep the change. She shrugged, turned and walked away.

'Seán, will you stop being such a git?'

We looked at the food. The woman came back to the table and left an untidy column of coins on the yellow oilcloth.

I heard the door open behind me. Emma glanced up, then immediately looked down again at her plate. Her hand went to her forehead and I saw a tear drop on to the white of her egg. I was just about to turn when I saw the woman behind the counter nod in our direction at whoever had just come in. The talking suddenly stopped. Footsteps came from behind. Then a hand was laid on my shoulder. It was firm but not grasping. 'If you'd like to come with us.'

Chapter 22

Bristol, 2008

It was six twenty – forty minutes before the meeting. I was now dressed in what I thought were the right clothes for the occasion: jeans and a shirt. I could feel myself getting edgy though, excitement turning to nervousness and then to dread.

I decided to drag the washing-machine from its slot to see if the instruction book had fallen down the back. It hadn't. But two small garments lay there, hidden under a carpet of dust. I was searching for something that was long enough to reach them when the door-bell rang.

I looked at the clock – six thirty. I needed to leave in five minutes.

When I opened the door, Roland was standing on the porch, grinning. 'Hi! I've been trying to call you. Your phone's off.'

I must have forgotten to turn it back on this morning. 'Come in. What's up?'

Roland squeezed his bulk past me into the hall. 'Look, I'm sorry to just turn up like this.' He stopped and looked about. 'Very quiet, isn't it?'

'Yeah, no one's in.'

'Oh! Really?'

'Lynn's away on a watercolour workshop and the kids are gone as well.'

'Place to yourself, hey?'

'Yeah. Sorry, Roland, I was just heading out. Was there something . . .?

'Allison knows.' He looked down the hall, then back at me.

'Knows what?'

'About the money. That I borrowed the money for the boat.'

'What? She's just found out?'

'Yeah, there was a letter from the bank today.'

'You mean you hadn't told her?'

'No.'

'Jesus, Roland!'

'I know, I know.'

'So what did she do?'

'Hit the fucking roof.'

'Christ!'

'Yeah. It's bad.'

'You can stay here tonight, if you like.'

He didn't respond, just stared at some middle distance between us.

After a moment, I said, 'You OK?'

'Yeah, no. I don't know. I could use a beer.'

'Look, I'd love to go with you but I'm on my way out.'

'Where are you going?'

'I'm meeting someone.'

A smile spread across his face. 'Oh, yeah, cat's away . . .'

'No. Not like that.'

'Oh, no? How come you're all kind of smart-casual, then?'

'Look, I'll tell you what. Have a beer and then drop me down the

240

town. That way we'll have ten minutes. You can come back here if you want and we can talk later.'

'OK.'

He followed me into the kitchen and slumped on a chair at the table. I handed him a bottle and sat opposite him. 'Cheers! What time are you meeting your fancy woman?' he said, with a hint of a smile.

'She's not a fancy woman.'

'She's a she, though?'

I looked at him. 'You've time to finish your beer.'

'A friend?'

'Yeah, an old friend.'

'That's nice.'

'I'm a bit nervous, actually.'

'Haven't seen her in a while?'

'No, not since . . .'

'So it is a "her"?' He was grinning now.

'Yes, it's a her, an ex from a long time ago.'

His eyebrows rose.

'No, not like that.'

He picked up his beer and shook his head. 'What have I walked into?'

'Nothing – nothing's going on, absolutely nothing.'

'Seán, you're as jittery as a juvenile just about to get laid.'

'Am I?'

'You are.'

'Christ!'

'So, where are you meeting this chick?'

'She's not a chick! It's not like that – she's an old friend. I went out with her in Ireland thirty years ago.'

'This is getting good!'

'We're just meeting for a drink.'

'So, what, you call her up in Ireland and say, "Hi! Remember me?"'

'No, I have a client who, it turned out, is her daughter.'

'One of your clients is your ex-girlfriend's daughter?'

'She's an ex-client now.'

'So this ex-client is the daughter of an ex-girlfriend?'

'Yeah.'

'Fuck!'

'What? I'm not doing anything wrong.'

'You sure?'

'Yes, of course I'm sure.'

'Lynn knows about this?'

'No, she doesn't.'

He sat staring at me.

'Look, Roland, I'm nervous. I don't know why I'm doing this and, at the same time, I don't see any reason why I shouldn't. To be frank with you, I haven't got a clue what I'm doing.'

'What time are you meeting her?'

'Seven, outside the Wills Building.'

'You haven't seen her in how long?'

'About thirty years – thirty-one, thirty-two, maybe.'

'Was she good-looking?'

'Yeah, gorgeous.'

'Really?'

'A bit of discretion here would be appreciated.'

'What do you think I am?'

'Yeah, sorry, we'd better get going.'

'Relax, I'll have you there on time.'

'OK. Thanks.'

'Yeah, I mean, I gotta see what kind of dogs you were sniffin' around when you were—'

'Roland, you can drop me there but you're not hanging around.'

'It's a public place.'

'Roland!'

242

'OK, OK. But you gotta tell me what happens. Every detail.'

'Fine.'

'You're something else, Seány boy, you know that? Tell me something, thirty years ago, were you fucking her?'

'We never got round to it.'

'You never got round to it? Shit! Glad I wasn't brought up in Ireland.'

Chapter 23

Wicklow Garda Station was small. The front gate was like the gate on any ordinary home. It even squeaked. Emma walked through it head down and angry. I wished I was too. But the only feeling I could muster, apart from numbness, was fear, and that was just an echo.

Once inside, she was brought to a bench, curved and shiny. She sat on it, bent low, hands between her knees, holding her bottom lip with her teeth.

I was marched through the room. I had to stop while they opened a door. When I turned back to her she was still in the same position. I wanted to say goodbye but she wouldn't look up. Suddenly I felt myself being hauled by the arms and led down a corridor and from there into a small room. It was empty but for a metal table and two chairs.

I was told to wait, someone would be with me shortly. Then the door closed. I was alone. I paced up and down the floor. They had me. This time it was the business, the boys in blue, backed by the judges with wigs and barristers in gowns, and behind their whole theatrical act were metal bars behind which they'd be happy to let me rot.

I put my hands in my pockets and then on my head. I had to think.

And this was the time to think. It was the time to organise everything, shore up every detail, because soon they'd be back and they had in their possession machinery designed to blow apart the most solid of stories. They were experts at it. They'd read manuals on the subject, attended lectures and honed their instincts. And the best of them would be through this door in no time and an interrogation would begin and I'd better have a solid story – granite solid.

The door opened. It was a garda, younger than any of the rest.

'The sergeant wants to know if you'd like a cup of tea?'

'Yes. Two sugars, thank you.'

I could tell them everything, nothing to hide but Scully. Tell them about Scully and you're dead, Farreller.

I tried to compose myself. This wasn't going to be difficult. What had I done? I was innocent of everything, except being a fucking idiot. And if that was a crime then at least nine-tenths of the population would be behind bars.

I wasn't going to do anything. Just sit on one of these fine chairs here and wait. The questions would pour in and the answers would pour out. A river of facts would flow from me and they could all be true except for anything about Scully. And they might not even bring him into the conversation. No, the river of facts would flow and the water would be sampled, tested for truth. It wouldn't fail because I could tell them everything. And, in the end, everything would be all right because everything was all right, basically.

This wasn't working. I couldn't even fool myself. What chance did I have against a machine specifically designed to detect liars and their wares?

The young garda came in with the tea. 'The sergeant wants to know if you'd like a change of clothes.' I looked at him in surprise. 'You know, you're wet and that.'

'No. No, thank you.'

'Right. It won't be too long,' he said, and left. Christ Almighty, what wouldn't be too long?

I was up again and pacing. Where was Emma? This was insane. I needed out of here. This room was too small. I needed air. I walked up and down again. One thing was for sure, I couldn't spend time in prison. I'd kill myself first. I'd go mad being locked up. But this was going too far too fast. I wasn't locked up. Sure, I was detained. But being detained was different. They had it at school, detention. They didn't use it much but they had it. Schools preferred to beat you. Funny that, the State using as its main deterrent something that schools ignored. But then they'd have to build detention wings on to the sides of school, or camps complete with barbed wire and guard dogs.

Christ! What was I thinking?

There was a commotion outside. Voices, lots of them. I couldn't make them out. I heard a woman's, but it wasn't Emma's. Then doors opening, shutting, more people, more voices. Then nothing. Silence.

I sat in front of the steaming cup. That must have been Emma being taken out of here. She was gone now, simple as that. But where would she be taken? Jesus, I hoped that wasn't her mother's voice I'd heard. It must have been. In the restaurant, when the police had arrived, one had leant down to Emma and told her they were going to take her to the station now where her mother would be arriving shortly. She'd looked up at him, all tear-stained, and shouted, 'Why don't you just fuck off?' and then, into the gallery of gaping faces, 'Why don't you all just fuck off?' I loved her for that.

But now they were separating us. They'd cut us off. It didn't matter. I knew, and she knew, we had strength and we were young, and all these fucking bastards would be dead and rotting when we were only starting to live. Except I'd probably still be sitting in solitary.

'And what do you do for a living?' asks the TV game-show host.

'I'm a detainee, Bob.'

246

'A detainee? Wonderful, wonderful! We've never had one of those on this show, have we?' The audience would all agree.

The door opened. Two guards came in. They were both big men. They stared at me but in an impersonal way. Farmers assessing a beast.

'Stand with your hands against the wall,' one said.

I just looked at them.

'Are you deaf?' the other said, but with added volume.

I walked to the wall and put my hands against it.

'Higher.'

I did this.

'Spread your legs.'

I obeyed.

Hands appeared on my wrists and patted down my arms to my armpits. Those hands, as deft as thieving mice, went over every inch of my body. When he had finished, the garda stepped back as though he might have ignited something.

'Turn around.'

I did.

'Empty your pockets on to the table.'

Out came the change, the roll of notes, a couple of receipts turned to mush from this morning's soaking, and a key to my parents' house.

They tried to unfurl the receipts, then thought better of it. They picked up the roll, looked at it, then dropped everything into an envelope and sealed it.

'Put your hands on the table.' As soon as I did, the one that had searched me had a pair of handcuffs on me faster than you could crack an egg.

The other was writing on the envelope. He said I'd get my property back in due course. They weren't exactly chatty. Not the kind who'd offer you dry clothes or a cup of tea.

I stood with one while the other opened the door and looked out. Almost immediately a man wearing a suit appeared. He shot a glance at me and at the garda beside me, then turned to the one at the door. 'Take him out the back, Jim. The press have got it. They're outside already.'

'Right you are,' Jim said.

At that, Quick Fingers and I moved into the corridor. I could now see into the room where Emma had sat. It was full of men in uniforms or suits. They were chatting and smoking like it was a sporting event.

I was turned in the other direction and, between the two big men, escorted down the corridor towards a metal door that looked as if it had come out of a different century and hadn't seen use in this one yet. But old Jim swung it open without much trouble. He looked out, then ducked back in, closing it behind him. 'Boss,' he shouted up the hall. 'They're out here too.'

The man he had spoken to was in the far doorway. He turned around. 'Jaysus, Jim, just take him out, will you, before they all get wind of it?'

With that, Jim opened the door again. There were about eight men standing at the base of steps in front of it. Jim shouted at them to move aside. The policeman behind me pushed my head down as I went out. The clicking of cameras started straight away. Looking at my feet I was steered towards a waiting car. They were bending down now to try to get a picture of me. Others were shouting, 'What's his name? Did he rape her? Was she raped?'

I was guided into the back seat. The non-Jim part of the pair kept my head down until we were moving. When we were clear of the station, he let go, and I sat up. I was in a police car with four uniformed gardaí. I looked behind. Another police car was following – two uniformed men in the front.

Non-Jim was looking at me. He had a smile on his face, but that was maybe too healthy a word for what he was wearing. 'Well, did you?' he said.

'None of that now, Conner,' said the one sitting in the passenger seat.

'Jaysus, did you see her? I'd have given her one, I tell you.'

'That's enough.'

Jim offered me a cigarette. I took it. Then he offered one to everyone else. Soon we were all smoking. The driver rolled down the window about an inch and said, 'Some jalopy this. Fuck me!'

'It was decent enough of them to supply it,' said the officer in the passenger seat. 'They didn't have to. If we'd had to wait for those other fuckin' eejits to get the wagon down we'd have been there all day.'

'I know, but still she's a crate.'

They rattled on like this through the sweeps and bends in the road. The Sugar Loaf appeared ahead of us. The last time I'd seen it I was hunched and freezing on the back of Max's bike. That was yesterday morning, a lifetime ago.

Ash was falling on to the trousers of the two beside me. They swept it away with their hands and rattled on. Their conversation was like an overweight plane trying to take off. Every time you thought they were up and away, one would throw in something and it would collapse back into silence. After a while, someone else would decide to give it another go.

At least they were leaving me alone. After the cigarettes, Conner produced a packet of mints. He only got two takers. I said no because the cigarette had made me feel ill. Besides, the handcuffs were taking the pleasure out of life. And, despite the window being cracked open, the car was refusing to give up its grasp on its own personal cloud.

Somewhere between the drone of their talk and the sound of the road disappearing underneath us, I fell asleep. I woke with a jolt when we took off from some traffic lights. We were deep inside the city now, a part I didn't recognise. The buildings were old. Dirt that had gathered in corners gave them the illusion of depth and sturdiness that they most certainly did not have. Kids on the street stopped their games to stare into the car.

We travelled through several more tight little streets with shabby buildings, then emerged onto Dame Street and drove into Dublin Castle. We pulled into what appeared to be the back of the building. The car stopped in front of a ramp that led up to double doors.

When I got out, I found my trousers had dried stiff with the salt. I tried to stretch but, between the handcuffs and the uniforms at either side of me, it was not possible.

We entered the building through a single door at the top of metal steps. Inside, I was led down a corridor, then through another door that shut heavily behind us. The paintwork was badly deteriorated and there was a strong smell of dirt. We passed doors at regular intervals. They had narrow sliding hatches at eye level.

We stopped in front of one of the doors and a guard opened it with a key that was on a ring with a thousand others. He stepped back to let me in. It was small, pale, like the room we had left in Wicklow. Except for the metal chair and table, it was empty.

'Hands on the table,' Jim said. He had the handcuffs off as quickly as he had put them on. He stepped back into the corridor. The door slammed.

I stood still. Overhead, a fluorescent bulb emitted a constant whine. The walls were smooth and featureless. This room could have been anywhere. Perhaps it floated about, visiting different buildings in different countries because every country needed rooms like this. Places where people too much for the peaceful running of society were put. And now I was here.

I walked back and forth, then stretched. After a moment or two, I sat. I put my head in my hands. I was tired to the bone. But there was fuck-all chance of rest here. I guessed that in prison, real prison, the one after the court, I could get all the rest I needed. There might be facilities there. I could become a dynamite pool player, or a historian, or a carpenter, or a painter. How long would I get? And for what, for fuck's sake? What had I bloody done? Steal a boat. Yeah, well, they had me there. Trawler-rustling, a hanging offence. John Sheehan would be having a head-fit, his big hands banging the kitchen table making the teapot jump and the cat cower. But they'd find it. They'd already know where it was. He'd get it back. One thing was for sure: now I could definitely not go back to the West Pier. So where else was there? Maybe prison was the place to go for a while. Perhaps it was designed to let the dust of crimes settle and the perpetrators shelter while the victims' desire for revenge faded. Maybe all those grim Victorian prisons were quite a sophisticated invention after all. 'Hoi, you there, criminal, why not duck in here for a bit while things calm down, hey?'

'No, thank you, I'm off to Barbados.'

'White man's grave? Better you than me son, better you than me.'

'No, it's a holiday resort now, all suntan cream and late-night drinking.'

'If you say so, son.'

With all the places they send people as a punishment now being used as holiday resorts, there's no choice but to lock people up at home. Keep them safe behind barbed wire – screws with truncheons and inmates with erections looking for tight young arses to ram them into.

I stood up and walked around the table. My heart was pounding. Small places didn't suit me. I needed air.

I had to calm myself. Apart from the boat, what did they have me on? 'Kidnapped' was what it said in the paper. But people were always saying you should never believe a word you read in the papers. So no one did. But someone must because they don't go walking to the shops every morning to get their paper thinking they're going home to read fiction. No smoke without fire. But I hadn't kidnapped Emma and she knew it. So did Liam and Plasma and loads of other people. So let's get on with it. Six months for boat-stealing, that was what I'd get. Six months, out in four. Leaking diarrhoea from a much-damaged sphincter

No, I couldn't go there. I couldn't. Look at me now. Ten minutes in this place and I was sweating.

The door opened. Two gardaí stood in the corridor outside and indicated I should step out. They didn't say a word. One stood in front of me, the other behind. I wondered for a moment was I being frogmarched. The idea made me want to laugh. Marching frogs, might be nice. If you lined up thousands of them, say ten abreast, and got the ones in front to leap, then the next row and the next and so on down the line, soon you'd have a rolling wave of slimy green. That's a frog march. What we were at here was nothing like it. This was a negotiating file, so called because we had to weave in and out of people coming the other way, or past other people just standing around doing nothing. Other things to avoid were boxes and those came in two types: cardboard and metal. The metal ones broke into other categories: filing cabinets made up the bulk and then there were nondescript ones painted cream with chocolate-brown lids. These hummed ever so slightly. And, as we negotiated those corridors, the one thing that struck me was the business of the place. Every room I could see into had people in it, all men in shirts and ties, standing or sitting at their desks and talking. Paper and typewriters everywhere, and shelves crammed with files and litterbins overflowing and the paintwork scuffed.

Finally, we turned into a room as big and shabby as the rest of the place. There was one large rectangular window at the back, too high to see through. It looked as though it had misted up from the weather outside. There were the table and the chairs, standard furnishings for rooms like this, I guessed.

One of the gardaí pulled up a chair for me, like you see men do for women in fancy restaurants on television. I sat. The chair was plastic and dipped down to the left side, where it had come unhinged from the metal frame.

I wanted to ask them what was supposed to happen now, but they had walked to the far end of the room and stood by the wall. I had my back to them. I wanted to turn and ask if I could change seats. I was afraid this one would disintegrate beneath me.

Then two men walked in. I presumed they were what people called plain-clothes police. One, the older and thinner of the two, dumped a bundle of typed papers he was carrying in the middle of the table, then sank into the seat opposite me. He looked at his watch, then at me. He was bald. Loose folds of skin hung under his chin. His eyes were pale blue, so pale the irises almost disappeared into the whites. There was a calmness about him that was disturbing. The other was small and stocky. He had raised the front of his hair into an oily quiff. He held himself very erect. When he sat, he began to shuffle through the papers, putting his fist to his face now and then to stifle a short cough.

Old Wattle-neck sat there as still as a lighthouse, his beamless gaze not moving off me. I tried to stare back without insolence. I didn't want to give him the impression I wasn't going to cooperate.

'Good afternoon,' he said, in a tone that was empty of interest. 'I'm Detective Inspector Connelly and this is Detective Nagle.'

I nodded. It felt wrong not to tell them who I was, but if there was one thing certain here, it was that these two knew my name.

Nagle found the piece of paper he was looking for. He passed it to Connelly, who finally took his eyes off me and directed them to it. He looked back at me, then stood. He walked around the table and continued to the back of the room. If I wanted to go on looking at him, I'd have to turn around, but the prospect of chair disintegration stopped me. Besides, he seemed to be off on some personal journey.

I focused instead on Nagle. He was examining his fingernails. When he noticed me looking at him he reacted as though I'd caught him picking his nose. He dropped his hands to the table and sat up very straight. Behind me I could hear Connelly coming back. Any second now he'd be in view, the great grey sails of his overcoat carrying him footless to the table's edge.

'What age are you?' he asked.

'Seventeen,' I said.

'Christ Almighty!' he said to the ceiling, and sat. He began the staring thing again. 'You're a real pain in the arse, do you know that?'

I wasn't sure if I was meant to reply to this. And if I did, how? 'Very observant of you, Detective Inspector, I can see you're a bright boy, one for the big promotion when it comes along.'

'Where's Scully?' Nagle asked.

This floored me. I had to answer, and answer now. 'I don't know.' It was all I could think of saying. Then I added, 'Have you tried his house?' I had to stay calm.

Nagle leant over the table. 'Don't get fucking smart with me!' His eyes were a deep brown and without warmth.

'I don't know where he is, I really don't.'

'When was the last time you saw him?' Connelly said, calm, without expression.

'Last night, when Emma and I were going down to the boat.'

'Who arranged that meeting?' Nagle asked.

'What do you mean?'

'Are you deaf as well as stupid?' Nagle's tone was heavy with feigned curiosity.

'No one arranged it. It just happened. He came into the pub. We were there.'

'What were you planning to do with the girl?' Connelly asked.

'Emma?'

'Yes, Emma.'

'We were going to get a flat.'

'Who was going to get a flat?'

'Me and Emma!'

Connelly looked at Nagle, then back at me. 'Listen,' he said, 'we can keep you here for a week if we like. And by the time that week's over we can have you swinging on the end of a rope for crimes you never knew existed, let alone committed. So my advice to you is simple. Answer our questions, here, now, in full, and we'll get this whole thing all sorted out. Do you follow?'

'Yes, right. I'm happy to. I want to.' There was something about this man that was frightening me. There was a callousness to him that was different to anything I'd ever seen before. He had power, he could use it, but he'd never have to feel its consequences. I was just one in a river of faces that flowed through rooms like this, past him, and into a maximum-security prison where I would stay until I was old and feeble. I was immaterial to him.

'So, what were you going to do with the girl?' Connelly asked.

'Listen to me,' I said. 'Today, we were going to go into town and get a flat. I didn't kidnap her. She's my girlfriend, has been since the end of the summer – ask anyone.'

'We know,' Nagle said. 'Handy that, isn't it?'

'I'm sorry, I don't get you.'

'Easier to kidnap someone when you know them,' he said.

I just stared at him.

'Tell us about Claire,' Connelly said.

'Claire?'

'Yes, Claire Traynor.'

'She was Hutch's girlfriend. He used to sleep with her in his bunk every night.'

'So, she was unknown to you before you joined the *Mary Jo*?'

'Yes. I mean no. I mean you're right. I didn't know her before that, no.'

Connelly's forehead became a ploughed field of creases. 'So, she was a stranger to you?'

'Well, she was, of course, when I first met her. I mean, everyone is when you first meet.'

This had Nagle out of his seat again. He was stopped by the rise of Connelly's hand.

'Listen,' I said, 'I never met her before she arrived with Hutch one night in Findlater's and after that she just stayed on the boat with us. I never got to know her. None of us did, except Hutch.'

'So why, in that case, did you all conspire to hide her when you were boarded by the Navy?'

'I don't know. We just did.'

Nagle came at me like one of that morning's waves. 'Just how fucking stupid do you think we are, Farrell? You were her gofer. What did she keep you sweet with? Bit of fucky-fucky? Well, your bit of fucky-fucky's inside now and will be till she's a very old lady. But since last Friday,' he pointed to the stack of papers, 'she's been singing like a fucking sparrow.'

I wanted to tell him that sparrows don't sing, they chirp. But there was no telling this man anything. He was travelling on a track well north of reality.

'We have you. We have those two and we have Doyle,' Connelly said. 'But Scully, who, I imagine, is the only one of you with any brains, has so far eluded us.'

'What are you talking about? What do you think we are? Look, me and Emma did something wrong. I know that. But it was nothing to do with any of the others.'

A broad smile spread across Nagle's face. 'I suppose you're going to tell us now that this has all been some terrible mistake?'

'I don't know,' I said. 'I don't know what to say. I'm very tired.'

'What was Claire Traynor doing on the *Mary Jo*?' Connelly asked.

'No one knew she was on board, except Hutch. Scully would have thrown her overboard if he'd known.'

Connelly turned to Nagle, then back to me. 'You just said she slept aboard every night!'

'Yeah, she did, but when we went out to sea she got off.'

'Why would she do that?'

'Because Scully would have thrown her overboard.'

Connelly's gaze was unflinching. 'Why?'

'Because women on boats are bad luck. Women and pigs.' Now they were both staring at me. 'Proper pigs, I mean, and priests. Yeah, women, pigs and priests.' I threw in the bit about the priests to dilute any unintended insult about the pigs but I knew I sounded like I was just ranting.

All that had happened before this interview was something I was expected to reveal, except now, it all sounded different, like I was making it up.

'Were you aware that Scully was once a guest of Her Majesty?' Connelly said.

'I knew he'd been to prison.'

'Do you know what for?'

'No.'

'Murder.'

Well, there was a fact that had nothing to do with me. Scully had killed someone. It didn't surprise me.

'So,' Connelly continued, 'let me see if I've got this straight. None of you knew Claire Traynor and Scully would have thrown her overboard if he'd known she was on board, yet when the Navy arrived, you all conspired to hide her. This doesn't make sense.'

I shrugged. 'We just did it.'

I could see their impatience mounting. 'I don't know what to tell you.'

'Try the fucking truth,' Nagle said, in a sort of sideways snarl.

'Look, as far as Claire Traynor's concerned, all I knew about her was she was Hutch's girlfriend. We took the boat out and Scully was skipper and one evening, after we hauled the gear, he said we should shoot it again. You know, stay out the night. Everyone was OK about it, sort of. Anyway, after dinner, Hutch is steering and everyone else is in their bunks and he gives me this bag of leftovers and tells me to take it to Claire. She's in the hold. I didn't believe him, but she was. She'd been down there all the time we were out fishing. I went back up to Hutch after I'd given her the food to get her a cigarette, and when I asked why she was down there, all he said was Scully would throw her overboard if he knew she was out with us because women on boats are bad luck.'

And you were satisfied with that explanation?' Connelly asked.

'Yeah. I didn't really think about it. Scully's crazy.'

'Go on.'

'How do you mean?'

'What happened then?'

'Hutch asked me to take the wheel while he went down to Claire, and next thing – bang! A light comes on. It's the Navy. They board us and Scully's up in the wheelhouse going mad wanting to know if she's aboard and I told him that she was.'

'And what did he do?'

'Made a plan to hide her.'

'Did you ever think about why he did that?' Connelly asked.

I shook my head.

'You didn't? That surprises me. With everything you've told us so far it just doesn't fit, does it? I mean, here he is, the man who would throw a woman overboard because she's bad luck, and he finds himself aboard with one and yet when the Navy present him with the perfect opportunity to rid himself of her what does he do? He hides her from them. Why?'

Connelly sitting there talking in this reasonable way made it all sound different. But, out there, at sea, it hadn't been like that.

'I don't know,' I said. 'He just did.'

'And you all joined in,' Nagle added.

'It's hard to explain. Anyway, none of it made any difference because they were arrested as soon as we docked.'

'And that,' Connelly said, resting his chin in his fingers, 'is when you decided to kidnap the daughter of the man Claire Traynor tried to kill.'

'No, I didn't! You make it sound different from how it was. I—'

'Oh. So you know Claire tried to kill Emma's father.'

I was silent. I had fallen into his trap. They had me. It was too late to act all surprised and shocked at the news.

'How did you know?' Connelly asked.

'We worked it out.'

'We worked it out!' Nagle mocked. 'You're too fucking stupid to work it out.'

'When did you find out that Claire Traynor was wanted for the attempted murder of Emma's father? When?' Connelly demanded.

'I told you, Emma and I worked it out.'

'You're not very good at this, are you?

'At what?'

'Lying.'

There was silence. I stared at the metal tabletop.

'Do you know where she is now, your girlfriend?' Nagle asked. I didn't even look at him. 'She's spread out on a doctor's table with her legs in the air while they probe her to see if she's still intact.'

The image numbed me. These people were animals. All fucking animals!

'All we wanted to do was get away,' I said.

'Sweet,' Nagle said, with a laugh. 'Sweet as chewed-up fucking toffee.'

'Shut up!' I shouted at him. 'Just shut up!' I surprised myself by the volume and the anger.

Nagle just sat there smiling. I wanted so much to smack his square podgy face. Why the fuck would they be doing that to her? They were bastards, all bastards, every last one of them.

'Those were pretty big seas you were out in this morning,' Connelly said.

I looked at him.

'No problem to you, though, eh?'

'They were plenty of problem to me.'

'Neat trick too, slipping through the bank like that?'

I shrugged.

'You must have built up quite some knowledge over the years knowing where that channel lies. Very impressive.'

There was something in Connelly's tone now that told me this game was almost up. He had decided to move in for the kill.

Nagle said, 'Three people were seen on the trawler leaving Howth this morning. When we spoke to the skipper of the boat you tied up to he said only you and the girl got off.'

'So,' Connelly said, 'why don't you tell us what happened to Scully?'

There had to be a series of words I could say that would get me out of this. There must exist some combination of syllables that would put these two to rest. The penalty for not thinking now was death, or prison, or both. Nothing came.

'Maybe you threw him over the side,' Nagle suggested, manufacturing a movement with the corners of his mouth that resembled a smile.

'I don't understand. What has any of this to do with Scully anyway?'

Connelly's seat made a barking noise behind him as he stood. 'Right,' he said, scooping up the bulk of papers from the table. 'If you want to spent the next twenty years of your life behind bars that's up to you. I have work to do.'

'I can't tell you where he is – I can't.'

Connelly ploughed his forehead again. 'You mean you know where he is but you won't tell us?'

No matter which way this worked out, I was a dead man. 'Scully said he'd kill me if I told you anything.'

Connelly put the papers back on the table. 'When did he say this?'

'Today.'

'On the boat?'

'Yes.'

'Where did he get off?'

'He swam for it after we got through the bank.'

Connelly and Nagle shared a look.

'You see, you don't understand. Scully will kill me.' I said this to Connelly.

'Oh, I doubt that,' he replied.

'What do you mean you doubt that? You've just told me he's a murderer. Well, the same murderer told me just hours ago that he'd kill me if I mentioned a word about him being involved. I just have, so I'm a dead man and you don't give a shit.'

'Involved? Involved in what?' Connelly said, settling back into his seat.

'What?'

'You said just now that Scully would kill you if you mentioned that he was involved. Involved in what?'

'Taking the boat this morning. He was afraid that if he was seen on it he'd be considered the ringleader for the whole thing.'

'What whole thing?' Nagle asked.

'I don't know. He was freaking out. I don't know what it was about. Well, I do, I suppose. See, he knew by then the trouble we were in.'

They were both staring at me.

'He told us about Claire and Emma's father. Then when we saw the headline in the café we knew this whole thing had gone mad.'

There was a knock on the door. One of the two from the back walked the length of the room and opened it. There was a fast exchange of whispers. Then the garda walked up to Connelly and spoke in his ear. Their exchange was inaudible and rapid. Connelly stared at me as he absorbed what he was being told. The garda straightened and Connelly spoke to Nagle with the same low-volume rapidity. Then he looked at me. 'It seems Miss Balstead's virginity is intact.'

Nagle laughed. 'With the amount of time you're looking at you'll be sorry you didn't fuck her.'

I stared at him. Someone just like him had poked about inside her until he was happy that this was a place that had housed nothing but his probing fingers.

Connelly leant back in his chair. 'I'm going to tell you a little story,' he said.

'I don't give a shit what you do,' I said.

'Well, listen, and you just might.'

I put my head in my hands.

'Kevin O'Sullivan,' he said, 'Scully as you call him, is a member of the IRA. He fell out of favour with them when a little job in Britain went wrong. The same incident had him residing in Wormwood Scrubs for seven years. We know this, it's a matter of record. John Hutchinson and Matt Doyle are also known to be members. All right so far? OK. One day, Scully is asked to provide temporary shelter for a Claire Traynor. She's just made a botch of trying to assassinate a British military attaché named Reginald

Balstead. She did manage to kill his bodyguard and permanently disable his driver – not what the organisation considered a success. But they had to hide her and, until a safe-house could be organised, Scully was the preferred choice. He's in an ideal situation for it and, of course, for Scully, it means he's back in. It's the first job they've given him since his spell in the Scrubs.

'Scully, as you know, is no fool and grasps the importance of this. It has to run smoothly. So when he learns, through Hutchinson probably, that you have been seeing Emma Balstead, he thinks all his Christmases have come at once. Here he is in a trusted position once again and, as a bit of added insurance, has access to the target's daughter, should he need it. Beautiful! All goes well at first, but then there's a problem. Claire Traynor, for whatever reason, does not want to leave the boat for her safe-house. Maybe she doesn't think it's that safe, who knows? Anyway, Scully decides to take the boat out to sea thereby giving her no option – she'll have to get off. But here he makes an error. He underestimates the effect she's had on Hutchinson. And he doesn't find this out until the *Mary Jo* is boarded. He has to hide her, of course he has to hide her, but he's mighty pissed off with Hutchinson – hence the débâcle on the deck once the Navy leave empty-handed. Enjoying this so far?'

I sighed and shook my head.

'What part of it don't you think rings true?'

'None of it, it's bollox. I was there as all this was happening. I mean, for a start, Scully took the boat out because the real skipper was too drunk. And the other thing, Scully offered me a berth on the *Mary Jo* before I ever met Emma. And this morning Scully didn't know who Emma was. Your story is complete bollox.'

Connelly was smiling. 'Tell me,' he said, 'what did you and Scully do after your interview in Howth Police Station?'

'We sold some of the fish in the hold.'

'Then what?'

'We went for a pint.'

'And that's when he funded you to go and get Emma?'

'No, he didn't.'

'So where did you get all that money?' Nagle chirped.

'Scully gave me the money but not to go and get Emma. It was my share of the catch.'

'It was when you and Scully made the plan to go and get Emma,' Connelly said.

'What plan? There wasn't a plan. I didn't kidnap Emma. Ask Carol, ask anyone.'

'We have, Mr Farrell, you can be assured of that. Tell me, you and Emma, that night in Wexford, who was it suggested she come back to Dublin with you?'

I had to think about this one. 'It was me.'

'As my colleague's already said, it makes it a lot easier to kidnap someone when you know them.'

I stared at Connelly. 'You're wrong. I didn't kidnap her.'

'You didn't even have sex with her,' Nagle said, grinning. 'How come? Something wrong in that department?'

I couldn't look at him.

'You didn't have sex with her because Scully told you not to. He didn't want the purity of the cause polluted by your grubby little needs,' Connelly said.

'You're mad – you're both fucking crazy.'

Connelly was giving me the gaze again. 'Well,' he said, 'why don't you give us your version of it, from the start right up until this morning?'

I looked down at my feet. The desert boots were wrecked. How old were they? Three days? Jesus, typical. Brand new shoes, three days on my feet and they're fucked. There again, it didn't matter what shoes I had on or what state they were in. Nothing mattered. A continuous river of souls flowed across the surface of the globe, coming in as babies, going out old and wrinkled. What happened to any individual made no difference, no fucking difference at all.

What had Connelly asked for? A story. Sure, why not add to their list of errors?

But trying to find a point of departure wasn't easy. There would always be too many unexplained circumstances to fill in so I'd go back a little further and on and on until I was almost at the point of getting expelled from school. As far as Connelly and Nagle were concerned, I was just being quiet.

'I don't know where to start.'

'Well, you could start with Miss Balstead. When and where did you meet?'

So that was where I began. Sitting on Carol Malcolm's couch, the house full of booze and empty of parents. Once the story was under way, it rattled out. Connelly would interrupt sometimes – clarification, mostly. Nagle, much to my surprise, began writing as soon as I began talking. My few brief silences were filled with the sound of his pencil leaving its trail of grey across the pages. I finished with the police coming into the café that morning.

Connelly just stared at me as Nagle's pencil scribbled on. Then, as though to get a closer look at what he was dealing with, he leant forward, parking his chin on the palm of his hand. This forced him to breathe through his nostrils. Finally, Nagle's pencil fell silent.

'Right, I think I got most of that.'

Connelly, still not taking his eyes off me, leant back on his chair and yawned. There was a row of metal fillings along his back teeth. He looked at his watch. 'Right,' he said to Nagle. 'Better get that lot typed up.'

Nagle gathered up the papers, hitting them on the table to get them all tight and neat, gave one of his little coughs, then left.

When the door closed behind him, Connelly got out a packet of

Sweet Afton and offered one to me. I lit up and, when I inhaled, I thought I was going to fall on to the floor.

'You need something to eat,' he said, then directed his voice to the two at the end of the room. 'This interview's over, lads. Maybe one of you would like to organise a bit of something for our friend here.'

Footsteps came up from behind. 'Something to eat like, boss?' said a voice.

'Yeah, a bag o' chips.'

'Right you are,' one said, as they both left.

The smoke flowed from the end of my cigarette in two separate columns, twisted and tangled itself before drifting into nothing. My head was reeling but I took another drag and hauled it in deep. My lungs erupted in a kickback of relentless coughing. When it subsided, it left me trembling. I thought my face must looked flushed now and that my eyes were probably all watered up with the coughing. Fuck it! I didn't want him to think I was crying. This was all so mad. Nagle's fat face saying that stuff about me wishing I'd fucked her. I wanted to stomp on his fucking head. I covered my face with my hands.

I didn't know what Connelly was doing on the other side of the table. Whatever it was, he wasn't making a sound. I didn't want to take my hands away now because I knew if I did there would be tears. And he'd see them and I'd want to explain that they weren't because I was frightened but because this was all so fucking mad, we weren't doing any harm to anyone. He wouldn't see that. None of them would. They'd go on making up complicated reasons for the things we did, reasons taken from their world, their logic, not ours. Well, fuck 'em, fuck 'em all.

Now they were rolling down and my whole body was shaking too. Christ! Of all the times. I put my elbows on the table and rested my forehead in my hands. In that position, the tears fell freely. Evidence. I didn't care. It didn't matter.

He coughed. I opened my hands and saw that he was offering me his handkerchief. A neat white square bordered with parallel purple stripes. I took it and blew my nose. Then I didn't know what to do with it. I couldn't give it back to him all crumpled and snotty. I held it in my fist and stared at the table.

The door opened and footsteps came in, along with the smell of vinegar. I hated vinegar. Whoever it was didn't speak. The footsteps went back out, leaving Connelly and me alone with the smell.

It stayed like that for a long time. Then he took a chip. I looked at him.

'Shame to let them go cold,' he said.

That made me want to laugh. Instead, I took a long deep breath and said, 'This is all so fucking crazy.'

'Have a chip.'

I did. They were already cold. But he'd take one and I'd take one and we were down to the snots in the grease-stained paper when the door opened again. Two uniformed gardaí came in and stood by the door.

'These two will take you to a holding cell. When there's any news I'll let you know.' I got up and went with them. Halfway down the corridor I realised I still had his handkerchief.

The cell they brought me to had been painted pale green but now it was chipped and scratched and smeared with finger-width lines of shit. There was a bunk protruding from the wall, not much wider than a shelf. Also, I realised when I tried to lie on it, it sloped downwards. No rest for the wicked. I sat in a corner, folded my arms and closed my eyes. Dreams came on strong. They mimicked reality to perfection until something so absurd and horrible happened that it bounced me awake. After several of these, I thought it might be better to walk around.

There was an emotion floating about inside me but it couldn't find the place where emotions are supposed to go. Instead, it visited organs that couldn't house it. It drew its energy from the essence of this place, the denseness of the walls, the sound of my footfalls, the motionless air that sat in layers, each with its own odour. It was an emotion seeking refuge from a threat. A strange threat. Like the sea, it held no malice yet it had the power to obliterate. And the nature of the obliteration would be fast, direct and utter.

The events that had me here belonged to a different time. And being here changed those events. The woman I had brought food to in the hold had tried to kill Emma's father. Thinking of the reasons would be pointless. It would be all bound up in politics and have nothing to do with people. Who had Scully killed? And why? I bet his reason would at least make sense. 'Fucker deserved it,' he'd say, and laugh. He'd probably say the same when he was asked why he'd killed me.

I parked myself on the bunk. All I knew was that I knew fuck all. Least of all about people and I was one myself. Sitting there, I didn't even know what I was supposed to be thinking, yet I was thinking. I couldn't stop myself. The thoughts were random and agitated and multiplied like insects to the point where there were too many of them in too small a space.

Facts! I needed facts. Facts had weight. They held you on terra firma. I needed them now. What were the facts? Emma was gone. That was a fact. I was here. Another. There were bound to be loads. Next one? Maybe there wasn't a next one. There had to be. There had to be loads of them, enough to fill a newsroom. And all I had were two. Emma was gone and I was here. I repeated them again and again until they sounded like a train running down the track.

The metal latch slid back followed by the clink of keys. The door opened. Connelly stepped into the cell followed by two uniformed gardaí I'd not seen before. He stood there with his gaze directed on me, feeling his narrow chin with the tips of his fingers. 'Seeing as their daughter was found to be intact, Mr and Mrs Balstead are not going to bring charges,' he said. 'In fact, they are both very keen that this matter be dropped as quickly as possible.' He spoke slowly as though pondering the wisdom behind this. 'So there's no rape charge.' He was almost smiling now. 'And since Emma's departure from St Helen's seems to have been entirely voluntary, the charges of kidnap and abduction can also be dropped. So, Mr Farrell, it would appear that we have no further business with you.'

I just stared at him.

'You are free to go,' he said.

'How do you mean?'

'I mean you can go.'

'But what about Scully?'

'Kevin O Sullivan has been apprehended.'

'Scully's been picked up?'

'Yes. In Bray, about an hour ago. So you needn't concern yourself with him.'

'Stop!' I shouted. 'I do have to concern myself with him. He threatened to kill me if I told you he was aboard this morning. I did tell you so now he'll kill me. It's that simple and you either don't understand that or you just don't give a shit.'

Connelly had propped himself against the wall and folded his arms. 'What do you think? That Kevin O'Sullivan has spies working in here? He doesn't know what you told us.'

'He'll find out. When he hears the evidence against him he'll find out.'

Connelly was shaking his head, smiling. 'If we have him, how can he get to you?'

'What, you're going to keep him locked up for the rest of his life?'

'These two men will escort you to where you can pick up your belongings.'

'You aren't listening, are you? When Scully gets out, he is going to kill me.'

The stare.

'You actually don't care, do you?'

'I work for the Special Branch, internal security. When it came to light that Emma Balstead had disappeared with a member of the crew that had hidden Claire Traynor, alarm bells rang in this building – and in a few others, I dare say. But it turns out that her flight with you was nothing more than a teenage fling, futile at that.' He smiled. 'It wasn't even consummated. Now I have work to do.'

One of the gardaí walked up to me. I felt a hand on my arm. 'Come along now.'

I shrugged him away. Connelly was off the wall and heading towards the door when he stopped. 'By the way,' he said, 'be somewhere we can find you.'

'The morgue.'

He smiled and walked out into the corridor.

The gardaí brought me into the corridor and headed me in the opposite direction to Connelly. I wanted to stop, turn around and tell him he was a bastard, a two-faced lying bastard. I wanted to stand over him and tell him it wasn't a futile teenage fling, and that when Scully did kill me I'd come back and haunt him fucking witless. He'd read everything wrong from the start. He'd never get it right because his mind was in the trough he'd dug for himself years ago. Same as it was for them all, the teachers, my parents, every bastard adult I knew: that was how they got old.

I was taken to the entrance hall. It was crowded. Men in uniforms merged with others who, I presumed, were the criminals. A large clock faced the tall double doors. It was ten past five. Rush hour and rain outside. Hard to believe that in just a few minutes I would be out there in it. Where could I go? Howth was out of the question. It didn't matter. I'd find somewhere. All I needed was food and sleep, and then I'd be able to think. Head to Paris on my own. Contact Emma from there.

One of the policemen escorting me tapped on a window beneath the clock. The man sitting behind it dropped his newspaper and slid the window open.

'Have you anything here for Farrell, Seán Farrell?'

'What's the case number?'

'It never got issued. Phone up Connelly if you have any questions.'

'No, thanks,' the man said, and walked off to some racks at the back of his booth. He plucked from it a brown envelope that had my name written across the flap. He brought it to the counter and handed it to me. Inside I found everything I had given them. I distributed the bits throughout my pockets. The roll of notes I shoved into the front one where I could feel it.

'Is everything there?' one asked.

I nodded.

'In that case, sign here,' the man behind the window said.

I was just about to do so when I noticed two figures by the door. At first I thought I was imagining it. I looked again. It was Walsh and standing beside him was O'Hare.

'Would you please sign here?' said the man behind the glass.

I signed and straightened. They were watching me.

'Goodbye now, and keep your nose clean,' one of the policemen said, and both walked away.

O'Hare stepped into the space they had just vacated. 'I must say, you're accelerating through the criminal ranks at rare speed, my boy!'

Walsh was smiling.

'All charges against me have been dropped,' I said to O'Hare.

'Oh, have they? Have they indeed?' He produced a folded piece of paper from inside his tunic. 'This is a warrant for your arrest, Mr Farrell. You'll come with us.'

They put on the siren and the cars in front of us peeled away.

They talked about Gaelic football. O'Hare was a Kerry supporter. Walsh backed Dublin. Walsh had a detailed knowledge of the players, their history and their form. He used it to try to convince O'Hare that his hopes of victory were seriously misplaced. But O'Hare was not daunted. He referred to the Dublin team as a bunch of upstarts and gurriers who wouldn't know a football if it hit them in the face, which, on the day, it probably would. They made no comment on the chaos they were creating in front and behind them. And when we were clear of the city traffic, we sped along the coast road where the peninsula of Howth could be seen resting in the distance.

I wondered where Scully might be. Probably, like me, sitting in the back of a police car, except he'd be on his way to the place I was being taken from. And Emma? On her way to the airport? Or would they bring her back to St Helen's? Hardly.

Everything was becoming distant. The voices in the front, the events of this morning, even the interview with Connelly and Nagle, all were fading. I knew only that I was tired. And those two jabbering in the front were failing to instil in me any sense of fear. Compared with the threats of this morning, they seemed comical.

We entered Howth Police Station through a side door. The few policemen there looked up when we arrived. Smiles and nods were directed at Walsh and O'Hare. I was told to stand in front of a desk. Walsh disappeared through a door as O'Hare walked around the desk and took a seat. He picked up some papers that were in front of him and made like he was about to read the news. 'Right, bucko, you're under arrest for the theft of the trawler the *Jasper*,' he suddenly said. 'Depriving a man of his livelihood is a most serious offence.'

I didn't say anything.

'Take him to Room Two,' O'Hare said, directing his voice to someone behind me. When I turned, I saw that he was addressing two policemen. They were both broad-shouldered, with thick necks and hair that ran in a carpet of bristles right up to the rim of their tight caps. They were almost the same build as Nagle. Maybe there was a mould in the basement of Dublin Castle where they churned out this stumpy model.

The room I was taken to was cleaner than any I'd seen so far. The paint was fresh, and the floor, although concrete, was spotless. There was no furniture. There were no windows either.

'We save this for our VIPs,' one of the stumpies said, with a grin.

'I'm a VIP now, am I?'

'You? You're nothing.'

I looked from him to his colleague. Surely if twins joined the force they'd be placed at opposite ends of the country.

'Sergeant O'Hare will be with you shortly,' the other said, as they left.

They even sounded alike.

I walked back and forth, then sat in a corner. There was absolutely fuck all to focus on.

Thoughts ran through me like ants through grass, determined and agitated. I had a feeling they might build up into something big, multiply into something grotesque and unmanageable. But they didn't: they remained singular, frantic searchers, disorganised and charmless.

From outside came the sound of keys, then the smooth metallic crunch as a bolt slid back. The door opened and there, smiling, arms folded across a row of silver buttons, stood Walsh.'How are we feeling now, Mr Farrell?' His smile broadened. The ants all went to ground.

'Fine thanks, Garda Walsh. By the way, I was wondering, when do you think they might issue you with your first bicycle?' In the silence that followed, I added, 'Of course, you'd have to be able to steer and pedal at the same time. Might be a bit of a problem, that.'

'I wouldn't be so smart if I were you, Farrell.'

'What are you going to do? Lock me up?'

'You haven't a clue what you're dealing with here.'

'I don't give a shite.'

'You will, Farreller, you will.'

The door clanged shut.

When the sound faded, I was alone again. The ants peered from behind the blades and the debris. 'He's gone,' I told them. 'But he was here.'

Somehow his visit had given me confidence. There had been an agitated excitement about him that he had tried hard to conceal. He had me exactly where he wanted me, yet he'd had to come in here and see it for himself. He was like a child staring at a parcel with his name on it under the Christmas tree. Was he afraid he might not have me for long?

I don't know why I felt this, but I did. I tried to dredge up some doubts to curb this optimism but nothing came.

It stood to reason. All the big charges had been dealt with in Dublin Castle. What was left over was the social mess. There was no doubt that Sheehan would be mad at me. He'd certainly have a go the next time we met but he wasn't going to drag me to the law. If he did, his crew and everyone else on the pier would think no better of him than they presently did of me.

What I had done was break the rules on both sides. For the fishermen, I was the one who'd had the West Pier swarming with police. Boats would have been searched. Christ knew what had been unearthed. That would not be forgiven. From the police's point of view I was a disruption, a new breed, as O'Hare had said when we'd first met. And what they didn't know they didn't like. But none of this would put me behind bars. So, if Sheehan didn't press charges, what did it leave? Nothing but a pile of misdemeanours that wouldn't amount to a decent fine. And if that turned out to be the case, I had the money to pay.

I lay down on the floor. The ceiling, which was white, had stains buried under the paintwork. Some were in the process of reappearing. So far, they were only faint brown outlines but you got the feeling they had the potential to blossom. But there was nothing organic about them. They were not growing, living things. The only way they'd get stronger was when the paint faded, which, in here, with the lack of natural light, might be some time.

I began to work out how many days there would be in my life if I lived to eighty-four. The problem was the leap years. I tried to remember when the last one was but I couldn't. So I guessed it. Every four years was three hundred and sixty-five plus one by four. The answer to that then had to be multiplied by how many sets of four there were in eighty-four. Easy: twenty-one. Twenty-one multiplied by four times three hundred and sixty-five, plus one was . . . was . . . The massive edifice of numbers was teetering. I just had to hold it steady, run around the side doing a little addition here, a little subtraction there, a few amendments. But it got top-heavy, wobbled and crashed. The entire floor was littered with numbers.

It didn't matter. I had other fish to fry. Let one equal red. Red and red is two. Two and two is yellow. Soon the blackboard was a patchwork of numbers and colours that I had to concentrate hard on so as not to lose their meaning. If this structure tumbled, the whole floor would be a rainbow of digits.

I got to my feet. Was I going mad? Was I mad already? Whatever the case, I wanted out of there now.

A long time later came the sound of keys. The door swung open and the twins walked in. I stood. They were coming at me with what seemed like purpose. Behind them, the doorway darkened with the figure of O'Hare. He stepped into the room and behind him was Walsh.

The twins took up a position on either side of me. O'Hare stood in front of me. Walsh lurked behind him.

'So,' O'Hare said, 'the Castle, in their infinite wisdom, have decided not to pursue charges against you. The girl's parents aren't going to charge you. Even John Sheehan has decided not to. Must be your lucky day.' He looked at the twins. 'What do you think, men? Should we drop all charges too?'

'What charges?' I asked.

His face was pure contempt. When he spoke, it was almost a whisper. 'The charge that you are a piece of living scum, an arrogant know-it-all, ignorant in the ways of how things work.' He straightened. 'And it's high time you were taught a lesson.' With that, he turned and walked to the door. There he stopped. 'You're not the first young lad to be so schooled.'

He was gone. Walsh walked towards me, his eyes more alive now than I'd ever seen them. A coldness spread through me. I couldn't believe that this thin-faced weed, with the aid of a pair of stocky twins, was about to beat me up.

'Walsh, you're a pathetic fuck,' I said.

An elbow came from the twin on my left. It buried itself in my guts and spread a deep, even pain across my abdomen. When I opened my eyes, Walsh was standing in front of me, fists clenched and sneering.

'There's just one thing I want to say to you.' I got the words out as his fist hit my chin. My teeth crashed together and my mouth filled with sweet liquid. When I spoke again it was through a gurgle. 'You're a fucking coward.'

I was glad later that I'd got it in because after the next blow I couldn't have spoken if I'd wanted to. The twins clamped me between them and Walsh used my face as a punchbag. When he stopped, they released me and I slid to my knees. Walsh planted a boot in my stomach and then in my crotch. I fell to the floor, unable to breathe. Pain, in all its different densities, ran around inside me looking for an exit. There was silence in the room. Then, without warning, came a blow to my forehead. It sent my head bouncing off the wall behind. Another went into my back and another into my knee. That one flared a pain so hot and white it obliterated all others. After that, it was rain soaking into something already saturated.

Some time later, I became aware of myself. I felt swollen, formless. Everywhere inside me was pain. Everything from the dullest sludge to the sharpest summits. I tried to grade it, place it, think about its causes. A splintered bone, a ruptured organ. My tongue found a tooth hanging by a thread. Thinking of this, I laughed. Now I knew what that expression meant. The laugh couldn't go beyond a desire to laugh. All voluntary bodily functions were out of the question. When I drew breath, sharp pains sprang about my insides. I tried to sit up against the wall. I couldn't move. I tried to imagine what I must look like. The back of my head felt as if it was still bleeding but that was as far as any external assessment could go.

I felt myself fall. Hot air rushing past me. I clutched my legs, burying my chin in my knees, ready for the ground to race up and hit me. Instead I saw boots. Black, round-tipped and shining, coming at me. I opened my eyes. Nothing. Just silence and darkness.

I heard the air leaving my body, listened to it run along the cold, clean floor. It encountered no debris, no dust. They did not come into this room to relax after their strolls through the housing estates, crunching broken glass and shattered fragments of brick underfoot. It was a room that seldom saw a smile save one born of malice. It was a room where revenge was inflicted and fear implanted. It was a room for branding the subconscious. The subconscious hates that: it can't stack up experiences as its mate consciousness can. Consciousness has logic and gravity and everything that keeps us sane. The subconscious has nothing. Things there – if they remain things – float, stretch, drift away, becoming something other than they were. Characteristics don't count for fuck here. They blend and bend sideways. Moist mud becomes a horizon and over it pops a tomato soon to be eaten by something that floated in here on a wave of guilt. The tattered leather of a stiletto heel, laughter at dawn on a gravel path. The stagger, the sway, the long stray into the damp grass. From the treetops comes thunder and the crows close rank.

I woke aware of nothing but pain. Everything in me had lost patience. No more analysis of what pain was where or why. All the strands had wound together and welded into a tight bar.

From outside came footsteps. I concentrated. These were real. They stopped at the door. I heard the key sliding into the lock and the bolt being slid back. I squeezed into the wall until my back was against it. I pushed and pushed. I couldn't go any further but my legs wouldn't stop. I was a child in a tantrum.

Light came in a long thin line. It broadened into a column. Into it stepped a form, square shoulders, a cap. I covered my head. Sounds came from me that I wished I could stop. The boots slowed as they neared me. Those feet were being used for transport only. I knew this but I couldn't stop my legs and I couldn't stop the whimpering.

The feet came to a halt. I heard the material of a uniform stretch as its wearer crouched. Then a voice. 'Dear God!' it said.

The words released me into a hot and alien place. My mind wanted to run in many different directions at once. Each one pulled against its opposite so I didn't move. I wanted his sympathy. I was angry with myself for this. He was the source of my terror and the source of its relief. I had to hug the beast that had done this to me before they would let me go. I couldn't do it. And if I didn't they would leave me here to congeal on their concrete floor.

He walked back into the column of light and closed it off behind him.

Later, the door opened again. This time there were two figures. By now I had talked a calmness into place. I had wall-to-wall carpeting over a floor thick with snakes. The two came close. I felt my wrist being taken with calm force. A voice ran alongside the movement. 'I'm Dr Alan Kelly. There's nothing to be frightened of.'

I wanted to crawl into his tone, make a pillow out of it and cry. His hand left my wrist and felt about my neck. 'Can you sit up?' he asked. I didn't move. I didn't know why. It was complicated.

I felt his hands feeling me. One stopped under my ribcage. He pressed the tips of his fingers into the softness there, then tapped them with his other hand. Then he felt my knee. Instantly, searing pain bleached out all other sensations. The mechanics for screaming rushed into place but something was faulty. What came out did so through my eyes.

'We've got to get him into Jervis Street.'

'Not on my shift we're not.'

The hands moved around my waist and up my back. I braced myself for another squall.

'We have internal haemorrhaging here. It's impossible to assess how much or how bad, but I reckon you may have a lot more explaining to do if you don't get him into hospital.'

There was a silence. 'Jesus Christ, then, go on.' This was followed by a pinprick just above my buttock and suddenly all pain was drifting away. I was up there with the tomato and the big guilty thing that wasn't guilt at all, just some trade-wind air that got blown off course bringing tropical scents to a coastline seeking sunshine.

Chapter 24

Bristol, 2008

Roland sat at the kitchen table, beer in hand, enjoying every minute of the interrogation he was giving me about Emma. At least it was keeping his mind off his own troubles. At ten to seven, I told him enough was enough, it was time to take me to my appointment.

'I said I would but now that I know what you're up to, I wonder if I should be a party to this.' He was smiling.

'Fuck off, Roland.'

'Well, I'm just saying I don't want to be used by the prosecution during the divorce proceedings.'

'The only divorce proceedings you're going to are your own.'

Suddenly he looked glum. 'Come on,' I said. I didn't want him dropping into a slump now of all times. 'It's not going to come to that.'

'I don't know, Seán. I've never seen her this upset.'

'Yeah, well, start threatening the bricks and mortar and you're asking for trouble.'

'I had to do something.'

'I understand that and I'm sure in time Allison will too. Now, come on, I really don't want to be late.'

We drove down Gloucester Road, each lost in our own world of fear, dread and expectation. I was off to meet a woman I hadn't seen for more than thirty years. And the sick, sad, worrying part of it was that I was hoping she could deliver me from the situation I was in now. And why Emma? I'd had plenty of other girlfriends between her and my marriage, most of whom I knew much more thoroughly than I had ever known her. Was it because she had, in effect, been delivered up to me wrapped in the little parcel of coincidence? Maybe. And if that was true, I was again taking the path of least resistance. But wait a minute! I was jumping the gun here. Nothing had happened, nothing was going to happen. I was only going to meet an old friend. Wasn't I?

'How long do you think it'll take her to realise I just had to do it?' Roland said.

'Who?'

'Allison!'

'Oh, yeah, right, sorry. I don't know. Talk to her, keep talking to her.'

'You're in another world completely.'

The traffic was crawling. It was two minutes to seven and we were nowhere near the Wills Building.

'Yeah, I'm a little distracted, that's all.'

'How bad are things between you and Lynn right now?'

'Roland, I don't want to talk about that, OK?'

'Jesus! That's bad.'

'No, what's bad is this traffic. I told you, I don't want to be late.'

To my amazement, Roland pulled out on to the wrong side of the road and raced down the length of it, past a set of roadworks that was holding everything up.

We arrived in front of the Wills Building at just seconds after seven. I looked as we drove by it but I couldn't see Emma. However, lots of people on the pavement were blocking my view.

Thanking Roland for his fine, creative driving, I leapt from the car as soon as we were going slowly enough and walked back up to the tall tower. She was not there. So, with one knee pointing outwards, I leaned against the light brown stonework, folded my arms and stared at the ground.

The minutes passed as slowly as they must for someone being stretched on the rack. Finally, I decided I'd wait no longer than ten minutes. By then, if she hadn't shown, I was leaving. Write it all down to one very bad idea.

At twenty seconds to ten past seven I looked up and there, maybe three feet in front of me, stood Emma Balstead. Her hair was shorter, darker, not curly now. Her face was thinner; there were lines at the corners of her eyes, two deep ones framing her smile. But it was her. She was standing in front of me, complete and real.

'Hi!' she said. Her eyes were so blue – how could I have forgotten? And the way she just stood there – it was her presence, solid and happy.

'Hello,' I said, and walked to her, then didn't know if I should hug or kiss her. I did nothing. 'I can't believe this,' I said. 'I really can't.' She was smiling. 'Should we get a coffee?' I asked.

'Yeah,' she said. 'Or let's walk first. Unless you'd like one?'

'No, walking's fine.'

In an awkward gesture, she took my elbow and leant forward to plant a kiss on the side of my face. 'I recognised you straight away. You haven't changed,' she said.

'Neither have you. You look great.'

She smiled and shook her head. 'And you're still full of it.'

'What are you talking about? You do.'

We started walking and suddenly I could think of nothing to say.

My mind flew to the shelves where subjects were kept but they were bare. Then I started to speak at the same time as she did and we both stopped. She laughed, and I drew a deep breath. 'Please, you go.'

'What are we like?' she said.

'I don't know. Look, this isn't easy for me. I'm really nervous.'

When she looked at me I realised I was taller than her. Yet I recalled feeling intimidated years ago because we were the same height. Had I grown? Had she shrunk?

'Why?' Emma asked.

'I don't know. I really don't.'

She smiled again and her eyes lit up. 'Well, I do. But let's not worry, let's just relax. We're two people walking down a road.'

I smiled. 'Tell me about you,' I said.

'Every detail since we last met?'

'I mean the filming thing, that sounds amazing.'

'What's amazing is you – a marriage-guidance counsellor.'

'I don't know why you're so surprised.'

'You, Seán Farrell, the man who was stomping about telling the world what was wrong with it. I thought you'd turn up screaming obscenities in a punk band, not in Bristol guiding couples through the rough.'

'Yeah, I suppose from the outside it must seem like a bit of a leap, but things happen . . .'

'They certainly do!' she said and, I don't know why but we both laughed.

We crossed the road and strolled down Park Street. The sun was lighting the buildings above us. The shops had closed but most of the bars had put tables on the pavement, which were full of people drinking and smoking.

'You make movies, Kate said.'

'Movies? No. I've just spent the day doing some last-minute editing on a piece about drugs for Channel Four.'

'A documentary?'

'Yeah.'

'And that's what you do?'

'Yeah, why?'

'I think that's great.'

'Well, you might not if you'd seen the shit I had to wade through today. Anyway, I don't want to talk about it now.'

'Fine, it won't be mentioned again.'

She took my arm again. 'So, tell me,' she said, 'how long have we got?'

'You mean this evening?'

'Yeah. You're married, kids and things, or doesn't your wife know you're out canoodling with an ex?'

'Canoodling? Is that what we're doing? How did you know I was married?'

'My daughter's been to your house, remember?'

'And?'

'One sweep around your hallway and she could tell you things about your life that even you don't know.'

'She's a smart girl.'

'She is, and what she's doing with that prat I'll never know. But,' she dropped her hand, 'I guess you're not allowed to talk about any of that, are you?'

'No.'

'So, your wife?'

'My wife is at a watercolour workshop. She doesn't know I'm meeting you.'

'Ah, secrets, not good, and in a marriage-guidance counsellor! You ought to be ashamed.'

'I'm doing nothing wrong.'

'Why didn't you tell her, then?'

'Because she's off canoodling with a paintbrush in the Brecon Beacons.'

'And the kids?'

'Gone too. Anyway, why all the questions?'

'Just curious. When Kate told me, you could have knocked me down with a feather. You, a marriage-guidance counsellor, it's just too funny, yet you're here and,' she looked at me, 'as far as I can tell, you're still the same, more or less.'

We were nearing Woodes. I looked at the chair I'd been sitting in when Kate first told me that Emma Balstead was her mother. A man with dyed black hair and a black T-shirt was sitting in it now. The Gothic script on his T-shirt read, 'Jesus sucks'.

'Well, can you imagine how I felt when Kate told me about you?' I said.

'And what did you think? I mean, had you thought about me?'

'Of course! In fact, just a few weeks ago, I came across those photographs – you know, the ones you took in Dublin. I was clearing out the basement – it was weird, there I was, surrounded by debris, and suddenly I was standing with you, watching that policeman and you telling me he was going to pick his nose and he did! Then you started snapping.'

Emma was silent. Then she said, 'It was such a very long time ago.'

We were almost at the bottom of the hill now. Its natural sweep would bring us right into the centre of town.

'Where would you like to go? Have you eaten?' I asked.

'No, but I'm fine for the moment. You?'

'I had a late lunch.'

'Let's keep walking.'

We crossed the road in front of the Marriott Hotel and continued down towards the waterfront.

'How's Manchester?'

'It's Mum that's keeping me there now.'

'She's still alive?'

'Yes!'

'Sorry, I didn't mean that in any . . .'

'No, you're right. She ought to have died decades ago. At the moment she's busy spending my inheritance on a fancy rest home.'

'So you two are still on good terms, then?'

Emma laughed. 'It just felt wrong to leave her alone after Dad died. Although I don't know why. She's perfectly capable. It's the Catholic guilt thing, I guess. It doesn't matter how much you despise them, they get to you.'

'Who? Catholics or mothers?

'Mothers and Catholics, and when they're rolled into one the mixture's lethal.'

'Well, mothers and daughters are seldom simple.'

'Is that a counsellor I hear talking?'

I smiled. 'Maybe. Jesus, not only have I become a counsellor, I've become a counselling bore.'

'If you have, I'll let you know.'

'Kind of you.'

We rounded the corner, crossed the road and walked into Queen Square. To the left of the path that ran diagonally through it, a hundred people, maybe more, sat in front of an orange and cream Volkswagen camper van. A woman in medieval costume was making a speech from a hole in the roof. In front of her, in similar dress, stood her suitor. She had just started the speech, 'Romeo, Romeo, wherefore art thou, Romeo?'

We slowed to listen to the words as they floated on the wind. 'Shakespeare in the park!' Emma said. 'That's so romantic.'

'You think?'

'Yes, of course. Don't you?'

'Brave, I'd say.'

We stopped at a bench and sat, Emma leaning forwards. She

turned to me. 'It's just so wonderful that you can take a bus and use it to stage a play written four hundred years before buses were even invented.'

'If you like, we can go closer.'

'No, it's been cordoned off. I'd hate to disturb them.'

Behind us, young men in baggy shorts spun frisbees and couples lay about the grass in absent-minded embraces.

'I wonder why they didn't do *A Midsummer's Night's Dream*,' I mused.

'Why?'

'Because it's midsummer night, the shortest night of the year.'

'Well, ain't that just great? We get to spent one night together in thirty years and it turns out to be the shortest one there is.'

It was difficult to make out her expression. The sun behind her was making a halo of her hair and I felt an almost overpowering urge to touch her face. She turned back to the actors.

After a few moments, she stood. 'Come on – otherwise I'll go all gooey. *Romeo and Juliet* does that to me.'

'I'd love to see you all gooey.'

'Come on.'

We walked out of the square and found ourselves on the bridge that overlooked Roland's yard. We stopped and, mimicking me, Emma rested both elbows on the rail, her chin on her knuckles, and stared downriver. 'Do you like Bristol?' she asked.

'Sometimes.'

'What does that mean?'

'Oh, you know, I'm settled here, the kids and schools and stuff. But do I like it? I don't know. I don't hate it. It's somewhere and as long as you're alive, you have to be somewhere.'

'That sounds a bit bleak. Do you ever have fun? Do you ever get excited by things?'

'At my age that might be highly inadvisable.'

'No, seriously, every life has to have a little something in it, otherwise you just crack like a twig.'

If that was so, then I was ripe for the cracking. I pictured Lynn's face, tired and angry. The children, vague and disinterested. Suddenly I was overcome with sadness. I looked at Emma's profile. Her mouth was slightly open, and I traced the curve of her upper lip as it rounded into the straight line of her teeth. Life was a combination of the thousands of insignificant choices you make all the time.

'Are you all right, Seán?'

'Maybe we should eat.'

'If you like.'

A man in a sharp suit and tight haircut greeted us at the door and told us we were in luck: a table on the terrace had just come available. With that, he led us to a landing-stage that overhung the river. He waited until we were seated in front of a single orchid, then produced two menus, bowed almost imperceptibly and was gone.

The terrace had only room for one line of tables so my fellow diners were hidden behind Emma's shoulders. This, to me, was perfect.

The river shimmered with the reflected light of the sinking sun. And, on the other bank, bathed in strong colours and deep shadows, was Roland's yard. Nothing in it moved.

'This is lovely. Dinner's on me by the way,' Emma said.

'Why?'

'Well, last time you paid.'

'That place in Wicklow before the cops arrived?'

'Well, yeah, there too, but I was thinking more of the hotel before the walk.'

'God, I remember. It was a lifetime ago. Do you remember all that?'

'Yes, I do.'

'I'm glad.'

'Maybe you wouldn't be if you knew why.'

I looked at her. She gave me a quick, cold smile, then put her bag on the table. From it she took a pair of glasses and put them on. 'These are new, for reading.'

'They make you look very elegant, very intellectual.'

'Bollocks!'

'They do!'

A waitress appeared and asked us what we'd like to drink. Emma asked for a gin and tonic. I ordered tonic.

'You're not driving?' she said.

'I haven't touched a drink for fourteen years.'

'You're joking?'

'No.'

'Fourteen years! I don't think I could go fourteen days.'

'I didn't have a lot of choice, really.'

'I can't imagine it. Life without wine?'

'Well, amazingly, such a thing exists, and not only that but it's highly liveable.'

'Well, obviously, but . . . you don't mind if I do?'

'Of course not. You know, the biggest pain in the arse about not drinking is how drinkers treat you.'

'How do you mean?'

'Well, sometimes people think you're holding them up to a moral yardstick. It's odd how aggressive they get. I haven't clarified my thoughts on the matter. When I do, I'll bore you stupid with them.'

'Seán, you couldn't bore me if you tried.'

'It's so wonderful to be out with someone who doesn't know me.'

'What are you talking about? I do know you.'

'Yes, I suppose you do.'

'You were such a wild thing, did you know that?'

'All I remember is feeling confused and scared, not that I would have let on at the time.'

'Being young is difficult.'

'I don't think we made it any easier on ourselves.'

She stopped and smiled. 'No, we didn't.'

The waitress came with two identical drinks clinking on a tray. She placed one before each of us and asked if we were ready to order. Emma chose the sea bass. I looked at the menu and ordered the first thing I saw: a steak.

She sipped in silence for a moment, then looked out over the river. 'It's a beautiful evening,' she said.

'Well, the gods have made us wait thirty years for this so the least they can do is put on a nice evening.'

'It was you who made us wait thirty years.' Her expression gave away nothing. 'Why did you never write?' she asked. There was a trace of annoyance in her tone.

'Why did I never write?'

'Some knight in shining armour you turned out to be. You rescue a damsel in distress only to leave her entombed in another dungeon across the sea.' She picked up her glass, stared into it, then at me again. 'You know, just now, before we met, I didn't want to stand on the street waiting, so I found a place for a coffee where I could see the Wills Building. When you came along, I stayed where I was and just watched you. Am I scaring you?'

I shook my head.

'You got out of a car and stood by the wall and I just sat there, thinking, There's the bastard who broke my heart.'

'Emma, that was—'

'I was amazed, I really was, at the sort of emotions the sight of you brought up.'

'OK, maybe I'm a little scared.'

'You don't have to be. I'm harmless.'

'Emma Balstead, you are many things but harmless is not one of them.'

Her expression now was a mixture of sarcasm and anger.

'I'm sorry I didn't write. I wanted to.'

'I just didn't inspire you enough to put down your pint and pick up a pen? I'm sorry,' she said, 'I suppose I'm being very impolite bringing that up.'

'You're being honest and direct. I should be honoured.'

'But you're not.'

'I'm ashamed, I suppose. Can I be held responsible for my actions way back then?'

'That's the excuse war criminals use.'

'God, you're right. But listen, and this isn't an excuse – for the first couple of weeks after you left I was in hospital.'

'Hospital?'

'Yeah. They beat me up.'

'Who beat you up?'

'The police. After they took you off, they brought me to Dublin Castle and during the interview I told them about Scully.'

'Christ! Scully! Now there's a name.'

'He's dead.'

'Did someone kill him?'

'No, cancer.'

'Why did you tell them about him? I mean, didn't he threaten to kill us if we said a word?'

'Yeah.'

'So why, then?'

'They tricked me.'

'What happened?'

'Well, the Castle dropped all charges and I thought I was free but then these two gardaí from Howth turned up and took me back to the station there and basically decided it was time I was taught a lesson.' I took another sip. Something in the intensity of Emma's stare was unsettling. 'So next day I was in hospital, all bandaged up and terrified that at any second Scully'd walk in and cut my throat with a scalpel he'd picked up from a theatre on the way.'

She smiled.

'I was. I couldn't sleep. I turned into a complete basket case. In the end they had to force-feed me tranquillisers and sleepers.'

'But he never showed up?'

'No. Plasma and Joey did, though.'

'Oh, Christ! Two more lunatics!'

'Yeah, but in a very different league. Plasma lectures at the University of Rhode Island now.'

'Plasma?' Her eyes widened. 'Lanky, long-haired madman?'

'That's the chap.'

'Incredible. What about Joey?'

'Dead.'

'Jesus! 'she said. 'All these people.'

Two waitresses arrived and spread dishes before us in a soundless display of poise, and the air was suddenly rich with the smell of garlic.

'Thank you.' Emma said. 'Could I order a . . .' She turned to me. 'This is difficult. Do I get a glass or a bottle?'

I held my hands up.

She turned back to the waitress, 'A bottle of house white. What about you, Seán?'

It was the way she had used my name: for a moment I was back on the clifftop at Howth. I smiled. 'A glass of water.''

The waitress nodded and stepped away.

Emma took a mouthful of fish. 'Hm, this is good, very good. Like to try some?'

'No, thanks.' I had just put a piece of steak in my mouth and flavours were racing into all four corners.

'So,' she said, waving her fork like an impatient conductor, 'Joey and Plasma came to see you.'

'Yeah, with a plan to go to Amsterdam. I didn't care where it was as long as it was somewhere Scully wouldn't be.'

'Why, where was he?'

'Well, that was the thing. He'd been arrested and charged but no one told me.'

'What did they get him on?'

'I don't know . . . perverting the course of justice, something like that. He got two years.'

'So, Scully goes off to jail and you go off to Amsterdam?'

'Yeah, well, I wasn't going to visit him in his cell, was I?'

'Poor man.'

'Emma, he tried to kill us.'

'He did not!'

'Well, he would have.'

'Yeah, but he didn't.'

The waitress returned, placed an ice bucket to one side of the table, lifted a bottle from it and poured Emma a glass of wine. When Emma nodded to her, she left, telling us to enjoy the meal.

'So, what did you do in Amsterdam?'

'Drugs.'

'Surprise, surprise.'

'It was Plasma, he managed to make a connection in the Chinese district. We were buying synthetic opium for ten guilders a bag, taking a hit each, then dividing the rest into ten parts and selling each of them for ten guilders. We were making a fortune.'

'As drug-dealers.'

'It was a living.'

'And to think I was in my room hoping for a letter.'

'Well, maybe you were better off. We all got strung out.'

'Is that how Joey died?'

'Yeah. One morning we found him in the chair where he'd jacked up the night before, stiff. Plasma went back with the body.'

'You stayed?'

'I couldn't go back.'

'What did you do?'

'Well, not having Plasma's acumen or charm, our little drugs business died and I found myself on the streets of Amsterdam, a full-blown smack addict.'

Emma laid down her fork, rested her chin in her hand and stared out at the river. After what seemed like a long time, she turned back. 'They brutalised us, didn't they?'

'You mean . . .'

'I mean all of them the police, the schools, the whole fucking shitbag.'

'They say what doesn't kill you makes you stronger.'

She looked out at the river again. The light, reflecting upwards, gave her skin a rich brownish texture. It illuminated her eyes and etched a line around her lips. She looked, at that moment, like a goddess.

'What happened when you got back?' I asked.

She smiled. 'It was like something out of a fairy story, but a grisly one. The first thing they did was lock me in my room. Then they got me into some awful convent. Mum had her driver take me there every morning and bring me back in the evening. She employed a whole series of nannies to watch me while I was at home. I think that's when I started to know how much of a bitch she really was.'

'How long did that go on for?'

'Till A levels. After that, I escaped, hitched to London, then Marrakech. I sent her a postcard from there, then nothing till after Kate was born.'

'Maybe you're right, maybe they did brutalise us. But sometimes things like that happen. You know, you and I meeting, running away.

It was like the movement of a rudder, changing the direction of both our lives.'

Emma had stopped eating. She picked up her glass and drank. 'I'm not sure our lives would have worked out much different if I'd said no when you asked me to come away.'

'Maybe. Anyway, I'm glad you didn't say no.'

'Are you?'

'If you had, we wouldn't be sitting here now.'

'You can be very sweet. So, just tell me one thing: how does a junkie on the streets of Amsterdam end up as a marriage-guidance counsellor in Bristol? Did you ever go back to Ireland?'

'Of course, loads of times. I even lived there briefly. But, to be honest, the place unnerves me.'

'And why Bristol and marriage guidance?'

'Well, I got out of Amsterdam by getting a job as a deckhand on a yacht. I bummed around on boats for a while but, to be honest, most of the seventies just disappeared on me. Then it was the early eighties and I found myself in London. I was clean when I got there but within a month I was using again. Then I met this drugs worker, Danny. We did a lot of counselling and I got clean. A year later, I was still clean and I started working with him. Lots of school stuff, you know, talks and things, and then I was working with other addicts. Danny said I was good at it, so I did some courses, got a diploma in counselling, then came to Bristol to set up the drugs project here. Eventually I realised I'd been ten years off dope and wanted to leave it out of my life altogether so I changed to couples counselling.'

'And why did you give up drink?'

'Because it's just another drug, and me and drugs don't mix.'

'Then you met your wife, had the kids and lived happily ever after.'

'If only life was like that.'

She leant forward. 'What is it like?'

With that one, almost whispered question, the walls with which I separated myself from the reality of my life crumbled. I took a deep breath. 'It's hard,' I said, 'harder than I want to admit.'

'Seán Farrell, you've come through slaughter to be where you are now. You're a great man.'

This was murdering me. She'd hit some emotional G spot and was now massaging it. I could feel tears rising but I couldn't let them show.

'Thanks.' I said and looked away.

Kittigani sat sleek and slender directly across the river from us, the sinking sun catching her varnished mast. Suddenly I was aware of something inside me changing, a gear slipping. I felt calmer. When I looked back at Emma, her eyes were fixed on me. It was hard to read her thoughts.

'It's so lovely to be sitting here with you,' I said.

'Same.'

That made me smile. 'What about you? Men, marriage, all that?'

'Men! I don't have a lot of luck when it comes to men. But at the moment my life's free of them, pets and children, and it feels great.'

'I'm glad to hear it. But you did marry – I mean, Kate's father.'

'Yes, we married but we were really just a string of one-night stands.'

'There must have been at least one significant . . .'

'Significant! They're all bloody significant at the time. But, yes, there was one. It lasted eight years. Looking back on it, they were probably the worst eight years of my life – I spent the whole time trying to facilitate what I thought was his genius.'

'He was an artist?'

'A writer – you may have even heard of him.'

I waited for the name but it didn't come. 'What happened?'

'Well, we always had difficulties when it came to sex. I thought he just wasn't that interested until one day I was working on his laptop and I came across videos.'

'What kind of videos?

'Standard sick shit.'

'What was he into?'

'Well, whatever it was, I wasn't doing it for him.' She laughed.

'Sounds intriguing.'

'That's exactly what it was not. He was just an arrogant arsehole – there are quite a few about.'

'What did you do?'

'I left. He made it as difficult as he could, which, ironically, helped me enormously. After a year or so, I realised it was the single best thing I'd ever done for myself.'

'It takes guts to leave. The number of hours I've spent listening to couples trying to sort their mess out when it's screamingly obvious that one of them should just stand up and walk away. But they don't, and mostly it's because neither of them has the balls.'

'Do you tell them this?'

'Are you mad? I'm the guy they come to so they have an audience for their problems. I'm the one they hope will bear witness to the fact that their life partner is an idiot. The last thing they want from me is practical advice.'

'Do you seriously believe that what you do is so useless?'

'Yes.'

'I don't believe you.'

'I didn't always, but I do now.'

'And is it the same with you and your wife – I mean the lack-of-balls thing?'

She was looking at me with the expression she'd used before: it had an intensity to it, an ability to burrow for things you wouldn't want aired. It unnerved me because I knew the answer to her question. I found myself nodding. 'You tell yourself lies – it's the kids, a bad patch – but the reality is you're there because you don't have the bottle to leave.'

'Maybe it is just a bad patch.'

I started to smile. 'Some fucking bad patch!'

She was still staring at me.

'Anyway, when did you break up with what's-his-name?'

'Four years ago.'

'And since?'

'I've been concentrating on me, not just my career and all that, but on me. First I tried to find out if I had the strength to stand on my own. I mean, everyone tells me I'm strong and independent but I'd never been on my own. And it's not until you do it that you realise you may as well rely on an empty bin-bag for support as a man. I think if most women won the lottery they'd leave their husbands.'

'Why do you say that?'

'Because for most women the only value the man in their life has is economic.'

'So most women despise their husbands?'

'That's not what I said. Look, for many what started out as love and orgasms has whittled itself down to his reliability in the bill-paying department.'

'That's a bit hard, isn't it? In my job I only get to see the wrecks but there must be plenty of partnerships, marriages, that actually work.'

Emma laughed. 'So how's your marriage, Seán?'

'Not fair! Anecdotal evidence is not admissible.'

'Says who?'

'Me! And I'm the judge here because I'm senior but, most importantly, I'm male.'

She laughed. 'Scumbag.'

'Good to see you haven't shred a trace of that charm.'

She smiled at me, then looked down into her glass. 'But, seriously, it's problematic, isn't it?'

'What is?'

'Men and women. Take you and me, old friends, sitting here. It's fun, and yet project that into an ongoing relationship and it would all end in tears.'

'Says who?'

'Me!'

'Why?'

'For all the reasons that none of my relationships have worked out. For the same reason you and your wife live the life you do. In fact, I'd say that you and me would stand even less chance than the average.'

'Look across the river. See that white yacht under the crane?'

'Yes?'

'Would you like to have a look aboard it?'

She laughed. 'I'm getting a strong sense of déjà vu here. You're not going to suggest we take off in it, are you?'

I smiled.

'Seán, why do you want me to visit that boat?'

'I just want to show it to you. I'm thinking of buying it. That's all.'

She was quiet for a moment. 'It looks nice.'

I found the key and slid the hatch open. As I climbed down I was struck again by the depth of the boat – it was like descending into a cave. I began to search for matches, something to light the oil lamps, when suddenly the place glowed with a dim light. I turned to see that Emma had flicked her lighter. 'This any use?' she said. When I'd lit the lamps, a warm yellow glow filled the interior. 'This is really beautiful – it's so cosy!'

'You like it?'

'It's gorgeous. Did you say you're buying it?'

'Roland – he owns the yard, the guy who dropped me off to meet you – he's offered it to me. Come on, I'll show you around.'

She put the half-full bottle she had brought from the restaurant on the chart table and followed me through the saloon. I showed her the sleeping quarters and then the master cabin. It was all wood, brass and bookcases with a large double bed.

'Wow! It's amazing, everything's so beautifully put together.'

'That's old-fashioned craftsmanship,' I said.

'Are you going to buy it?'

'Well, for the price he's asking it would be silly not to, but, Christ, what am I going to do with a boat this size?'

'Sail the high seas!'

I shut the door and suddenly we found ourselves standing close. I could feel her breath on my lips. 'I should get you a drink,' I said.

She smiled, then walked ahead of me into the saloon where she sat on the sofa by the table. In the galley I found glasses, and tonic in one of the lockers, which I poured for myself, then brought the drinks to the table. 'Cheers,' I said.

'So,' she said, 'here we are again, on a boat.'

'Indeed. We haven't had the best experience on them, have we?'

Her eyes were shining, and suddenly I had a vivid memory of her face in the galley aboard the old steel trawler. It was the light, almost exactly the same, and here it was allowing age to evaporate.

'Oh, I don't know,' she said. 'Sometimes I think of that thing Scully did, when he made you drive us through the sandbank. Remember? Was that as crazy as I think it was?'

'It was pure desperation. Our chances of getting wrecked were an awful lot higher than our chances of survival.'

'That's what I'd imagined. So was he crazy or clever or just lucky?'

The tonic was flat. 'I don't know. I've never met anyone like him since. I was in Howth last year seeing my sister and I met some of

300

the old boys from the pier. We were talking about this and that when someone mentioned he'd died. I was really sad. I was surprised by that.'

I felt her hand stroking the side of my face. 'Seán, you were never very good at emotions, were you?' I turned towards her. 'How does it make you feel, sitting here with me now?' she asked.

'Like a little boy,' I said.

'Like a little boy?'

'Yeah – excited, anxious, fretful, terrified. I don't know.' She was gazing at her drink. 'How does it make you feel?' I asked.

She rested her head on the back of the sofa. 'I don't know. I'm a mess. I think tonight I expected to find a dead-in-the-water, slightly bloated, middle-aged man but I should have known better.'

'How do you mean?'

'And you're still completely frustrating!'

'Tell me, then.'

'Oh Seán.' She turned and our lips met. The kiss was tentative and it was consuming. When it stopped, she rested her head in the crook of my neck, her hand around my waist. 'It's so nice when life stands still like this. It's delusional but sweet.'

'Is that what's happening here?'

'I don't know what's happening here, do you?'

'I'm showing you the boat?'

'Oh, is that what we're doing?'

'Yeah, and now we're having a drink.'

'Why did you bring me here?'

'To show you the boat.'

She smiled. 'You know, had you been that slightly dull middle-aged man none of this would have been a problem. We would have had dinner, shared a few memories and said good night.'

'But now?'

'Seeing you again is jarring. And I've had too much wine and shouldn't be saying any of this.'

She was looking straight at me. I leant forward and we kissed again. This time there was nothing tentative about it. 'This is wrong,' she said. Her breathing was hard. 'This is wrong.' Our lips met again and I felt her fingers sink into the flesh of my thigh. My hand went to her breast and, beneath her blouse and bra, I felt her nipple harden. Her hands began to move on my thighs, finally coming to rest between them. Suddenly she stopped. 'Seán, we shouldn't being doing this.'

My heart was racing now. 'Why?'

'For a whole load of reasons.'

Several of her blouse buttons had opened. I fingered the black lace of her bra strap. 'None of them matter.' I slid my hand over her breast. 'Emma, I don't want to think about anything. I just want to go to bed with you.'

'You and I should know better by now.'

'Yeah, well . . .'

She kissed me, it was gentle and soft, and I felt sure when it finished that she would tell me it was time for her to go. But instead she whispered, 'Take me to that cabin, then.'

What happened was not at all like the mad erotica I had fancied making love to Emma would be. Everything about her was gentle. Her fingers flowed over my skin like water. We seemed to know each other's bodies instinctively, each unafraid of the other, each trusting the other. It was like that first conversation we'd had over the arm of a couch, scary and exciting but safe, too, because this was Emma and somehow we fitted perfectly together.

Afterwards I lay beside her, bathing in sweetness. 'So that's what making love to Emma Balstead is like.'

She opened her eyes and smiled. 'You're very lovely, you know.'

'Emma, come away with me.'

Her face left the folds of the pillow. 'Oh no you don't. Not this again!' She was almost laughing.

'I'm serious.'

'No Seán.'

'At least consider it.'

'Excuse me, aren't you Seán Farrell, the marriage-guidance counsellor who has a wife, kids, a mortgage, not to mention clients and a business?'

'Correct.'

'And what would happen to all of those if you disappeared?'

I turned towards her, resting on an elbow. 'I've been thinking of it for a while now, before I even knew anything about you coming to Bristol. I was going to do it for a holiday but, really, a holiday would have been no cure for what's ailing me.'

'Seán, what happened tonight was great, it was fantastic, but what you're saying now is just plain crazy.'

'Why?'

Emma lay back on the pillow and stared at the ceiling. 'I need a cigarette.'

'I'm not sure that's allowed down here.'

'I don't believe this! I'm cruising along doing just fine and then I bump into you.'

'What have I done?'

'Let me know how lonely I've been.'

'You? Lonely? Your life must be crammed full of people.'

'It's crowded and it's busy, and I've managed to convince myself that I don't need anyone to share it with when I get home in the evening, but tonight, thanks to you, I got a glimpse of what I'm missing.'

'But that's just it. I did too.'

'Jesus, Seán, we're not kids any more – we can't just up and go because you look good through a filter of evening sunlight and too much wine.'

'Emma, it's more than just the physical, you know it is. Did you ever think that Fate might have an agenda when it comes to you and me?'

'I'm sure Fate, if there is such a thing, has a lot of agendas.'

'I'm sorry. I didn't mean to make you angry.'

'I'm not angry, I'm lonely and vulnerable and I hate seeing those things in myself.'

'Do you know what the name of this boat is?' She didn't say anything. 'It's Kittigani, which means, in some African dialect, the marriage of destiny and love.'

She began to laugh. 'You talk some bollocks.'

'OK, what about this? Where we are now is called the floating harbour. You can only get in and out of it when they open the lock, which they can do for an hour either side of high tide. So what if I go and look at the tide tables and see if the gods are with us?'

'Seán, I don't understand you. You're asking us both to swap the lives we know for some fantasy based on the whim of the tides?'

'You're lonely – you said so yourself. I've been running around the inside of my life like a caged rat on a wheel for what feels like an awfully long time. What would we be losing? I'd still see my kids. You'd still have your life, your filming.'

'You don't know anything about my life.'

'I know you, and I know that something sparks between us when we meet. It always did. Thirty years on, and it's still there.'

'All I know is I need a cigarette. You go look at your tide tables if you want to. I'll be in the cockpit.' She swung her legs out of bed and stood. 'I think you'd give old Scully a run for his money in sheer madness.'

I smiled as I watched her put on my shirt. 'We'll let the gods decide.'

When she'd gone, I pulled on my jeans and went to the chart table. From the rows of manuals I picked out Reed's Almanac and sat down. I leafed through the pages to find 21 June. I could hear Emma above me, pacing the cockpit, and even down there I caught the faint, sweet aroma of her cigarette. Then she came into view, just her head and shoulders. She was sitting in the corner, her face lit by the screen of her mobile phone. She was either texting or reading a message.

I searched down the columns of figures. Low tide was at 22.08. Quickly I turned the page. The first entry for the twenty-second was high water for Avonmouth at 03.37. This meant the gates would be opening at half past two. My watch was on the floor of the cabin but the clock in the saloon was showing twenty-five past one. My first thought was, How had it got so late? Then I realised that the timing could scarcely have been more perfect.

I waited for a rush of excitement to fill me. It didn't happen. All I knew now was that we could go if we wanted – the gods were allowing it. I looked up at Emma. Her face was still illuminated by the pale blue light from her phone. She was beautiful and she was here. She had said she was lonely and that I had made her aware of it. So, surely, sailing away with me now would mean an end to that loneliness. There was a risk, of course, but this was Emma. She had done it once before.

I looked back at the tables. Those gates would open in an hour. Had I been a prisoner my heart would be leaping at the knowledge. Whether Emma came or not, I had a perfect escape route laid out in front of me. The gates would swing open and beyond them there was a channel and then open water. There, the possibilities were endless. I had to smile. It was like when Scully had given me all that cash from selling the fish – the possibilities had been endless then, too.

And what of life on this side of the gates? Up the Gloucester

Road, left onto Berkeley Road and there, at the corner, the tall house where there was a washing machine I couldn't work, an office with new furniture in the basement, Mark's bass boom and Karen's demands for everything she was told to want. There were the books, the paintings, the furniture, a home, everything I had created, or helped create with Lynn. Could I turn my back on it? And what about Lynn? We had drifted, that was all. I'd seen it a thousand times in couples. It was seldom more than a slight change of course from one or the other but, given time, it was enough to have them inhabiting different worlds. It happened because of kids and bills and the pursuit of some notion of a better life. I knew, too, how much work it would take to get everything back on track. Did I want to do all that? Would I be capable of it? Even if I was, would Lynn? I pictured her on the couch, her glasses at the end of her nose as she wrote furiously across some child's effort to please her, and doubted it.

There was no disguising the fact that life at home was a mess. So, what, then? Sail out through the gates simply to avoid it? I supposed that was what those faces that had appeared down the West Pier looking for a berth on a fishing-boat had done. And here I was, thirty years later, contemplating the same. I sighed. Sailing through those gates would change almost everything except the one thing that had caused the problems in my life. Myself.

Movement came from above. I looked up and saw Emma's long bare legs descending the stairs. When she reached the bottom she stood looking at me.

'Well?' she said.

'Those gods, they're smiling on us.'

She walked to the saloon table and leant against it folding her arms. 'Great! '

'Yes.' I said.

'So?'

'The gates will be opening in an hour.'

'And then where? The Canary Islands, Antigua, Barbados?'

'They're all there, waiting.'

Her mouth curled into a smile. 'But we're not going to any of them.'

'I don't know what to say.'

'Then it's usually best to say nothing.'

'Emma, seeing you tonight has changed everything for me. I thought that all I wanted to do was run away with you, and there is still a big part of me that would love to, but I've also realised there's something else . . .' She was walking towards me, an index finger to her lips. When she reached the chart table, she kissed me on the lips. 'Don't say any more,' she said. She was smiling but her eyes were sad. 'Tonight, talking to you and listening to you, I realised two things. The first is that a big part of my life is empty because I don't have anyone like you in it, and the second is that I never would have you because, although things might seem a mess for you at the moment, I know you'll sort them out.' Her tone was sorrowful.

'All you have to do is speak to me Emma and I feel better about myself. I get hopeful. It just seems so crazy that we have to part. It seems wrong.'

Emma stared at me, then smiled. 'Well, maybe someday it won't seem like that but right now we have to, regardless of what we think about it. You know that.'

All it would have taken was to slip those mooring lines and glide out through the gates. By dawn we would have been in the Bristol Channel and, after that, anywhere. But it seemed that instead we were going to turn in the opposite direction and slip back into our individual lives. 'Would you go, Emma? I mean if I started up the engine now and took off would you—'

'Seán, sometimes it takes making love to someone else to realise what you really want.'

'What? You think that's what happened here?'

'All I'm saying is we both came close to a fantasy becoming real. And that's a scary thing.'

'But we are real, you and me, we're not ghosts.'

'From each other's pasts we are.'

'Emma stop it. The woman I just made love to was very real.'

She leant forward again. 'It was lovely. But you know as well as I do that it was not part of our lives, it can't be, no matter how we feel at this very moment.' She spoke with calmness and certainty.

'I know you're right. I know it. I just wish it was different.'

Twenty minutes later we walked onto Redcliffe Bridge. Almost immediately we saw a taxi coming down the opposite side of the road. Emma raised her arm and the driver flashed his lights and continued towards the roundabout at the end of the bridge.

'Will we see each other again?' I asked.

'Let's not plan anything.'

'But some time in the future.'

'That's planning.'

'You're right.'

The taxi pulled up a few feet ahead of us. 'Look, I'm a very lucky woman to have met such a sweet soul and then to have met you again.' Our kiss was strong and forceful. As we broke from it I saw that Emma's eyes were heavy with tears. 'Leave it to that Fate you're so sure of,' she said, then stepped into the cab and shut the door.

I watched as the taxi swept over the bridge and past the restaurant where we'd eaten.

The sky over *Kittigani* was lightening to a delicate blue. Beneath it everything was sharp and dark in silhouette. On the water only the swans sailed. I watched two float downriver together in silence. I turned and began to walk. It was time to go home.

ACKNOWLEDGEMENTS

Many people helped in many different ways to put this story together: Steve Barnes, Hilary Fannin, John Moran, Marie Fannin, Giles Newington, Rynagh O'Grady, Gael Rowan, Becs Monks, Denise Fannin, Foina Hance, Danny Kushlick, Faith O'Grady, Peter and Jill Rolt, Caroline Davidson, Anne Rawnsly, Ciara Considine, Terry Heron, Karen Edwards, Breda Purdue, The Bristol Classic Boat Company, Margaret Daly. To these and the many others, my heartfelt thanks.

TB